SURVIVAL GAME

Books by Philip Kerrigan

Dead Ground

Survival Game

SURVIVAL GAME

Philip Kerrigan

Crown Publishers, Inc.

New York

Grateful acknowledgment is made for permission to reprint selections from *The Watcher in the Shadows* by Geoffrey Household. Copyright © 1960 by Geoffrey Household. By permission of Little, Brown and Company, in association with The Atlantic Monthly Press.

Published by Crown Publishers, Inc., 225 Park Avenue South, New York, New York 10003

CROWN is a trademark of Crown Publishers, Inc.

Manufactured in the United States of America

Library of Congress Cataloging-in-Publication Data

Kerrigan, Philip, 1959–
  Survival game.

  I. Title.
PR6061.E794S9   1987   823'.914   86-32983
ISBN 0-517-56582-X

10 9 8 7 6 5 4 3 2 1

First American Edition

I believe that for the animal always, and for man sometimes, fear is only a vivid awareness of one's unity with nature.

GEOFFREY HOUSEHOLD
Watcher in the Shadows

1

Rumors of the War

1

He needed a gun, so he was walking up Argyle Street in a pouring October rainstorm. He walked quickly and deliberately, as if he had to give thought even to simple actions. Cars whipped by, heading toward Glasgow's Central Railway Station. Their headlamps made diamond stars of the rain.

A side street took him down toward Broomielaw and the river. Under the hood of the old blue parka he wore, his eyes were like camera lenses.

He came to the Glengavel public house and stepped into the bar. It was hot and noisy. The Thursday-night clientele had been supplemented by people sheltering from the rain. A jukebox full of oldies pumped out "River Deep, Mountain High," and cigarette smoke wafted like cloud cover two feet from the ceiling.

He shook the rain off and flipped his hood back. No one noticed when he came in. He elbowed his way to the bar, grimacing as if close contact with others were a disease, and ordered a pint of bitter. The landlord asked him to speak up. He repeated it louder, staring at the landlord's cracked, wooden face.

He rubbed the back of his head, touching the short bristles of hair. He glanced at the crowd in the bar. His beer arrived. He paid for it uncertainly, like a tourist who had no idea of the price. There was nowhere he could sit alone, so he stayed there, searching the faces.

Finally, he saw one that looked as if it could be the man

who had been described to him. A short, greasy rat of a man in an old lumber jacket and faded jeans. The rat was drinking some kind of orange cocktail and holding forth to a small circle of friends.

He approached the rat through the jostling crowd, homing in on the thin Falkirk scrawl of his voice.

". . . So I told him, 'If that's all the evidence you've got, I'll be making my way home now.'" One of his little claws was curled around the bottle blonde next to him. "I mean, I don't mind helping the forces of law and order about their business, but I'm no' a charity."

The friends laughed as he swigged at the cocktail. The blonde gave him a nudge to alert him to the intruder. The others turned uncomfortably and stared.

"Can I be of any assistance, squire?" The rat eyed him sideways on.

"Are you Donald Bishop?"

"Depends who's asking. Has he won the pools?" The rat winked at his girlfriend and let the others know everything was easy.

"It's a business matter."

The rat glanced at his watch. "It's half-past eight, mister. I don't know what hours you work, but I'm strictly a nine-to-five boy myself."

"I've been looking for you. Mr. Squires told me you sell."

"Buy, sell. The whole world does that, my friend."

"Hardware," the stranger said, sweating. He was conscious of the curiosity in the faces around him, the stink of sweat and cheap perfume and aftershave.

"What, like bath taps and stuff?" The group sniggered as the jukebox changed to Springsteen's "Glory Days." "Ah, I don't know about all that, squire. I'm right out of bathroom suites and bidets just now."

"I heard you sell guns."

The rat paled suddenly. His friends breathed in sharply, as if a matter in bad taste had been raised. He put down his glass and stepped close to the stranger. He was holding his anger down.

"Come with me," he said.

They went toward the toilets in the back of the pub. The rat waited while a drunken youth peed over the urinal on the wall, then slammed the door and leaned against it, right hand in his pocket.

"If you like to stay healthy, don't ever do that again," he said. "If I wanted the world to know my business, I'd advertise on the radio."

"Go on the box, for all I care. And stop fingering that knife or I'll break your fucking arm."

The rat drew his hand, empty, out of his jacket. When he spoke, his voice was less confident. "So, you've got my undivided attention, right? What's your problem?"

"Do you sell guns?"

"What's that? I didn't quite catch you?"

"Don't fuck about with me."

The rat peered at him nervously. "What's wrong with you?"

"Nothing. Tell me if you want to make some money or not."

"Who sent you?"

"I told you. Your pal Squires. I've been looking for you for a while. What about guns?"

"You've never done this before, have you? Coming in like that. You could get yourself killed."

"Think so?"

Someone bumped against the toilet door. The rat hissed over his shoulder, "Wait a minute, all right!"

The other stood by the dirty sink, saying nothing.

"What d'you want the tools for?"

"That's my business."

"Going to rob a bank, are you? Or is it your wife's boyfriend?"

No answer.

The rat scratched his chin, coming to a decision. "Okay. But you'll have to meet me later. I don't do business here."

"Where?"

The rat named a place. "Eleven o'clock, okay?"

"Why so late?"

"The pubs'll be letting out. The coppers'll be busy picking up drunks. Safer that way."

"Twenty-three hundred. I'll be waiting for you."

"'Course you will." The rat relaxed a little. He took out a pack of cigarettes and offered them.

"By the way."

"What?"

"What sort of tool is it you're after? I don't carry my entire stock with me."

"Rifle. And a handgun."

"Fine. I'll see what I can do."

2

THE MAN WHO WANTED TO BUY A GUN TURNED OFF KING'S Drive into the Gorbals. He parked the car in a street that had the dull smoothness of black leather in the rain. He sat behind the wheel, clutching it every few seconds in a steady, nervous movement. He kept his eyes on the deserted street, on the dustbins by the roadside and the rotting warehouse doors.

A rusting yellow Ford Transit van turned the corner and drew up in front of him. The headlamps went out. A face appeared, sculpted by the dim interior light. The rat beckoned.

The van's back doors opened as he walked round. He tilted his head, as an animal does when scenting for danger, but there was nothing to fear. Inside, the rat crouched in a tumble of old sacking, dirty cushions, and discarded fast-food boxes.

"Welcome to my wee emporium." The rat grinned. "It's no' Forsythes, but it does for me."

He could not recall what Forsythes was. He put down an old red carryall, knelt awkwardly in the van, staring at the rat. "What've you got?"

"Well, my friend, for you I delved into my stock. I've got some lovely tools here." He lifted a portion of the sacking and revealed the weapons.

"Is that all?"

"All?" the rat said. "Did you want a bazooka or something?"

"I want a rifle, a good rifle. Don't you have an L1A1 or an L42?"

"What the hell for? There's no call for them. No one ever did a security truck with one o' those. Too long and clumsy."

"They're accurate."

"I'll no' argue with you there. If it's good enough for the army, it's good enough for me. But there's no demand for them in civilian life."

He reached down and turned some of the weapons over.

"That's the M-3A1," the rat said.

"I know what it is. I don't want a machine gun. Christ, this stuff's junk."

"If you know someone else who'll do better for you . . ."

"Never mind." He picked up a couple more, but threw them aside. At the bottom of the pile, he turned up a neat, snub-nosed rifle.

"Ah." The rat sighed like a true connoisseur. "You're holding the most successful small arm since World War Two in your hands now. Designed by Mikhail Kalashnikov. Rugged, high rate of fire, accurate—"

"Only to three hundred yards."

"So, what sort of game you after?"

"Mind your own business." He lifted the rifle, squinting down its pillar and tangent sights as the rat went on with his sales talk.

"As used by the U.S.S.R., Egypt, Syria, Yugoslavia, the Vietcong, and, of course, the IRA. Nice little tool, that."

"I wanted something with a longer range."

"You've seen the stock."

He checked the inside of the barrel. "It must be thirty years old."

"Reliability means longevity, as my old man used to say."

"Ammo?"

The rat dug behind the passenger seat and produced a banana-shaped magazine for the AK47. "I've plenty for this one. Popular little number."

He fitted the empty magazine and swung the rifle up on his

shoulder, getting the feel of it. Then he broke it down and reassembled it.

The rat watched, fascinated. "You've had experience."

"I read the gun magazines. What about a pistol?"

The rat showed his wares. It did not take long. The stranger chose a Browning 9mm automatic. It was slightly rusted, like the AK47, but he knew these were cosmetic faults.

"How much?"

The rat took a deep breath, considering. He mentioned a figure.

"You're joking."

"With plenty of ammo thrown in, naturally."

"It's still fucking robbery."

"Depends how much you want them. You'll no' get them cheaper anywhere else. Besides, I don't think you've got the time."

"What do you mean?" Cold eyes turned to fix on him. The rat shuddered. He was suddenly aware of how small the van was, how lonely the street was. He saw the bony hands flex on the rifle.

"Nothing. I don't care what your game is. If you want the tools, you have to pay, that's all."

The stranger gazed at him. The rat's insides swirled like water going down a drain.

"So what's it to be?" he managed to ask.

"You're a fucking crook."

The rat tried for a smile. It came out weak and unsteady. "That's really funny, coming from you."

A wad of twenty-pound notes appeared. The rat licked his dry lips, watched the notes peeling off the roll. He gathered up two more magazines for the rifle, then stacked several boxes of ammunition: 9mm for the Browning, 7.62mm for the AK47.

Money changed hands. He stashed it in his jacket as the guns and cartridges went into the red carryall. The stranger appeared to have some difficulty fitting the automatic inside.

"Well, it's nice doing business with you." The rat offered his hand. The stranger recoiled as if it were a lizard on a rock.

The rat did his best to stay calm. "Hope the tools come in handy."

The stranger moved toward the rear of the van. He picked up one of the cushions to get it out of the doorway. A car turned the distant corner at the end of the road. Relief came over the rat's thin body in a shiver. "Who knows, maybe I'll read about you in the papers," he said.

The car roared past in the wet, empty street, stereo blasting. The other turned back for a second with the cushion held up in front of him.

"Oh, you won't be doing that," he said.

The cushion exploded in a burst of rotted feathers.

It muffled the report of the gun. No one in the street heard it, the people in the car did not hear it. Only the rat heard it.

And he did not hear it for very long.

3

HE WENT THROUGH THE DANK LOBBY OF THE RUN-DOWN
house where he lived. A light was on under old Carlisle's
door. The BBC World Service blared out. Carlisle was sitting up, deaf ear pressed to the radio set, waiting for signs of
immoral activity from the house's other occupants. It was
something to do while senility set in.

He reached the first floor and let himself in. A fog of cigarette smoke and whisky fumes hit him. It was like being
back in the pub. He coughed.

"That you?" The old man slouched like a corpse in front
of the television, glass in one hand, cigarette in the other. By
the blue light from the TV he looked pickled and bloated.

"Yes, it's me." He walked toward the back bedroom,
keeping the bag out of sight.

"Have a nice evening? Wine, women, bit of song?"

"It was all right."

"Where'd you go?"

"Oh, some pub. I don't remember the name." The carryall
was safe in the bedroom. He turned back to talk to the old
man. "It was all right."

"Good. You should get out more with people, my lad. Can't
get yourself better sitting around here keeping an old bugger like me company. Youngsters should be out on the town."

"You're not so old yourself."

"Oh, I'm on my way out."

"Don't talk like that. You should have come along tonight."

"Oh, no," the old man said, fingering his glass. He spoke with the exaggerated clarity of the permanently drunk. "I prefer being here with the television. You know, I never watched it much before. Now I know what I've been missing all these years." He stared at the screen. Walter Pidgeon, trapped in a cave, was making a bow and arrow from a brooch and some twine. "I saw this when it first came out, you know. The Empire, I think, nineteen forty-one or -two. George Sanders doesn't know it yet, but he's about to get one in the eye. Literally." He began to shake with silent laughter. He took another drink.

Now was as good a time as any. "Listen," he said, "I'm going away for the weekend."

"What?" The old man lowered his glass. "The weekend? Again? I know I said you should get out more. You don't waste time, do you?"

"It's only for the weekend."

"Don't tell me. You're taking some young lady to Edinburgh's bright lights."

"It's just a bit of camping."

"In October?"

"Why not?"

"No reason, I suppose. You're trained for it, after all. How to survive in open country in the depths of winter with naught but a penknife and a ball of string." The old man laughed and sighed and drank again. "I could come with you, you know. Where you going?"

"Up country. But you wouldn't—"

"Don't worry, you won't catch me getting wet socks and a lumpy bed at my time of life. I'm too busy raging at the dying of the light—at least, I will be when I've finished this drink."

"I'll be off early in the morning," he said, trying to keep relief out of his tone. His head was hurting with noise. It felt blown up like a football. "Before you're up, probably. I won't wake you."

"And when do you plan to return from this little expedition? When can I hope for the pleasure of your company again?"

"Afterwards—after the weekend."

The old man turned a congealed eye toward him. He was suspicious. "Can you not be more precise?"

"Monday, then."

"You are coming back, aren't you? Aren't you?"

The rhythm of pain increased. "Of course I am. What else would I do?"

The old man's suspicion changed to something afraid. He reached out with a trembling hand, but the other stepped back. "You're not leaving me, are you?"

"No, for Christ's sake. I told you."

A tear rolled down the old man's flabby, sallow cheek. "Only I want to know, see. You mustn't just trot off without a single word. I know I'm not much use anymore, but you're all I have now. You understand, don't you?" The hand reached, begging to be held.

"I'm only taking a trip," he said, squirming in his clothes. "Don't get worked up over nothing."

The old man let his hand drop. He took up the glass again, held it to his lips. "Well, you be careful. I don't want to see you on the box, being brought down by the mountain rescue service."

"No chance." He moved toward his bedroom again. The sound of Carlisle's radio pierced through the floor.

"Hey?" The old man roused himself.

"I'm here."

"You're all right, aren't you, my boy?"

"Fine," he said. "I want some time to myself, that's all."

"Good, good. As long as there's nothing wrong."

He smiled through the throbbing pain. "I'm great."

He slipped into his room, leaving the old man sprawled before the ghost light of the television.

It was a large room. The single window frame was twisted out of true and the floor dropped to one corner because of subsidence. It overlooked a weed-choked yard. In the house's good days, it might have been the children's bedroom. Now it was more like a shrine. The shabby walls were covered with posters from army recruiting offices, pictures from military magazines. Camouflage colors and uniforms, faces smeared with dirt, stretched in battle cries. Fold-outs from magazines showed all types of weapons, from tanks to heavy artillery, rocket launchers to handguns. Black-and-white photographs of the Parachute Regiment in the Falklands conflict had a place over the bed: Brigadier Julian Thompson walking into Port Stanley with his bodyguard, Camilla Creek House, Darwin Settlement, the raising of the British flag at Government House. Books were scattered about, most of them piled on a chipped sideboard by the old fireplace: James Jones's army books, Hemingway's *Across the River and Into the Trees*, Manchester's *Goodbye, Darkness*, and Major General Frost's *Two Para Falklands*. There were stolen library copies of expensive histories of the Paras and S.A.S. Under the sideboard, a stack of videotapes labeled "The Paras" and "Behind the Lines." A Gurkha knife hung on one wall.

He stripped naked and lay down on the bed. He massaged his forehead slowly, breathing regularly, trying to keep himself locked up. He stayed there until he heard the old man switch off the television and go to bed. Then he got up and stared out at all the lighted windows he could see. All those people out there, carrying on as usual. They were coming home from pubs and clubs, watching dirty films on the video, screwing, and going to sleep. Oh, they were in for a surprise. Everyone was in for that.

He turned and opened the big wardrobe. There was not much inside. A best suit that had been fashionable five years ago, some jackets and cord trousers. And a uniform. Combat fatigues. He stood for a long time, leaning, touching the rough, heavy materials, the pouches and pockets, straps and buckles. He lifted the uniform out and laid it flat on the bed. It looked very professional.

"I'll be professional," he said. "Oh, yeah."

He dressed carefully, with a certain air of solemnity. It was important to be accurate and correct in this. He would be professional throughout, because anger—no matter how much he felt—had no place in his task. Where he was going would be cold and damp. So he wore several layers of clothing. Nothing too heavy: army-issue underwear; then a pair of woman's tights, which were useful insulation when you were tabbing over rough country, fording streams, and wading in bogs; then a wool-and-nylon teddy-bear suit—the kind used so often by the S.A.S. in freezing climates; a "Mao" quilted jacket; and finally, the uniform.

He took a pair of boots from the wardrobe. Not the usual D.M.S. boots, which had put more men out of action during the Falklands campaign than the Argentinians, but Arctic boots. They were already broken in by numerous recces in the past few months. They fitted comfortably over the thick socks he wore.

Outfit complete, he stepped in front of the mirror and stood to attention, inspecting himself. He had done this before, many times, but not for a long while with this good, sweet sense of purpose.

"Good turnout, Sergeant Major," he whispered. "Thank you, sir. Stand at ease." He smiled. He picked up the carryall and took out the parts of the rifle and the handgun. He proceeded to clean both of them. The Browning was exactly what he had wanted. It held a thirteen-bullet clip, which might come in handy. The AK47 was less than the perfect choice. He would have preferred something he was familiar with. But you could not argue with the AK47's record. It was light and small, even with the stock extended. Easier to carry and conceal.

When he was done, he walked back to the window. Most lights were out in the windows nearby, but one remained. It showed a bedroom wall, the soft spread of light from a pink shade. A woman was tucked up safe in bed, reading a book. Nice and safe.

He raised the rifle, sighted on the window. Then he swiveled slowly, turning back into the room, until the rifle was pointing straight at the only picture in the room that was not concerned with the military. The photograph was from *The Mail on Sunday* Headlines column. It showed a man in his late thirties and a young woman doing some kind of dance at a party. The caption under it read: "Dan Goldman, famous for his love of all things culinary, shows his assistant (?), Georgina Lawrence, how to make a dog's dinner of the last waltz."

He centered on the laughing, suntanned face of the man. He pulled the trigger, listened to the hammer fall.

"Fuck you," he said.

He left at four o'clock in the morning, going down the stairs with an old coat on to disguise the uniform. The guns, ammunition, and a little food were in a rucksack slung over his shoulder. He wanted to get an early start, because there was a lot to do before the big day.

As he reached the downstairs hallway, Carlisle's door creaked open and the starved old face peered out.

"Who's that?"

"Me, Mr. Carlisle. From upstairs."

"Upstairs? What're you prowling around at this time of night for?"

He grinned at his own audacity as he went through the front door.

"I'm going hunting," he said.

4

DANIEL GOLDMAN PICKED UP A COPY OF THE *FINANCIAL Times* and studied the previous day's headlines.

"I can't see where this is getting us, gentlemen," he heard Ashe's legal adviser say. "We could talk all night but we remain as far apart as ever."

Dan rose stiffly from his chair and went over to the window. "We *have* talked all night," he said, and pulled the curtains. Faint dawn light blushed against the glass. He opened the window and breathed deeply. The air was damp and cold. A London cab chugged past in the street below.

A fine atmosphere of weariness hung over the suite. At half-past six on a Friday morning, even the Dorchester looked drab. The men who had come in fourteen hours ago to do business seemed grayer and smaller too. Roland Ashe in his city-slicker suit, lots of gold on fingers and wrist, tie pulled loose, shirt unbuttoned to show his fat, hairy belly. Ashe's legal adviser, a cold fish named Harker. Ashe's managing director, Stephen Miller; full of ideas and desperate to please the boss. They were ranged on one side of a long coffee table piled with papers. On the other side—the good guys' side, as far as Dan was concerned—was Peter Bailey, his managing director. There was no need of a legal adviser with Peter around; he knew all they had to know. Peter was down to shirt and waistcoat, the coat unbuttoned and the chain of his gold pocket watch hanging loose on his chest. With spectacles perched on the end of his long nose, lean face screwed up in apparent concentration, he peered at the opponents now and then like something from Dickens. That was Peter's disguise. He came on like your old-fashioned, middle-aged English businessman, all airs, graces, and feigned incompetence, then sandbagged the enemy from behind. Peter was, apparently, giving all his attention to a sheaf of Xeroxed reports. Dan knew better—at least, he hoped he did. Peter seemed unusually tired. But he had been following Dan's blueprint for these negotiations, tying Ashe and his advisers up with detail, gaining time.

He turned from the thought that Peter might be losing his edge. The night had been long, and all his energy had to be directed toward this deal. It was important that he integrate the U.K. side of his enterprise. Ashe's business would enable him to do that in one move—and cheaply, if things went according to plan.

He glanced at Roland Ashe again. Ashe, shoes off, lounged across a couch between his two men, smoking his fiftieth cigarette since the meeting began. Sweat glistened on his bald, bullet head. He had been drinking steadily through the night. He was getting pissed off and suspicious under all the North Country bluff. But that was fair enough; he was losing his business, which was his life. Dan knew enough of the similarities between himself and a guy like Ashe to know how he would feel in the same position. Son of a dirt-poor Yorkshire mining family, Ashe had built his meat business from the ground up. He had a public face—the ordinary, average guy made good—which he used to great advantage. Dan played the same game; only his disguise was the rough, good-hearted Brooklyn boy. In his case, it was close enough to the truth so he never felt he was faking it. As for "from the ground up," that was simple fact.

Daniel Goldman was born in Ditmas Park, Brooklyn, in 1946. The son of Max Goldman and his wife, Mary. As a young man, Max had some large ideas and tried all kinds of ways to get rich. He had a hot-dog concession on Coney Island, then tried running a bar. The bar was on the way to closing when he went to fly bombers over Germany. He knew enough of what was happening to the Jews in Europe to make World War Two something of a personal matter between himself and Hitler. He was accurate and brave, and when he came home, something of a hero to the neighborhood. He also had a sizable amount of back pay stashed away.

The first thing he did on returning was marry his childhood sweetheart, Mary Campbell. Mary was the daughter of the local cop on the beat. He made a big deal out of their Scottish ancestry, and it was well known that he did not take all that kindly to his eldest daughter marrying into the Goldman clan. Still, Mary was not as impressed about their heritage as her old man. The marriage took place toward the end of 1945.

The only son of the Goldman family came along in 1946. It was not an easy birth, and the doctors made it clear that they had better look after the boy, because he was all they were getting. Max said the kid looked like a heavyweight contender, all crumpled up in his crib with hands in front of his face. His mother said he was an angel. Neither of them was right.

As all these domestic joys were taking place, Max was busy with his back pay; he bought a delicatessen business from an old friend of the family and swore to give Mary gold bath fittings and a palace on Long Island before the end of the decade.

Of course, it did not happen like that. By the time the son, named Daniel George, was old enough to run errands for his father on the old bike they kept in back of the store, Max had still not gotten out of Brooklyn. He never did. And for a long time, it looked as if his son would not either. Dan scuffed along at school, always popular but never head of the gang. He laughed a lot. He flirted with the kind of criminal activity that kids in the city will flirt with. He gave his mother and father some heartache. In 1966, when he was nineteen, he received his invitation to Vietnam. He attended the party, did his year, and came back in one piece. He seemed remarkably unscathed by the things he had done and seen.

However, what he did on arrival home surprised everyone, including Max, who would live two more years before his heart gave out one afternoon during a New York Mets game on the radio. He bought a burger concession on Coney Island ("Going into the family business," his mother remarked, only to be silenced by a meaningful glare from Max). When the concerned father asked the son what had brought on this sudden access of purpose, the son smiled his charming smile and said: "I have to do something with the back pay." Dan made deals for himself and his father. He had a certain savvy that Max never had. The concession made money. The next thing he did was move on to an eatery near Prospect Park. And after that he went into partnership with an old army buddy, opened a small chain of burger joints which, in time, became a large chain. He bought the partner out after five years, and by the end of the seventies, he was several times a millionaire. His business interests covered restaurants, leisure facilities, hotels, even a small record company. He moved into England and, in a small way, Europe. His company, Goldoor, was not an ITT, he was not a Getty; he was more like a Richard Branson. But as he said to Branson one time when they appeared together on a television talk show, that was no mean thing in these difficult times.

So he knew how Roland Ashe must be feeling now as he was forced to sell his business. His was one of the most successful privately owned meat producers in the country, and it was all his own work. His major contract at present was supplying to the WonderBar hamburger chain. But he had become interested in other aspects of the business, particularly soy meat substitutes, and stretched his resources too far. He had put a lot of personal money in soy futures. The price had risen suddenly over the last few months due to drought in the Midwest, and he suddenly found himself in a hole for the several million dollars required to meet the increased margin in Chicago. He was having to sell just to keep from going under personally. But he obviously hated it, and the American who might save his skin. They had been arguing all night over price, and Ashe was beginning to suspect Dan of protracting negotiations deliberately. He just couldn't work out why.

Dan raised his arms and yawned widely. "I could use a coffee right now. Anyone else?"

There were murmurs of agreement from all concerned, except for Ashe, who sat puffing on a cigarette, swilling his whisky, and staring fiercely at the window.

Dan glanced at his watch. If Bob Townsend didn't ring soon, Ashe might ruin it all by closing the meeting down. "Fine. I'll get them to send up some sandwiches while they're at it," he said. "If you'll excuse me, gentlemen . . ."

He opened a door and went into a bedroom, closed the door quietly. For something like half a minute he watched the woman who lay asleep on the bed. She was fully dressed, but had pulled the counterpane over her in sleep. She lay on her side with knees drawn up, face half-concealed in the pillow. He studied the delicate orb of the closed eye, the gentle color of her cheek, the curve of her nose, and the soft line of her mouth. Dark hair spilled over the pillow. One hand was under her face, like a child in a sentimental picture. Her breast rose and fell under the cotton of her blouse, her hip molded the counterpane into a curve.

He remained by the door, watching her, hardly breathing. There was a light in his eyes that was not often there.

She sensed someone in the room, turned over restlessly. She groaned, and the sound was close to fear.

He stepped forward before she could wake, spoke her name:

"Georgie . . . Georgie, come on, kid, wake up." He stood over her as she opened her eyes. She came out of sleep then like a cat: fully conscious and knowing exactly where she was.

"I fell asleep."

"Only for a couple of hours."

She sat up, touching her disheveled hair. "Have I missed anything?"

"Not a thing. Bob didn't call yet?"

"No." She swung her legs off the bed and slipped her shoes on. She was neat and businesslike again in a second.

"Well, wait on his call, and while you're doing that, send down for some coffee and sandwiches, would you?"

"For you, anything." She picked up the phone and dialed the desk. "How's it going in there?"

"About as well as you'd expect." He yawned again. "That guy Ashe won't go without a fight."

"Which is why you need Bob to come in."

"Peter's marshaling the forces for another attack. We're holding our own."

"If not somebody else's."

He gave her an old-fashioned look. "Why, Miss Lawrence, I do believe that was a *double entendre*."

She gave her impression of a bubble-headed secretary: "Ooh, no, Mr. Goldman!"

He watched her put in the order with the desk. "Hey, thanks for sticking around. You didn't have to, you know."

"And miss a team like Goldman, Bailey, and Townsend in action?"

"If Townsend ever shows up."

"He will," she said.

"He'd better. Ashe's been a bug under my hide too long. Besides, I want this all wound up so we can get to Edinburgh tonight and be on Scorba in the morning."

"The game." She nodded. "I've been getting fit for it."

"I can see that," he said.

"Why, thank you."

For a moment he was staring at her and she knew it. He couldn't help himself. Finally, he broke away.

"I'm going to freshen up," he said. "If you hear the war start up again in there, try to limit the bloodletting."

She was smiling as she turned to the phone again. "Okay."

He flicked the light on in the bathroom. The fluorescent hurt his eyes. He turned the taps on full and filled the sink, took his shirt off. When the sink was full, he bent low, ducking his face in the water. He washed, then picked up the razor Georgie had put out for him, shaved quickly. He gazed at his face, noticing the lines and wrinkles. They weren't too much to scream about. But what was the old saying? After forty, you spend ten minutes every morning shaving your father.

—Who'll be shaving me in forty years' time? he thought. Mama was always telling him he should have a wife and kids by now.

Dabbing his face dry, he watched Georgie through the partly open door. She was brushing out her hair in quick strokes, unaware of him. Where had she been all his life— apart from growing up? And when would all this unspoken stuff turn into reality? When she was ready, he guessed.

The thought that he, Daniel Goldman, could be made to wait for what he wanted would have been funny if it caused him less pain. He was acting like a kid, but when a man is in love for the first time in twenty years, he is allowed to be- have out of character.

He reached for the fresh shirt she had laid out for him, put it on, thinking about the deal they had to make, wondering how much longer it would be before Ashe really blew his cool. He was waiting for that with a kind of professional in- terest. He was sorry for the guy, who wouldn't be? To lose it all was a terrible thing. But the all-night meeting had shown Dan two fatal flaws in Ashe. One was arrogance beyond the point where it was useful, the other was impulsiveness. No one who really prized his business would have risked it to that extent just to save a little on soy.

Humming lightly, he brushed his teeth with the brush also provided by Georgie, and went out to begin what he hoped would be the final phase.

Georgie was already in the room with the others. She sat in a chair some distance away from the main gathering, causing the usual discomfort among the men. Dan noticed Ashe's leer as he came out of the bedroom. They all thought Georgie was something more than a personal assistant to him.

Which she was. But only, so far, in his head. They wouldn't believe it if they knew.

The coffee and sandwiches arrived. The only person to eat with any real enthusiasm was Dan. He sat talking to Stephen Miller. Ashe went on drinking whisky.

"So this 'survival game' thing is actually yours?" Miller said. He was holding a glossy brochure marked *SURVIVAL GAME—The Ultimate Test*.

Dan nodded.

"We got it in the post the other day," Miller said. He opened the brochure. "Same kind of thing as *Skirmish* or *Survive* I take it?"

"Better," Dan said.

"A few of our lads go down to some place in Surrey to play it . . . The Isle of Scorba. Where is that, exactly?"

"Argyll, northwest of Scotland." Dan picked up another sandwich.

"And you hold these . . . adventure-game things up there?"

"That's right."

"Isn't that rather remote?"

"Worth the trip, believe me." He had bought Scorba almost three years ago. An old Scots family had put it up for sale along with big slices of their mainland estate. It remained unused until Bob Townsend, who had gone wild over survival games, suggested it could be made to work for a living. "Look at it," Bob said, foxy eyes sparkling. "Close to the winter sports, perfect site for a really rugged game. And there's a hotel in the town up the coast that could go big with investment. You'd be a mug not to use it." Bob always had a quaint way of advising him.

So, after the idea had been around long enough for it to become his own, Dan looked into the company leisure business. Plenty of corporations back in the States were using survival games as tests for management potential; even in backward little Britain it was catching on. It was a gold mine waiting to be dug. The little town was glad to have its faded hotel brought into the twentieth century; what had been a cute but run-down bunch of cottages and fishing boats was now becoming a summer resort. And it just so happened he was taking Georgie and Peter and Bob there for a first visit this weekend. But he wasn't about to tell Miller that.

Miller was saying that he might give it a try some time, when Peter brought them back to the point.

"Right, gentlemen." He arranged some papers on the table. "Shall we return to the business at hand?"

"If you think it'll do any good," Ashe muttered, sitting up.

Peter frowned in a way that the unprepared might have taken for vague. "I'm sure we can hammer this out."

"We bloody won't if you stick to that pathetic offer."

"Which one would that be?" Dan asked, sitting down. Peter handed him some sheets of hastily written notes. He scanned them for the relevant details. "We've made about fifty different offers since we came in here. You know, Mr. Miller, I'm starting to wonder if your boss really wants to sell."

"Me?" Ashe cried. "If you'd stop bogging us down with bloody details we might get somewhere."

"Let's not get all het up, Rolly." Dan grinned.

"Don't call me Rolly." Ashe glared.

There was a moment of uncomfortable silence. Harker, clearly pained by his client's ill-bred attitude, broke it: "As far as I can see, Mr. Ashe, even if we can agree upon several major details, and reflect that in the price, the opening offer is still insufficient."

"I'll tell you one thing," Ashe muttered. "I'll not sell for fifty million. It's not enough."

"With all details taken into account," Peter said, "we feel that fifty million's quite adequate."

"My back's against the wall, but I'll not give it away." He drew himself up slightly with obvious pride. "I'm worth sixty."

Peter nodded. "Your business is presently heavily reliant on a single contract with the WonderBar company. A contract they have consistently refused to extend beyond a term of three months. Evergreen—unless either side gives three months notice. If that contract were to be canceled, the value of your company would drop quite considerably. Something in the order of twelve million pounds, I'd say. We have to take that into consideration."

"There's plenty of people who'll pay what I'm asking," Ashe protested. He knew Peter had spotted the major weakness in his business. He was trying to bluff it out. "WonderBar have been taking my stuff for over five years. Where else would they go?"

Peter referred to Dan. They started gathering up their papers from the table.

"Hang on a moment, gentlemen," Miller said. They paused. "I think we can make this work, if we're all prepared to give a little."

Dan watched Peter going through all the motions. When he was hot, it was a joy to watch him work the trick of appearing to be older than his years. He glanced questioningly at Dan for permission, then slowly resumed his seat. He rippled sensitive fingers over the papers newly spread on the table. He took his watch out and flipped the cover, shook his graying head slowly, clicked his tongue.

"Well, let's see. We might, of course, be prepared to go a little higher. What do you say, Dan?"

"It all depends," Dan said. No one would have guessed how much he wanted this deal to succeed. "We've already established asset value and your average profit. Admittedly, we're offering less than a look at the PE ratio might lead anyone to expect. It depends how you judge PEs. But" —he clapped his hands slowly together—"like Peter said, we have to consider that one contract is almost half your business."

"And there's still this matter of Mr. Ashe's warranties," Peter said.

"Oh, not those again," Ashe groaned.

Peter squinted over a column of figures. "I'm still not happy about the pension funding. To be honest, I think your actuary miscalculated. The pension scheme . . ." He seemed to lose his thread for a moment. ". . . is underfunded by something like two million pounds."

"Three million," Dan said.

Peter blinked. He shifted uncomfortably. He fumbled for the papers. "Ah, yes. Three million. I think we ought to just go over the details of your calculation of that shortfall."

"This is bloody time-wasting," Ashe said, bitterly.

"We can just go over it again." Miller took up a calculator and notepad. "It shouldn't take a minute."

Just then, the phone bleeped. Georgie rose and picked up the receiver. She spoke quietly into it, then replaced it. As Peter and Miller began working over the figures, she came to Dan and muttered something in his ear. He betrayed no more than polite interest.

"What's up?" Ashe inquired.

"Bob Townsend's coming up. He's got some stuff for me."

Ashe watched Georgie as she went round, refilling their cups. The calculator buttons clicked.

"What about the money, Goldman?" he said, draining his glass. "Have you got the brass?"

"Look, Mr. Ashe, you're in a buyer's market. You know I've got the money. I'll pay the going rate. But I don't pay a cent for hope value."

"So you're looking to make a profit out of my bad luck?"

"Bad luck?" He raised an eyebrow. What had Papa always said? "In business, you don't have bad luck, you have bad judgment."

Peter took off his spectacles, pointing with them to his own calculations. Miller and the legal adviser hunched over the table.

Ashe scratched his head. "Come on, come on. Get the bloody thing sorted out."

There was a knock at the door. Georgie went into the hall to open it, but Bob was already making his entrance. Dan looked up to see him swagger in. There was no other word for the way Bob walked. From the top of his beautifully barbered head to the brilliantly polished shoes on his feet, his figure crowed youth and vitality at the world. It was part of being successful beyond the dreams of most twenty-eight-year-olds, and if some of it was overconfidence, that was okay; Dan had no use in his business for people who did not believe in themselves. Bob gave Georgie a big wink as he passed, threw his coat on a chair, and came across the room. He did not look as if he had been up all night. His dark eyes were clear, his face had that look of sharp, foxy alertness Dan knew so well. He was neat, well groomed, everything the young executive should be. He nodded curtly to the assembled company, then made straight for Dan.

"News," he said.

Dan stood up, trying to appear curious. "News?"

"Can I have a private word?"

Dan shrugged. "Gentlemen, if you don't mind. Georgie'll look after you. Peter . . ."

The three of them retired to the study. Dan rested his back against the door. "Got it?"

"What else?" Bob produced several sheets of paper like rabbits from a hat. Peter took them, read quickly, nodded, and passed them to Dan. "We'll take a loss to start with, but we make it up later."

"After we get Ashe," Dan said.

"I was sweating I wouldn't get here in time."

"You could've phoned it," Peter remarked.

Dan shook his head. "Let him play the Seventh Cavalry if he wants."

Bob glowed under the boss's approval. "How's it been going, anyway?"

"I think Rolly wants our blood more than Dan's money," Peter said. "He's taking it all personally. When he finds out about this, he'll put two and two together."

"You been keeping them confused?"

"He's all over them." Dan folded the sheets and put them in his pocket. "That's it. Well done, you little bastard."

"That's the kind of praise I like," Bob said.

"Shall we go in?" Peter asked.

"Wait a minute longer. Ashe already smells something. Let it build."

Bob was almost hugging himself. He put a hand on Peter's shoulder. "I can't wait for this."

"Hold on to your enthusiasm for a minute," Peter said.

"And remember, when we go in there, try not to look too pleased with yourself. It's this man's life we're pulling out from under him."

"You're all heart." Bob assumed a poker face. "I'll try to look sympathetic to the old bugger."

Dan listened to them as indulgently as a father to his children. He yawned again. "Okay, let's get to it, boys."

They went back to the sitting room. Ashe was on his feet. His eyes were bloodshot.

"What's going on?" he demanded.

Dan, Peter, and Bob sat down. They were calm personified. Dan felt a surge of happiness.

"If you'd like to take a seat," Peter began.

"I'm fine here," Ashe said.

"Well, gentlemen, we've just had some news that rather changes things."

"What's he on about?" Ashe barked at Miller.

"I came over as soon as I heard," Bob joined in. "Thought you might know already."

"Get to it," Ashe growled. "I've had about all I can take tonight."

Peter coughed. "It would seem that your company has lost its contract with WonderBar."

Ashe jerked as if he had been shot. It took him a second to recover; then he snapped his fingers at Miller, who went off to the study. Dan relaxed against the couch, listening to Miller's hurried voice on the phone in there.

"We're not the only ones who've been up all night," Bob went on. "Seems a company by the name of Durrell-Eliot sneaked in behind your back and undercut you."

"I never heard of them," Ashe cried, casting around for someone to explain all this. Harker was examining his nails.

"Small American outfit," Bob said. He oozed sympathy. "Trying to start big in the U.K."

"Wait a minute." Ashe stepped close to him. He was a big, powerful man. "How d'you know all this?"

"I've got friends," Bob said blandly. "They thought I'd be interested in the news."

Ashe's face was dark. "I bet they bloody did."

Miller came out of the study. He was dumbstruck. Rubbing at his stubbled chin, he whispered a few words to his boss. Ashe muttered, "Christ Almighty," and sat down heavily. He remained there, alone on the couch, hardly moving. Miller hesitated for a moment, then sat too.

Dan waited for Peter to move in. He became aware that Peter was not speaking. He glanced across. Peter was staring at Ashe. Suddenly the extra age did not seem feigned. Bob noticed. He nudged Peter's arm.

Peter snapped out of it. "This obviously changes matters to a great degree," he said, readjusting his spectacles on his nose. "I think you'll find that our previous offer is now no less than exceedingly generous. After all, with the WonderBar contract gone, the present worth of your company drops twenty percent. In fact, it may make it very difficult to find a buyer at all."

There was near silence in the room. Roland Ashe was breathing hard.

"The question now is, does Mr. Ashe still want to sell?"

Miller looked at his boss. Ashe snarled: "I've bloody well got to, and they know it."

Peter was unruffled. He was back in normal gear; the expression of shock he had worn a moment before was gone. "So, I think, as long as we sort out the matter of the pension rights to our mutual satisfaction and you give the warranties I've asked for, our offer as made stands."

Ashe remained still. Then he bowed his head. He was beaten and he knew it. The word came out like a hiss of steam. "Yes."

There was no demonstration of triumph on Goldman's side. They all kept their peace. But Dan rose and went to the window, leaving Peter to deal with the paperwork. It was all over now.

"Georgie, will you send down for a full breakfast for me and anyone else who wants it," he said. "I'm hungry as hell."

Ashe stood up. "You bastard, Goldman."

The room was hushed again. Dan turned. "Pardon?"

"It's your fucking company, innit?" The Yorkshire accent made all the words ugly. "American firm," he sneered. "Durrell-Eliot, my arse. It's yours. You put 'em up to it. That's why you've been pratting me about all night—waiting to hear."

Dan shrugged. "Peter, do we have anything to do with Durrell-Eliot?"

"We've had some dealings with them, I believe."

"What a load of bullshite," Ashe said. "You'll get my business, still have the WonderBar contract through Durrell-Eliot, and do me out of ten million quid."

Bob was ready to grab Ashe if he tried anything, but Dan waved him off. "I've done nothing you wouldn't do if you had the chance."

"Mr. Ashe," Miller said faintly, "perhaps we ought to leave."

"I'll leave when I'm good and ready," Ashe said. There was spittle on his chin. "I'll get you, you bastard. No one does this to me. I'll get you."

He spun unsteadily on his heel and left the suite. The door slammed behind him. Miller and the legal adviser were left fidgeting.

"You guys better go," Dan said. "We'll deal with the paperwork later today when your boss sobers up."

When Ashe's men were gone, Georgie came up and shook all three of them by the hand. "If you were footballers, we'd've won the World Cup."

"Thanks to my team." Dan gave Peter and Bob a ghost of a bow.

"Your master plan," Bob said. "We're just your werry 'umble servants, Mr. Copperfield."

"My God," Georgie said, "he's showing a glimmer of culture."

He smiled charmingly at her. "Snotty bitch."

Dan touched Peter's arm. "You okay?"

"I was just thinking," Peter said. "When Ashe said he'd get you just now, he looked as if he meant it."

Sunshine was breaking through the window.

"What's to worry?" Dan said. "You ever hear of a York-shire Mafia?"

Over breakfast, Dan noticed two things. First, that Bob, despite being up all night like the rest of them, was bright and alert, while Peter looked absolutely shattered. Second, that Bob was having a hard time concealing how he felt about Georgie. He was unsure which bothered him more.

"So," he said, polishing off a plate of ham and eggs, "all we have to do is transfer the mule work, and we can all give our minds to the game."

"I hope you've been in training," Bob said, quaffing orange juice by the pint. "It's going to be hell out there."

Dan lifted his cup in a mock toast. "Peter, you ready for it?"

"What? . . . Oh, certainly. All I need is forty-eight hours sleep, and you'll suddenly realize I'm a fully primed killing machine."

"Watch out, Sylvester Stallone," Georgie said.

Peter stifled a yawn. He was still going over some of the paperwork. It lay before him among the debris of crockery and marmalade jars. Dan wished he would put it away.

"What's on the menu before I can call my time my own?" he asked Georgie.

She reeled it off from memory. "You have a lunch appointment with John Baxter and the new presenter on *After-noon People*. He wants to get your approval."

"I'm just the TV chef," he said.

"And a star to millions of ironing boards across the country," she replied. "Then *Options* want an interview at eleven thirty. And you're supposed to be meeting Harrison King for drinks at four."

"Okay. Cancel the *Options* thing. Tell them I've lost my voice." He pressed his palms against the table edge, pushing away. "See, drinks with Harrison at four. Can we all be down at the airfield by six this evening?"

The others nodded.

Bob got up from the table. "I'm going back to the office to set things up for next week. Georgie, want to get some exercise later?"

"I'll catch you in your office," she said.

Peter also rose. "I'd better follow suit. There's some things I ought to do."

"Forget it, Peter," Dan said. "Go home, get some sleep."

"But there's all this paper to be dealt with."

Dan reached across and took the pages. "I'll give them to Kevin. You did great. Go on."

Peter's shoulders sagged. He glanced at Bob, who looked that much younger and fresher beside him. He seemed to think about it for a long time. "All right," he said. "If you're sure."

"Sure I'm sure. Just wake up in time to catch the plane."

Bob and Peter left together. Bob was full of talk; Peter had little to say. Dan watched them leave, then resumed eating as Georgie came back from the hall. He felt that she could read what was on his mind.

She dumped a bundle on the table. "The morning mail," she said. "I had it brought over in case you don't have time to go back to the office."

"What begging letters do we have today?" he said.

"New York postmark," she said, tossing him a blue envelope. "Not your mother, is it?"

He opened the letter, flicked over its contents. "No," he muttered, and threw it back.

She picked it up. "Veterans' Association? . . . Oh, Vietnam. They want you to speak at their next convention. That's some sort of honor, isn't it?"

"I'll be busy," he said.

"It's not until next April."

"I gave a bundle to the VVMF," he said. "And I've been to the wall." This was a lie. He knew several of the names on that long chevron of black granite in Washington. But he had never visited it, any more than he sought the company of other veterans. It was so long ago: other guys might still be neurotic about it, but when he came back, he left it on the shelf. A year of his life was enough to have given. "Write them a polite refusal."

"Okay." She went on sorting the mail.

"And get on the phone and arrange the plane for six tonight," he added. "Then get Jack and tell him to have the car out front in twenty minutes."

"Yes, *sir*, Mr. Goldman."

5

THE SUN WAS UP OVER THE HILLS OF GLEN RHEISDALE WHEN
he arrived at the abandoned crofter's cottage. He pulled the
car into the shed beside it and switched off the engine. He
felt curiously peaceful inside. His ears still seemed to ring
from the gunshot in the close confines of the van. The bag
with the guns and the ammunition was on the seat beside
him.

He got out of the car, locked it, and went outside. The hills
were dark and shadowed beneath an overcast sky. He bent
to touch the rubble-strewn ground.

The rat had gone down looking so surprised. As if he had
never realized that a man who sells guns for a living is in a
dangerous profession. He laughed gently. The rat was small
time; he had served a purpose.

He reached in his pocket and took out the picture of Goldman and the girl. He held it by the edges, as someone who
is disgusted by spiders will hold a nature-book photograph
of a black widow.

—Preparation, he thought.

6

IT WAS STILL ONLY 8 A.M. WHEN DAN AND GEORGIE LEFT THE Dorchester. As the car took them into the Park Lane traffic, she said, "You do own Durrell-Eliot, don't you?"

"My dear girl," he said, unseriously pompous, "when you're as diverse as Goldoor, you can't keep track of everything. Maybe I do have a finger in their pie, maybe not. Who knows, who cares?"

"Roland Ashe," she said.

"Roland who?"

"I'm not being outraged or anything," she explained. "I'm just trying to learn."

"You planning to squeeze me out?"

"Not for a couple of years." She flicked her hair back. Her gaze was level. It was also beautiful, but she couldn't help that. He was just susceptible to gorgeous young women whose names were Georgina Lawrence.

"I wondered how you felt about it. Taking his business away," she said.

"Ah, the moral element."

She laughed. "You're making fun of me."

"Heaven forbid, dear. Who else could organize my time so well?" He rubbed his eyes. "If you're asking do I feel sorry for Ashe, sure I do. But it's a jungle out there, just like they tell you in all the books. Ashe has done all kinds of dirty things in his time. Anyway, you call fifty million pounds taking his business away, I wish someone could take a few things off me."

She leaned toward him. "Now you sound as if you'd pack it all in, given half the chance."

It was his turn to laugh, as he wondered how she had divined even this. "Are you kidding?" He put his head on one side. "I've been thinking about taking some time off, though."

"You take a holiday? I don't believe it."

"No. More than that." He watched the cars jostling near the windows. "You know, I started in on this nearly twenty years ago, and I never really took a break since then. You can get tired even of being a millionaire."

"When I become one, I'll let you know."

"There's all kinds of things I wanted to do back then. I thought I'd get a little cash together, then take some time off. Do a little traveling maybe."

"You travel all the time."

"From one meeting to another. You know why I bought Scorba?"

"Tell me. I'll put it in your biography."

He was amused at the memory. "Because it's on the Northwest of Scotland, and Mama's name is Campbell, and I had some crazy ideas about living on an island for a while."

She did not laugh at him. He had half expected it, but she just waited for him to continue.

"Sounds dumb, right? But scratch a city kid and you get a guy who wants some space around him and a boat to sail and all that horseshit—Pardon me."

"No matter," she said.

He found himself talking on. It was not something he should have been discussing with anyone yet. But he wanted to tell Georgie more than anyone. "In fact, I've been thinking about putting it all into practice sometime soon. The new year, maybe."

"But you wouldn't sell up, would you?"

"Not at all. But it's no big thing for the head of a company to take a couple of years off, even semiretire."

"Who runs things for him?"

"The best men he's got. They keep it all running smooth,

and he just puts his nose in when a big deal has to be made. Call it a lessening of the workload."

She sat there, biting her lip. "Are you serious?"

He raised his arms helplessly. "How should I know? Maybe, maybe not. After a bout like last night, everyone thinks about a hut in the South Seas. But I've been thinking it over, wondering who I'd trust to look after it while I'm gone."

"It'd be Peter, wouldn't it?" she said.

He found himself avoiding her eyes. "Yeah . . . I guess so." He thought of Peter's slipups through the night, his tiredness this morning.

She turned glum.

"What's the matter?" he asked.

"I just thought. If you go off on an extended holiday, what becomes of me?"

He was sure he blushed as he said: "I'd still need you." Then, after a short pause: "Good P.A.s are hard to find."

"Two compliments in the same morning," she said. "I like you when you've succeeded."

"What was Bob saying about exercise?" he said.

"Oh, jogging. He hates to run alone. No one to compete with."

"Oh," he said. He settled back in his seat. Now he was annoyed as well as worried. Annoyed because Georgie made him feel and behave like some kid. Worried because he was more serious about taking some time off than he let on, and this trip to the survival game was beginning to look as if it would be less about fun, more about using it as one more way of judging Peter and Bob's potential for heading Goldoor while he was away. He had always thought Peter, but lately doubt was setting in.

There was an increasing possibility that someone would get hurt by this weekend.

7

HE LAY ON A HILL WITH A LINE OF FIR TREES BEHIND HIM and watched over the town and the shallow bay where it sheltered from the Atlantic winds. The morning was fine and dry. Heavy clouds were etched into an arid blue sky. The jumbled rows of graystone cottages shone in the northern light. It was very peaceful, lying there randomly against the dark green rises of the land, the sudden rips and outcrops of the cliffs to the north. He could see it all: the road going down to the harbor and the narrow lanes that came off it. Two cars stood outside the post office. Some men were down on the shore, working by a red fishing boat. It was not what an Englishman would have called a town. More of a hamlet, a few houses making their stand against the bitter Highland weather. Nor did it possess the kind of beauty tourists used to come looking for. But it was beautiful, all the same. Like a sword or a gun.

He took his field glasses and focused on the largest building in sight. It was a three-story Victorian house, neo-Georgian style. It rose on a hill above the town like a minor attempt at a castle. It had always dominated the scene, but recent changes made it stand out more than ever. Wings had been added, modern extensions increased its size. It was fresh-painted white, windows gleaming. The gardens were landscaped, and several old cottages had been demolished to make a better car park. On the street running down from it new shops were open.

He looked from the hotel to the bay, where one small party of men toiled by their lone fishing boat.

Guns began to sound in his head. Faintly, far away, like the rumor of battle. No louder than the gulls scudding high in the cold sky.

—Calm, he told himself. Calm.

But he could already smell death in the air.

8

AFTER MAKING LOVE, BOB AND GEORGIE LEFT HIS FLAT AND started jogging toward Regent's Park. It was eleven-thirty.

"You know, you're going to have to develop your technique," she said.

It came out of the blue. He was astounded. "What?"

"Your sexual technique, big boy." Her tone was sarcastic, to say the least.

He was not up to this kind of thing so soon after bed. "Nobody's complained before," he said.

"If you will sleep with virgins to avoid comparison . . ."

He turned toward her as they sauntered up Devonshire Place and turned left. "Do you have to start that here?"

"Don't be such a prude," she said. She was mocking him.

Marylebone Road was clogged with traffic. They crossed, went easily along by the Royal Academy of Music, and turned in through York Gate. The air was cool and misty with last night's rain. An old geezer with a bicycle stared into the water below York Bridge, looking for fish.

"Anyway," he came back on the attack, "I might have more technique if you ever let me do anything."

"If you don't like it, you know what to do," she said.

He picked up speed. She was deliberately needling him. He could not figure her out. He never could. She enjoyed herself in bed with him—seemed to, anyway. If he rarely did anything inspired, it was because she did not allow it. Her and her drawer full of gloves and her tart act. Why did she start up like this all the time?

He had never meant to get close to Georgie at all. The first months she was around, they were as cold and distant as they could be. He figured her for some empty-headed glamour girl playing up to Dan's infatuation. Then he began to respect her work: she could organize a hurricane. As for the thing with men, she would have the same effect if she went around in a sack, but she played up to it like murder. Especially when she was alone with him.

The sense of challenge she threw out had finally overcome his resistance a few months back. They slept together fairly often. He had no idea what she thought of him. Sometimes she was warm and tender, other times as cold as if he were paying for her. He would not for anything have her know it, but she had him very confused.

Such confusion fitted badly with his upbringing and attitudes: military tradition and a life-style that placed heavy emphasis on manly domination. He did not actually join the army. After he was deported from the United States for a minor drug offense, when his father was military attaché at the embassy there, he declared that the real cut and thrust of the modern world was in business. His father, relieved that he showed any kind of direction, used family contacts to get him started.

Later, having proved that it was more than a passing whim, Bob went to Goldoor. He had been going from strength to strength ever since.

Georgie left him alone as they ran to the Inner Circle. He began to get into it, the good, hard feeling of running with the rush of the city around him. He forgot business and determined not to go home until he had covered at least five miles. He needed to clear his body of the bad air accumulated in the all-night wrangling to get the WonderBar contract.

They circled Queen Mary's Gardens, cut off over the lake to the southwest, and turned right onto the Outer Circle by the zoo. A few leaves sifted down as they passed. Georgie tried to get ahead of him.

He was nuts to mess with her anyway. By rights, she was Dan's. Except Dan seemed to have problems getting at her. He worried that Dan would find out what was going on, but Bob could not stop it. Of course, it never occurred to him that she should not belong to somebody. That was also part of his upbringing.

As they passed the zoo's main entrance, Georgie said, "Did you know Dan's thinking of taking a sabbatical?"

"You must be joking," he panted.

"You don't think so?"

"He'll never pack it in. He loves it more than my old man loved the army."

"You're full of opinions this morning. Must be getting that contract."

"While you were kipping down at the Dorchester, some of us were putting in the hours, Georgie Porgie."

"Don't call me that!" she snapped. Her reaction to the nickname was, as usual, way over the top. There was something weird about her, he was sure of it. One thing to Dan, another to Peter. If he had been given to deep contemplation, he might have tried harder to find out.

He kicked enough to put himself out in front. Sebastian Coe versus the world. No competition.

She came up behind him, legs beating the tarmac, breathing evenly. And passed him.

Bob started to get annoyed. She gave him a sneaky little smile as she overtook. Not on at all. No woman in a yellow track suit was going to run him out.

He poured on more speed and began to pull up on her. Closing in on Gloucester Gate, he drew alongside.

"Bandstand?" he suggested.

Georgie nodded. "But don't wear yourself out, big boy."

He dodged right at the second turn, leaving her the Outer Circle. He figured the distance by separate paths would be about the same. They pounded away from each other, dodging the strollers. Turning the corner by the zoo, he glanced across and saw her through the trees, running parallel by the

Danish Church. Now it was truly a race, and neither was trying to hide it anymore. Last one to the bandstand was a loser.

They almost collided as they hit Chester Road, ran neck and neck for Queen Mary's Gardens, split again to take different halves of the Inner Circle. He poured on the speed, forced his breathing to remain steady, keeping a rhythm. The warmth of exercise spread through his body. He passed the open-air theater, looking to see Georgie reappear on the sweeping curve of the road.

There she was. Both of them swerved through the gap in the railings, past the ice-cream kiosk toward the bandstand. Georgie was flagging, while he still had something in reserve. This would teach her a lesson.

He was all ready to let it loose—when she just pulled up. He wanted to go on and touch the railings by the stand with a whoop of triumph, but there was no point. Not with her standing by, resting easy and taking in the interested stares of passing men. He faltered and came to a halt, feeling as frustrated somehow as he did when she refused to let him touch her in bed.

She approached him with that superior smile all over her face. He met her, bent over and catching his breath.

"You bitch," he panted. "You . . ." The words failed him.

"Come on," she said. "If you're good, I'll buy you an orange juice."

As she drove home to change and pick up her gear for the weekend, Georgie tried not to think of everything, but felt her mind beginning to turn in the same tight circle as always. There were times when her head almost burst with it, but she never showed it, not even to herself. She drove toward her flat through the teeming traffic, completely alone.

The recent sight and sound of Bob enjoying himself hung in her mind. He was so obsessed with looks that he never questioned the things that happened between them. Why did she treat him like that, why did she play the Queen Whore to him? Why bother at all? He was as shallow as a plate, but charming in his own way; he was a bit of a bastard. Maybe that was it: they were equally worthless, so it did not matter what they got up to. Except it did matter. She rubbed her hands on the steering wheel, reminding herself to take more gloves with her to Scotland. If there was to be any bedroom contact between them, she wanted to make sure she had gloves. He could think whatever he liked about her wearing them to bed. She knew the real reason.

She had Bob where she could control him, although she wanted nothing of him, and she knew how Dan felt about her. But she would not let anything happen with him. It was nothing to do with pride or fastidiousness about using a relationship with the boss to further her career: Dan just did not deserve to be stuck with her, not the way she was. He was better than that.

Stopped at traffic lights, she used the driving mirror to study her makeup. Naked eyes stared at her through the careful composition of her face.

"Daddy's pretty girl," she whispered, and wanted to wash all Bob's sweat and sex from her skin.

The lights changed. She felt worse and worse.

—Go and see Peter, she thought. He should be awake by the time you're ready. Go and see him.

The idea lifted her spirits a little. She put her foot down.

9

ALL AFTERNOON, IN A WIDE DESERTED STRETCH OF HILLS above the River Aude, he concentrated on getting the rifle zeroed in. A low wind moaned in from the ocean. The sky was full of voices.

He used a flat-faced outcrop of granite on a steep rise for a target. He marked rough circles with chalk, then walked back two hundred yards to try the rifle, checking between each shot to see how high, low, or wide it was. When he had zeroed in, he proceeded to find out what the effective range actually was. He walked back ten yards for each shot. At three hundred yards he was still hitting the inner circle, which was the size of a man's head. At three hundred and ten it was less certain.

Good enough, though.

10

PETER HAD NO IDEA HE WAS ABOUT TO BE SHOT. HE SAT IN his workshop at the bottom of the garden, surrounded by gleam and rust. The frame and engine parts of a 1923 Norton motorcycle were piled in one corner. In others were pieces from various machines, picked up from junkyards and garages all over the country. These were the raw materials of his hobby, which was the restoration of vintage motorcycles. A fan heater pumped out warmth to take the chill off the air, filling the cramped space with the smell of oil. An old cassette recorder on the bench played middle-fifties Sinatra classics. He could have afforded more comfortable surroundings, but this was his little corner of peace. It reminded him of the shed where he and his father used to tinker with machinery when he was a kid. If he needed to relax, this was where he came. And he needed to now. Ashe's face when he knew the truth was on his mind.

He was sitting at the workbench, spectacles on the end of his nose, cleaning the Norton's carburetor. So he did not hear the workshop door open behind him.

He picked up a small pin and stuck it through the needle jet, working the dirt out.

The door continued to open gradually. An inch, two inches. Damp air disturbed shreds of cloth on the floor.

Peter bent his head over the valve, turning the float unit gently in his fingers. Brass gleamed in the lamplight.

Under cover of Sinatra's rendition of "Pennies from Heaven," the door gaped wider.

"Ah, that's got you," he said. He reached for a clean rag.

A gun barrel slipped into the gap between door and jamb. The blue metal of a .44 Magnum glimmered. It rose slowly until it pointed at a spot between Peter's shoulder blades.

He replaced the float unit on the bench and leaned back, stretching lazily.

The hand holding the gun trembled for a second, then steadied. The forefinger applied pressure. It pulled the trigger.

Peter had time to grunt in surprise. He fell forward on the bench, scattering the parts and a coffee cup on the floor.

"You're hopeless," Georgie said. She stepped into the workshop, laughing.

Peter levered himself off the bench, glaring at her.

"You lunatic. If you were Sarah or Liz, I'd put you over my knee."

"Threats, threats." She wagged the gun at him. "I wanted to see how your reactions are. You won't last five minutes tomorrow, you know."

"And you won't last five minutes today, if you do that again." He took off the dirty anorak he wore in the workshop and studied the bright scarlet paint splash down the back. He was annoyed, but pleased to see her. "What a child you are."

"Pretty hot shooting, though?" She stood like a naughty schoolgirl waiting to be told off.

"Bob would be proud of you." He took the gun from her. It was a very good replica of the Magnum handgun. "It is his, isn't it?"

"I stole it from him—in his office this morning. He wants to take it to Scorba."

"We're not allowed to take our own guns, my dear. If we were, I'd borrow a twelve-bore and make a decent shoot of it."

"Oh, you don't go shooting. You're too gentle."

"Rubbish. Haven't you noticed I beat my wife and children?"

"That'll be the day."

He hung the anorak on a nail and bent down to search for the float unit. "Tell you what you could do for me."

She played the child again: "Yes, Daddy?"

"Go into the house, make me a large cup of coffee—even have one yourself if you must—and bring it out here for me."

"I don't think that's in my contract."

"I said please."

"No, you didn't."

"Go, child, before I put you over my knee anyway."

She bowed out, leaving him feeling rather happier than he had been before she arrived.

He had been out in the shed for several hours. "Go home, get some sleep," Dan had said, and he had gone. But he had known he shouldn't all along, so he could not rest when he got there. After spending a fitful morning in bed, he had come out here and started eating away at himself.

He kept thinking about Bob's little performance with the WonderBar contract. How young he had looked, how much like some predatory beast in its prime. And Bob had performed brilliantly, while he had made mistakes. Only small ones, yes. But mistakes nonetheless. And then to sit there paralyzed with sympathy for Ashe when the trick was turned. Dan had noticed. He had sent him home.

—Why did you do it? What's it to you if Ashe goes down? You should have gone back to the office and done what needed to be done. Not retired the field like some old man.

He knew he was obsessed by the comparison between himself and Bob. He tried not to be, but couldn't help it. He sensed that Dan was watching, that Bob was trying to do him down.

He had always hoped it could be otherwise. He had recommended Dan to take the boy on in the first place. They worked so well together in the beginning, when Dan was expanding into the U.K. Bob was like a pupil being shown the ropes. He had grasped everything so fast. Peter would never have admitted it to his wife or children, but he enjoyed the almost father-son relationship they had.

—Showing him the ropes? he thought. Rather accurate. Is it any surprise that he's trying to hang you with them now?

He heard Georgie call from the house: "Nearly ready."

What was wrong with him? It was part of the system. Your

subordinates were no good to you unless they wanted your job. Any bloody fool who didn't catch on to that lasted about five minutes. When he started in the offices of a catering firm twenty-nine years ago, he had waited his turn with all the other young men. Except he had a little more drive. He put in the hours and was noticed. When he rose, he did so on the back of a superior, who had, as the old saying goes, been promoted to the level of his own incompetence. That had been all right, because he was young and hungry to get out of the dreary streets of his childhood, and the manager was some old fool of fifty.

—I'm forty-eight now, he thought. He was thinking it a lot lately. I'm forty-eight years old and Dan is forty, and Bob is twenty-eight.

No matter how many times he told himself that he was fine, that Dan knew how much his experience and knowledge of Goldoor was worth, he kept coming back to the numbers. Bob was twenty-eight.

"Coffee," Georgie said. She kicked the door shut and carried the cups in. "Are you still looking for your bits? Sorry."

He growled, "Never mind," and went on searching.

She sat on the edge of the bench. "Where is everyone? I wanted Sarah to join in shooting you."

"Vickie's gone down to Oxford Street to ill-treat the credit cards. Sarah, I hope, is studying hard at college. Liz is at school."

"We're all alone?" she said. "The neighbors may talk."

"You're here so much I tell them you're my long-lost third daughter."

"You don't mind me coming, do you?" She sounded almost anxious.

"Of course not. Anyone who can stand this family is welcome to it."

"Well, I like it."

"Quite a mutual admiration society, aren't we?" He bumped his head on the bench.

She took a survival-game brochure from her jeans pocket and perused it. "Do you understand the game?"

"It's Capture the Flag, isn't it?"

"It says here it's the ultimate thrill."

He straightened up, rubbing his head. "I rather hoped there was more to life."

"Want to know more about Scorba?"

"As long as there's brandy and a hot bath afterwards, I don't care."

"You sound as if you'd rather stay at home."

He sipped his coffee. "Not at all, not at all. Everyone should relax after a demanding year by running about the Highlands in army surplus boots."

She lifted the gun. "Bob can't wait."

"Bob is naturally disposed to the physical jerk side of life. I'm more suited to the contemplative. As for you, child, I hope you fall in a bog."

"Thank you very much."

"I'll push you myself, if necessary." He felt better for this playful talk with Georgie. It was rather like the conversations he had with Liz and Sarah. Playing the old curmudgeon improved his humor. Most of the time, anyway.

"All I'll say about survival games," he remarked, "is what my eldest daughter said when she heard I was going along. There's something creepy about the idea of grown men playing soldiers, she feels. It encourages violence and leads people like—say Bob—to think that war is just a huge adventure playground. She thinks there's something fascist about it. Then again, she's at that age."

Georgie sighed. "Maybe she's right." Then a twinkle came into her eye. "What's the time?"

Sighing indulgently, he took out the half-hunter pocket watch that traveled with him always. It was an exquisite nineteenth-century gold timepiece. Tiny emeralds marked the Roman numeral hours. Engraved inside were the words:

TO PETER
INSTEAD OF A RING
LOVE, VICKIE

As Georgie leaned closer to admire it, he ran his thumb

over the tiny scratches that crisscrossed the words. It had belonged to Vickie's grandfather, who liked Peter a great deal. The scratches were Sarah's attempt, when she was three years old, to add her own inscription. According to Sarah then, and ever since, they actually meant: "I love you, from Sarah." Over the years, they had come to mean as much as the original inscription.

"That's a beautiful thing," Georgie murmured.

"You say that every time you see it," he said. "You also never fail to ask me the time, despite the fact that you're wearing several hundred pounds' worth of Patek Philippe on your wrist."

"I like antique timepieces," she said defensively.

"You're a magpie."

She was disconcerted. He missed it. "Who says so?"

"Vickie does."

Her poise slipped another half degree. "Why?"

He continued insensitive. "It was just something she said. You like pretty things."

"I do not."

"You do. If this watch wasn't chained to my belt, you'd be away with it."

"That's not true!" she said. "I'd never hurt you. Not any of you."

He finally realized. Something naked and terribly hurt was in her eyes. His immediate thought was to do what he would have done if she were Sarah or Liz: take her in his arms and say sorry. But she was not his daughter. At the moment he should have said something, he felt most uncomfortable, most incapable of breaking out of the reticence that childhood training and her attractiveness printed into him.

As if they were someone else's, he saw his hands rise, mock-defensively. "Only joking, you know."

She was not mollified. She turned away and brooded over the survival-game brochure again. He began sorting the intricate pieces of the carburetor, abruptly recalling what Vickie had said about Georgie after they first met. They were lying in bed in the dark, talking as they often did after the day was over.

"She's a nice girl," Vickie said. "At least, I think she's nice. But she makes me feel . . . uncomfortable."

He was unwise enough to suggest that his wife did not like the competition of another beautiful woman. Vickie looked down her nose.

"Not at all," she said frostily. "But she tries so hard to make everyone love her. Especially—"

"Especially who?"

"Men. It's as if she can't stand anyone not lusting after her."

"Even me?" He raised his eyebrows.

"Not you."

"Thank you." Now *he* was offended.

"You don't understand. I'd say she had a crush on you—"

"Oh, please . . ." he cried, secretly rather flattered.

" but she's not the type."

"What type is she, darling?"

"I don't know. What's her family like?"

"I don't think she ever mentioned them."

"Mmm."

"Perhaps it's just that she's young and unsure of herself. Last year, she was a university graduate in an uncertain world, now she's personal assistant to a millionaire. Didn't you want everyone to love you at her age?"

"Do other women—at work and so on—do they like her?"

"I think so. I don't know . . . Perhaps not all of them. Why are we talking so much about her?"

Vickie rolled into his arms. "No reason. Let's go to sleep."

Since then, Vickie had obviously overcome any reservations. Georgie was a regular visitor. His crack about her being his third daughter could have been serious. But Vickie's initial reaction had stuck in his mind. He thought of it at times like this.

He shoveled all the machine parts into a drawer.

"I could do with another coffee," he said.

She pored over the brochure. "Fine. I ought to be going."

"I thought we were driving out to the airfield together? It's half-past three, by the way."

"Good."

In his discomfort, he fell back on fatherly authority. "Georgie. Stop sulking."

It worked. She grabbed the gun and waved it at him. "Promise not to be a grouch over the weekend."

He considered the coming days with less enthusiasm than he should have mustered. "As you wish, my child." He gave her his cup and set about tidying the shop. She went back to the house, leaving him with his own preoccupations.

Such as how to stay cheerful when the whole weekend was putting his neck on the block?

11

DANIEL GOLDMAN, GEORGINA LAWRENCE, PETER BAILEY, AND Bob Townsend were at the airfield by six that evening. They were in Dan's Edinburgh apartments for a late dinner by nine, and in their beds by eleven. Tomorrow was an early start. They needed all the rest they could get: they were going to war.

And out in the dark, drizzling night of the west coast, sleeping restlessly in his car, one man in army uniform with a Russian assault rifle by his side.

They were going to war.

2

Phony War

12

THE WATCHER ON THE SHORE THOUGHT ABOUT THE KILLING
he had to do.

He touched the focusing wheel on his Zeiss field glasses
and brought the image up as sharp as the early-morning mist
would allow. The two men on the island were over a mile
away across the sea, but he knew who they were. Williamson, the head warden, dressed in an imitation of army combat gear, was talking to the boatman. The boatman sat in a
peeling sixteen-foot dory, mending something. They were on
the end of the jetty, and the jetty stuck out from the island
into the sound, and there was no one else in sight.

Which was just as it should be.

He put the glasses down and wiped a thin sheen of drop-
lets from his face. He was huddled into a cleft in the rocks.
The cold, plus the icy, windblown mist, made things pretty
uncomfortable.

—So, big deal. What were you trained for anyway? You
don't go off to battle expecting central-heated foxholes and a
coffee machine in every dugout.

Waiting had never been his game, especially waiting for
action to commence.

The thought of coffee made him twist round in the
cramped hiding place and reach for his gear. He took out a
Thermos and poured himself a cup. The coffee had the
strange, creamy taste that a Thermos always gives it, but it
was hot and it warmed him all the way down as he sat there,
blinking the little needles of moisture out of his eyes.

The sky was gray almost to black in the north, although the sun had been up for half an hour. He had seen that kind of sky before, clouds swollen and racing by on high winds above. Hard rain would come before the weekend was over but, with luck, not until his business with Mr. Goldman and friends was finished. The rain might add an interesting element to certain aspects of the hunting, but it would also reduce visibility. When you were hoping for a large proportion of kills with a rifle, you needed all the clear weather you could get. So the clouds must carry on scudding overhead, threatening all they liked, but not let go. Not for a little while.

Sipping the coffee, he stuck his head out of cover to check the terrain. There was no chance he would be seen from the island. He glanced round quickly, eyes passing over everything in sight.

He saw what had been there before men came from Ireland with flint arrows and tools stuck in their reindeer belts. Old Gaelic legends said that when God finished making Britain, a few crumbs of earth and stone were left in his apron. Like any craftsman when the work is done, he flicked them out, and they fell into the western sea, making the islands of Argyll and Bute. It was a story he liked to believe. Looking out from the bare hillside, he could see the shores of five islands. To be precise, he stood on one himself. Laing was joined to the mainland by no more than a bridge, but the strait was so narrow that no one thought of Laing as any more than a narrow peninsula. To south and north was gray-green coastline, formed and scarred by glaciers, not a sign of human presence. The low, crippled hump of the tiny outcrop, Rubh Aird Laing, marked the peninsula's southern tip. A hundred feet down the hill was the rough track that formed Laing's only road, the way back to Baldrick. Wardens' cars were parked haphazardly in a graveled clearing. A sign by the landing stage said: KINLOSCH FERRY—TO ISLE OF SCORBA SURVIVAL GAME. After that it was the sea, the heavy, freezing expanse of the ocean. It thundered down the Sound of Laing, scouring the peninsula and all the islands on the other

side; rolled into the Sound of Jora, brushing the great mainland forest of Knapdale; and later the seven tides that met at
Mull of Kintyre would beat the sea up the channel once
more. Its voice was a low, constant mutter, like the words of
the dead from the mountains. All his life he had been hearing them.

Only Scorba showed itself to be an island. The rest were
tumbled close together, but Scorba crouched like a dog ready
to fight. Tall and ragged to the north, smoother with the
coarse grass of the moors in the southeast. It rose steeply,
sides clad with the deep green of conifers, to a finger of stone
at the summit. It looked small, but that was a trick of the
weather. It had been big enough, a long time ago, for people
to scratch a living. Thirteen hundred years before, the Gaelic-
speaking Scotti had colonized it, and their descendants
carved the intricately marked crosses that signaled God's
ownership. Norsemen came raiding in their dragon ships. For
centuries afterward the island lay under the rule of warring
clans. Then came the clearances, crofters evicted to make
way for sheep. A mad old laird built the folly, tried to establish a religious retreat. And now it would be large enough to
hold a battleground and a graveyard.

He closed his eyes. The wind cut over his hiding place. He
was safe from that. But sitting in the cold and dark for so long
had given him pain behind the eyes that got worse when he
thought of the enemy. He held on to the ache as it spread
through his skull, drumming in his ears. This was the old
problem. Worse lately. It never left him alone anymore.

—You're in control, he told himself. You have the hang of
it now, you can deal with it. Get back in line and stop
bellyaching.

It began to move off. He screwed the cap back on the
Thermos and put it away. His hand lingered for a second on
the working parts of the rifle, which was broken down, ready
for assembly. He ran his fingers over the smooth, oiled surface of the barrel, watched the island and the two figures on
the jetty. They were only flickers of movement without the
field glasses. It was tempting to put the rifle together now,

but that was against orders. And no well-laid plan of attack was worth a bag of shit if some element went off before orders. By the book was the way to play it. Besides, he was not thinking well. He could not reach the island with a crummy Russian rifle. Not even with the old L1A1.

He left the gun and picked up the glasses. It was 0731 hours Zulu Time, and he figured the guests of honor would arrive soon. Not like the Yank to rise late, and he would not let his arse lickers do any different. They would all be running in circles, chewing their tails off to please the big man. Those idiots on the island had come before first light.

"When the big chief's around, all the Indians start dancing."

That was something Goldman had said, on one of those television shows where his grinning, deceiving face could often be seen. Another of the sayings of Big Chief Goldman, which he remembered like everything else about the bastard, was: "I like to be up early, so nobody can surprise me."

—Well, Mr. Goldman, he thought, flexing his cold fingers, this morning I was up really early, and I've got a fucking surprise for you.

13

"THEY'VE PICKED A BLOODY ROUGH DAY FOR A WAR," LOGAN said, chewing thoughtfully on a cud of tobacco big enough to sink a yacht. He had a sour, meaty face that looked as if it had been rammed by a trawler.

Williamson pulled his collar up against the wind and lit another cigarette. "Looks fine to me," he said.

"To you it would, aye." Logan spat a clot of brown juice at the water, watched it thin and disappear. "You don't know yon weather from your backside."

"Maybe it'll rain off the VIPs—the weather, I mean, not my backside."

"VIPs," Logan growled disgustedly. "All this bloody malarkey for the boss."

"Never mind that, Jocky." Williamson grinned. "You just make sure he doesn't notice that fishing gear of yours. Don't want our esteemed owner seeing that you can't forget your glorious seafaring past, do we?"

Logan's scarred old fingers worked in his net. "It's nae fit work for a man," he muttered. His leathery face crinkled up until his eyes disappeared. "Nae, it's not."

Williamson laughed. "You old sod. You've got it damned sweet down here. A little bit of ferrying, little bit of private enterprise with the fishing, then home to the old woman for tea. You try it up there with the customers some time. It's like basic training every bloody day."

The boatman scowled under his cap. "Soldier boy."

Williamson left the old man mumbling about his forty years fishing off Colonsay and Mull, and sauntered back up to the lodge. He drew the last half-inch from his cigarette and threw the butt away, ran a practiced eye over everything. The lodge was spick and span from a recent coat of paint, the parade ground—a partially concreted clearing beneath the trees behind—was nice and tidy. All was well.

Just then, MacNeice came out from behind the generator shed. The sight of the big, brawny Scot with the sensitive face put his teeth on edge.

"What've you got there?" he called.

MacNeice came toward him with cupped hands outstretched. "A wee rabbit," he said.

Williamson eyed the tattered mess of fur and blood. "Looks as if it was in a fight."

"Kestrel dropped him," MacNeice said.

Williamson stared. He was sure there were tears in MacNeice's eyes. He felt his irritation growing. How could anyone so big, who looked so right in the warden's uniform, be such a damned sissy? MacNeice was all conservation and birdwatching.

"Well, get rid of it, there's a good man," Williamson said. "Somewhere out of the way. Don't want important guests fainting at the sight of gore, do we?"

"It's a shame," MacNeice said.

"You're the one who's all for nature in the raw, aren't you? Can't get much rawer than that."

"I hate to see a little thing die, that's all."

Williamson flexed his hands. "Couldn't agree more. By the way, did you get up to the cliff path yesterday?"

MacNeice went on gazing at the rabbit's body. "There wasn't the time."

Williamson tutted. "Well, that's no bloody excuse. If some big wheel falls in the sea because we forgot a bit of fencing, we'll look pretty stupid, won't we? You'd better get up there now and deal with it."

"Won't I miss them arriving, then?" MacNeice said.

Williamson looked at the big man with his hands tenderly covering the dead rabbit and felt a sense of hopelessness rolling over him.

"I'm certain we can manage without you."

"Well, all right."

"Good God, man, will you put that rabbit somewhere before you stain your uniform."

MacNeice nodded sadly. "All right."

MacNeice watched his boss walk briskly away. He smiled faintly. He took the rabbit off into the trees and buried it quickly in the shallow earth. He whistled gently to himself.

From the first day, Williamson had shown a particular sort of condescension for him. He was always talking about teachers knowing more of theory than fact. He always gave MacNeice the dirty jobs. If a safety fence was needed on a dangerous bit of cliff, or a carcass had to be removed from the rocks—it happened now and then; a cow or sheep would float up on the tide from the mainland— you could guarantee Williamson would give it to MacNeice with an insulting grin and some snide comment. "Oh, MacNeice can handle that. He's seen service with Her Majesty's Finest— What comprehensive was it, MacNeice?" That hurt a bit; the only reason he had given up teaching was the low pay. He still regretted it sometimes. Better to teach physical education to growing lads than watch flabby businessmen fall about in the heather. But then there were Mrs. MacNeice and the three kids at home, and his wife was still a teacher. So he bore the taunts with stolid dignity.

It had taken him a while to get Williamson's measure, but he knew how to handle him now; pretend you didn't want to do something, and he would make you do it. There was a lot of the child in the Englishman's behavior, and MacNeice prided himself on knowing how children thought. So, unwittingly, Williamson had told him to go and do exactly what he wanted to do.

He checked his binoculars, made sure his pencil and

notebook were secure in his pocket. He could be up on the cliffs in something over an hour and get in a good spot of birdwatching before returning to join the VIPs.

He scratched his head. Williamson and the others, they were all right, but they missed the beauty of the island. To them, it was a job. He saw himself as an unofficial representative of those who cared about nature. Hadn't Mr. Goldman himself, in one of those magazine articles, declared that he wanted the island environment to be undamaged? That was what he, MacNeice, was there to ensure.

He started off for the cliffs, whistling happily but still quietly mourning the rabbit.

Williamson went inside the lodge, down to the staff room, sniffing a rich odor of bacon and eggs. The other wardens were lounging around, reading papers, listening to the radio.

"What a heartwarming scene of domestic bliss," he said, smiling beatifically upon them. "Everyone comfortable, are they?"

Ellis, the Welshman, paused in chewing on his bacon to nod.

"I'm so pleased, lads," Williamson said. "Big man's arriving in the next ten minutes, so let's bully the place up a bit, clear?" There was a relaxed buzz of agreement. Williamson did not think this was quite enough. "Smarten up!" he roared. "PDQ."

Everyone moved at once.

He walked back to his office and sat down at the green metal desk where he did the little paperwork that was required of him. He opened a drawer, pleased with his display of authority. He could still muster up the old power when necessary. Civvy street had not taken it away. He poured himself half a cup of brandy and gargled it deep in his throat before swallowing. Then he considered the level in the bottle, poured another one, and went over the message from the hotel once more:

FRIDAY—OCTOBER 8
MR. GOLDMAN AND PARTY ARRIVING FROM EDIN-
BURGH BY AIR APPROXIMATELY SEVEN THIRTY SATUR-
DAY MORNING. PLEASE ENSURE FULL COMPLEMENT
OF STAFF ON SCORBA FOR PLAYING OF SURVIVAL
GAME.
REGARDS
GEORGINA LAWRENCE
P. P. DANIEL GOLDMAN

He gazed out of the small leaded window at the craggy hill
above the lodge. Coming in by air, was he? Well, it would
be bloody interesting trying to put a helicopter down around
here. Of course, it was just like Mr. D. Goldman to fly in, instead of driving out from the hotel like normal people. And
all this rot about a full complement of staff—for four people.
There was nothing to be done, so far as Williamson was concerned, with Americans. Especially Americans who had
come up from Brooklyn or the Bronx or wherever it was
Goldman had come from. They would flash their wealth at
you until you were sick, and still drag out more to impress
you with. It was the upbringing.

Williamson himself, being the child of an old English
family that had, of recent years, been somewhat short of cash,
knew all about being discreet where money was concerned.
Throughout his expensive private schooling, training at
Sandhurst, and stint in Her Majesty's forces, you would never
have guessed that his old pater was straining every bloody
nerve to find the readies.

And here he was, after a fairly distinguished ten years in
service of his country, reduced to drawing a salary from D.
Goldman, Esquire, Britain's favorite American.

—Not my bloody favorite, he thought, swigging the brandy
and fumbling for his cigarettes again. He may please the ladies on afternoon television with that smooth act, but we'll
see just how hot he is today. Once I get him and his execu-

tive types out in the field, we'll soon see if he's got any legs for hard slog, or whether it's all put-up stuff.

Richardson barged into the office with the sugar tin in his hand. "'Scuse me, Nick."

Williamson frowned at the familiarity. He also hid the brandy bottle. "What is it?"

"I think they're here. Plane's coming in from the east."

"Plane?" He grabbed his beret. "Let's get to it, then."

14

THE PLANE, A RESTORED DE HAVILLAND OF CANADA DHC-6 Twin Otter seaplane, came in over the hills. It had been audible for some time but the watcher, waiting on the hill above the ferry, was still surprised when he saw it. He had expected a helicopter or a power boat, something in keeping with Goldman's image. He had forgotten those articles in the Sunday magazines about the man's love of old airplanes.

It banked over Loch Milfort toward him. He followed it through his field glasses, beginning to tense up the way he always did when an attack was about to start. His heart beat faster, starting the ache and the noise again.

The plane roared overhead some way up the shore. It was still high. He remembered another sight like this—the overcast sky; wind cutting fast across heavy seas; cruel, treeless waste of mainland. It made him smile bitterly. Plenty of people had died there too. The difference was that this time only the bad guys would get it.

15

"WILL YOU LOOK AT THAT," BOB YELLED, PUTTING HIS CAMERA right up against the window.

They were out of the cloud. Below were the irregular hills and valleys of the mainland, dotted with lochs that shone like gunmetal under the morning sky.

Dan, sitting up next to the pilot, turned in his seat. Peter, tucked away at the rear of the cabin, shuffled the papers he was reading out of sight. "Baldrick's a few miles north," Dan said. "That's all. There isn't a house or a human being along this whole stretch. See down there. That's the road to the ferry."

"Road?" Bob adjusted his focus. "It's a cart track. No one's going to run his Roller down that."

"Mostly the players come out on the hotel bus," Dan said. "You've got to remember, Bobby boy, we're not talking amateur night here."

Peter took off his spectacles, wishing to God he could get rid of his headache. It had been with him ever since he woke, which was hardly surprising: they had been up at four this morning to catch the plane. What sort of cure for a headache was the rhythmic drumming of aero engines? Not to mention trying to read pages of detailed company law by half-light in the freezing cold?

"Look at it," Bob cried. "Talk about the back end of nowhere."

Peter rubbed his eyes, wishing Bob would tone it down a bit. He was too much so early in the day.

He put the papers in his case and unzipped his parka. It was difficult to move in the confines of the seatbelt but, after twisting around a little, he got hold of his watch and flipped the cover. Seven thirty-eight. He supposed he should not have brought the watch when violent exercise was on the cards, but he would as soon have gone anywhere without it as Arthur without Excalibur.

They circled the island so Bob could use up film. Peter looked down and was struck by the beauty of the view below. It was better than a detailed map at this height. Scorba and the islands to north and south were all peaks of the same submerged mountain range. He decided that Scorba itself slightly resembled the decapitated head of a rhinoceros. The bodiless beast stared west into the Atlantic. It was about three miles across, the highest point being on the northwest side. Dark green and brown, with gray patches of rock tearing through the surface here and there, it was threaded with water. A small loch glistened in the south; silvered streams wandered between low valleys and tipped over cliffs in white plumes. But the strangest thing was the trees. It had two great spreads of evergreen forest. The smaller one covered the east side, the larger clad most of the great hill that formed Scorba's summit. It surrounded a stunted tower there by the high northwest cliffs and grew almost to the sheer edges. The rest was scrub grass, gorse, and rock, with piles of stone here and there that marked ruined cottages.

The plane banked again. A red building on the mainland-facing shore must be the lodge, and there was the jetty. A boat, a chip of duck-egg blue in the water, motored slowly toward the center of the channel.

He watched Bob chattering to Georgie.

—I'm forty-eight, he thought.

Dan touched the pilot's forearm, signaling to land. He looked happy with the plane's performance. It had not let him down. But he usually looked pretty pleased with himself. Sharks smile as they make a meal of you. For all that he liked the man, Peter knew that no one gets to be a millionaire by being nice. He lived with that knowledge like Damocles with the sword: make a mistake, and eventually you are back on the street with all the plastic removed from your wallet.

He shook his head gloomily. "Relax," Dan had said, when he suggested the weekend. "Don't think about work anymore." But he knew there was more to this trip than just pleasure. How could he relax when the entire weekend would be spent trying to prove himself against a whiz kid half his age? Refuse the invitation? That would be worse than going and making a fool of himself.

—Oh, grow up, he thought, snapping his watch shut. This is a social weekend. We're all friends, we're just having a good time.

But he knew, right down inside where he couldn't sleep at nights, that in business you had no real friends who were not your peers. The higher you were, the fewer were your peers. He was socializing with his boss and his ambitious protégé: he would need to be very sharp today.

Or he would be deader than any game could make him.

16

THE PLANE CAME IN TO LAND. IT WOBBLED CLUMSILY, AS IF blind and searching for a foothold, then the flotation booms touched, striking foam like sparks from the water. It skimmed, settled, and began drawing four great lines into the swell.

The watcher picked up his field glasses, scanned the water for the boat. It was sputtering away from the island, pointing up the sound to compensate for the driving current. The plane swept round to rendezvous. Someone aboard opened the cabin door. It flew back and a young man jumped out on the boom.

—A little closer, the watcher thought, and I could take you out right now.

He checked the time, realized now why this place reminded him of the other one. It was because he was getting ready for action, and what was ruled by nature most of the time was about to become a battlefield.

His battlefield.

17

"COME IN HERE," GEORGIE SHOUTED ABOVE THE ENGINES' roar.

"Power-assisted surfing," Bob yelled, spray jumping all about him as he clung to the support strut one-handed.

"The lad's had a hard year," Peter said, unbuckling his seatbelt. He stood carefully, bracing his feet against the plane's wallowing. He stretched his arms above his head.

"Feeling your age?" Georgie asked, and was surprised by the hard look he gave her.

"I'm fine, thank you."

"Peter, you promised you wouldn't be a grouch." She began gathering Bob's camera gear into his bag.

Dan climbed out of his seat, one of his I'm-an-American-millionaire cigars clamped between his teeth.

"Collect your belongings, men," he growled. "We're going into action. Peter, my man, you look the part."

"A study in military chic," Peter said, coming forward. He stuck his head out of the door, glanced at Bob, then at the weather. "Not so serene once you're down, is it?"

"You kidding?" Dan put an arm round his shoulders. "This is a good day."

"It's pneumonia weather."

"I know. Wonderful, isn't it?" He pulled himself through the door and clambered out on the boom, waiting for the boat to come alongside.

Logan scowled at the plane. "Mr. Goldman?" he called, slinging a rope for Bob to tie around a strut.

Dan pulled the boat in close. "You're talking to him."

The boatman's face showed surprise. "I've seen you before. On the telly, is that right?"

"Could be," Dan said.

"He's a star of stage, screen, and afternoon TV," Georgie said, handing out the camera bag.

Logan touched two scarred fingers to his cap in the presence of a lady. "Aye, afternoons," he said. "My wife, she could tell you what program it was . . . Aye, it's that one with the fat lady, right?"

"Jackpot." Dan flashed the public-relations smile while trying to keep steady in the rocking waves. "The Fat Lady Show."

"It's nae called that."

"Close enough, my friend. Take this bag, will you, and hold her still while we come down."

Georgie climbed onto the boom. "See how it is?" she said to Dan. "No one cares about a millionaire, but get on the box and everybody loves you."

"Just because it was her idea," Peter said.

"Not that I watch." Logan back-pedaled from his uncharacteristic burst of good humor. "Not my cup o' tea, yae know?" He helped them into the boat. His eyes grew more and more weary at the sight of their parkas and combat gear. All this mock battle dress made his blood simmer. He leaned over the side to eject a parcel of phlegm at the water, then realized Dan was watching him.

"Touch of flu." He coughed, thumping his chest.

Peter was last in. The pilot came down to untie the boat and secure the door. "Have a good time," he said.

Dan nodded. "Back here, Monday morning."

The door slammed and the boat started to drift. The plane's engines kicked up again, showering them with spray. It slid into clear water and turned toward the gusting wind. The pilot waved as he raced past them, picking up speed, booms skipping off the surface. The boat reeled furiously in its wake, then the plane was rising, climbing toward the mainland.

"Stranded," Bob said.

"Marooned a thousand miles from civilization," Peter agreed.

The boatman stared at them with an eye like a boiled pebble. "Would you care for a trip round the island, Mr. Goldman?"

"Better take us straight in, Mr. Logan. It's a little rough for sailing."

Logan put his hand to the throttle. The boat labored over the freezing sea toward the island, Logan muttering under his breath about the currents.

"Are they bad?" Peter asked.

"Terrible, sir."

"So, if we want to retire the field early or the boat decides to give up the ghost, we can't swim for it?"

"I would nae advise it even in fine weather, sir. The sea round these islands is a treacherous thing. Sweep yae down yon channel and out to sea in no time."

"That's reassuring," Peter said. "Still, I don't foresee any real problems. I see this as a test of experience over brawn. Dan and myself, being fully blooded in combat—"

"Weekend exercises on Salisbury Plain," Bob jeered.

Georgie laughed out loud.

"North Wales, if you don't mind. National service took me to all the exotic locations," Peter continued, unabashed. "As I say, we have the edge, do we not, Dan?"

"Oh, the best man'll win," Dan said. "And before we begin, let's understand which man we're talking about here."

"I'm not a man," Georgie protested.

They squabbled and joked on as Logan steered in toward the jetty. The island bulked huge under a stained sky. It rolled gently away, first to the lodge nestling in a cup of hills, then to the small plantation of pines and firs. Beyond, so misty that it looked more massive than it was, the high center shrouded by the large plantation, the upraised finger of the broken tower.

Bob sat up, peering through his viewfinder. "Hey, the parade's out to greet us."

The boat ran up against old tires lining the jetty. On the leveled ground at the other end stood Williamson, tightly at attention. Behind him, less well drilled, a rank of five wardens. They were uniformed, complete with berets sloped on heads, plastic eyeshields around their necks, guns holstered at their belts.

"What's the betting," Peter whispered to Georgie, "that the tall one gives Dan the salute?"

Georgie gave one herself. "Ready to take inspection, sah!"

"Will you lay off," Dan said. "Williamson—former Captain Williamson—runs a tight ship. The idea is, impress the customers with a smell of military authenticity."

"*That's* what the smell is." Bob picked up his camera bag.

Peter jumped out of the boat before Bob could do it, and tied the boat up.

Williamson marched down the jetty, boots clanking on the wood. He stopped in front of Dan, snapped a salute. "Welcome to the Isle of Scorba, Mr. Goldman."

Georgie spun around, suddenly becoming deeply interested in the gulls winging overhead. Her shoulders trembled gently while Peter waved an open, money-grabbing palm in front of her.

Dan tried to ignore them. He shook Williamson's hand. "Nice to meet you, Captain."

Williamson flushed with pleasure at the use of his rank. "I brought the lads down to show themselves off, Mr. Goldman. Thought you'd like to see them all lined up. MacNeice is out clearing things up a bit. You'll meet him later." He led the way back to the path like a commander showing chiefs of staff around an important installation. Pausing before each man, he offered a few details of personal history. Dan responded in kind, coming on like the President of the United States crossed with General Patton. He discovered that two of the men were, like Williamson, ex-army. Three had been game wardens on private estates before times got hard. Only MacNeice, the absent teacher, was a Scot.

Dan shook each man's hand, then made his own introductions. Williamson went around with the same fast handshakes. When he came to Georgie, however, it was a slight bow and a kiss to her hand. She would not have been surprised to hear the click of heels.

"Miss Lawrence," he said. "We get a number of ladies playing the survival game these days, but none of them quite as beautiful as you. You used to work at the Edinville, I gather?"

"In the old days, before Mr. Goldman took it over." She nodded. "A holiday job."

"Did you ever visit the island?"

"Oh, no. I only worked at the hotel for a few months. Never had time to explore before I was snatched away to a life of wheeling and dealing."

"Mr. Goldman's very fortunate to have you as an assistant. I think I speak for the lads when I say we're glad to have you with us." His face, in the biting wind, was like a side of cooked ham. "Now then, *lady* and gentlemen, I expect you'd like to warm up after your journey. Coffee in the mess, perhaps?"

The two great leaders moved off together, Georgie between them.

Bob shook his head happily. "This is going to be great."

"Why's that?" Peter asked.

"It's so military. That bloke Williamson, he's really seen it, you know?"

"Seen what?"

Bob shrugged. For a moment he seemed almost embarrassed. "War. Fighting."

"Killing," Peter added.

"Yeah. You'd think there'd be some sign."

"A mark on his forehead, perhaps?"

"I don't think you get my meaning."

"It's all a joke, isn't it? That's the impression I got."

"How can you say that? It's serious." Bob grinned widely. "Deadly serious."

18

LOGAN WATCHED THEM GO, ROLLING A BALL OF PHLEGM around in his mouth. He finally got to hawk it into the water. After that messy declaration of free speech, he untied the boat and put his hand to the throttle.

Bloody foreigners, he thought, the whole crowd. And one of them a girl. There Williamson had been, bad-mouthing the Yank for all he was worth, then he lay down to have his belly stroked when the man arrived. It was disgusting, no matter if Goldman was on the telly. Forty years, Logan was thinking, forty long years earning his living in boats, and he'd come to this—ferrying bunches of weekend soldiers about so they could shoot paint at each other.

He motored toward the middle of the sound, feeling the need to put some distance between himself and them. Out on the water he could mumble and curse them as much as he liked. Out on the water it was something like old times.

He stopped the engine, leaned over the gunwales to look down in the dark of the sea. He sat back, gargling another mouthful deep in his throat.

—I'll spit, he thought. Right enough, I'll bloody spit where I please, and no millionaire business types tell me otherwise. By God, not this year.

He pursed his lips for a long throw, but as he wound up for it, he saw someone else on the ferry. Whoever it might be, he was waving frantically. Logan started getting angry again. He delayed the spit.

Another one. Some fool who didn't know the island was

closed, probably. Well, whoever it was, it'd be about right if he left him there till his feet froze off. But what if Goldman could see what was going on from the lodge? There would be trouble for ignoring a customer. Besides that, the man on the ferry looked to be in a state about something.

With a deep sigh, he restarted the engine, turned the boat, and headed in.

A thin prickle of rain began to fall.

"What the hell d'you want?" he demanded, when he was in hailing range. He glowered at the man standing at the end of the landing stage.

"You've got to take me over to the island." The man could not keep still. His long coat was filthy and the rucksack on his shoulder jangled with every movement. As the boat came close enough, he jumped in.

"Now, wait a minute—" Logan said.

"No, you don't understand. I ran my car into a ditch over the hills back there. I've got to get to a phone."

"I can't just take you over," Logan grumbled. "We've got important people today."

"For Christ's sake. My car's a write-off. My—my wife's hurt. Please."

"All right, all right," Logan puffed. "Just hold your horses."

He twisted the throttle over. The boat's prow reared up as it sped into the heavy-rolling water, cutting away from the long dragon back of the Craignesh peninsula.

"Why couldn't you walk to Baldrick?" he yelled over the churning row of the engine.

The man clasped the back of his head. "You want me to spend three or four hours doing that while my wife takes ill?" The rucksack slipped from his shoulder and fell into the bottom of the boat. Something heavy inside rattled.

"What're you doing on yon hills this time of day, anyway?" Logan asked.

"Would've been walking," the man said. "We're on a walking holiday."

"In October?" Logan spat in the sea. "You must be mad,

man." The boat jumped across the swell. "Don't I know you, though? You look familiar."

"Maybe."

"Been in Baldrick at all?"

"A bit. Hurry, will you."

Logan bit his lip, thinking hard. He wasn't so good with faces, but this young feller had a look about him, as if he was thinking something awful while he sat staring at the island. Then again, if his wife were hurt . . . He noticed the man's boots were army issue. Under the greatcoat were khaki trousers.

"We're not going into the jetty," the man said quietly.

"Beg your pardon?"

"I said we're not going in by the lodge."

"What the hell're you talking about now?"

"Round that outcrop to the south and into the cove. Just drive the boat. I'll tell you where."

Logan smacked a palm against his forehead. "Are you a reporter? Is that what this is?"

"What?"

"Williamson said there might be reporters following the Yank. Is that what you're about?"

"You stupid old bastard."

Logan throttled back and switched the engine to neutral. "I don't know what your game is," he said, "but that's about as far as you go." The boat slowed and began to drift through the gulf between Scorba and Jora. The tides made a race between walls of stone.

The man flushed. He began to tremble, and his voice came out tight and low. "You thick-headed old fart. You'd better take me in."

"I'll tell you what we do, son. First, you show me what's in yon bag of yours. Then we'll think about where to go." He bent over, wheezing, to pick up the rucksack. The man stood up, but Logan went ahead. He was not about to be threatened by any young bastard reporter. He drew the cord on the rucksack and forced it open with his fingers.

Inside, dismantled and shining with oil, were the working parts, barrel, and stock of a rifle.

He looked up, starting to be confused, and noticed two things. First, the stranger's greatcoat was open. Underneath was the combat uniform of the Parachute Regiment. He did not take note of which battalion because of the second thing. He was looking down the mouth of a Browning 9mm automatic pistol. He did not actually know the caliber or brand, but he was certain this was no jumped-up, pellet-firing air gun.

"Don't give me any more trouble, you old fucker," the watcher said unsteadily. "Get me over to that cove."

The gun was steady enough. Logan stared into its darkness. He had lost all desire to spit.

19

THEY WERE ON THE PARADE GROUND, HEMMED IN BY STEEP hills and trees.

"This," Williamson said, tapping the weatherproof map on the wall, "is the Isle of Scorba."

"Do you happen to know what Scorba means?" Georgie asked.

Williamson shrugged. "Anybody's guess." Which meant that some historian chap, or any local who knew his Gaelic, would have the answer, but he had not bothered to find out. "If MacNeice were here, he could tell you. However . . ."

Bob yawned and stretched. He was eager to be off and running. As for the history lesson Williamson was giving them, he knew it from the research he had done. The island managed to support a reasonable community at one time. Then, a century and more ago, the fourteenth laird of Brynair decided to retreat into a life of religious seclusion. Scorba was his choice for an earthly paradise (rainswept northern variety), where he and his followers—if any—could meditate in peace on God's work.

The old boy was a mid-nineteenth-century version of the loons who went to India seeking enlightenment when Bob was a kid. But he wasn't satisfied with the Lord's work on Scorba. First of all, he chucked off the few peasants who had survived the enclosures and the 1848 potato famine, leaving their cottages to fall down from neglect. He wanted dark forests to walk in, so he brought in young trees by the boatload, thousands of them. It was no easy work—the salt winds of the

Atlantic blasted the island all the time—but the cliffs in the northwest formed a natural windbreak. The trees survived.

It was funny. They all felt as if they were out in the wild, yet the place was manmade.

The lodge, a cross between red-brick bungalow and castle, was another of the laird's eccentricities. A bungalow with battlements and arrow slits, front and back entrances like church doors. The modernization had left the exterior largely unchanged: a gesture to the laird's memory.

Privately, Bob was amused by the parallels between the laird and his employer. Dan had bought the island without a practical reason. And now, according to Georgie, he was thinking of getting out. Bob was suspicious of impractical decisions. He wouldn't be surprised if the next thing Dan did was purchase one of those manorships that came up for sale in job lots at Sotheby's every now and then. But what if she was right? Who would run Goldoor?

He lifted his camera and snapped a picture of Georgie and the others. He felt wound up, tensed for a good day's exercise. He and Georgie against Dan and Peter. It would not take long. Maybe they would arrange other games to compensate for the absence of full teams.

Williamson was speaking to him: "You've played the game before, Mr. Townsend?"

"An authority on the subject. What I don't know about this game—"

"Would fill a set of encyclopedias," Peter said.

"With supplements," Georgie added.

Bob mimed firing a pistol at them. Bronson in *Death Wish*.

"Perhaps you'd be good enough," Williamson signaled two of the wardens, "to give us your opinions on the equipment."

The wardens passed out four sets of the bug-eyed goggles and a pistol each.

Georgie took hers and weighed it in her hand. "I may be able to shoot it," she said, "but can someone else carry it for me?"

"They've got decent weight," Bob said. "Specially designed, by the look of it."

"I take it you've all had experience with some kind of air gun?" Williamson said.

All nodded. Bob smiled at Georgie's confident air. Until last Sunday morning, when he took her out to the country for some shooting practice, she'd never fired anything stronger than a water pistol.

"Here's your ammunition." Williamson stepped forward and handed each person a transparent plastic box containing twenty of the dye-filled pellets. Two batches were yellow, the others were blue. "The ammunition packs clip on your belt, like so. You can decide which colors to take when you pair off. Put your goggles on, please."

They did so. Georgie glanced at Bob and started to giggle. He raised his gun.

"Mr. Townsend, if you wouldn't do that, please." Williamson sighed.

—I'll get you too, Bob thought. Right between the shoulder blades. Bam!

"From now on," Williamson said, "when your guns are loaded, you must wear the goggles. The guns won't kill anyone, although a pellet on the exposed skin at close range will sting a bit. But if you take one in the eyes, you could be blinded. We go for body shots, obviously, but we want no unfortunate accidents. Household!"

The warden ran to a spot some twenty yards away. The jacket he wore had been daubed with color so often that he looked like a Jackson Pollock canvas. He faced them.

Williamson took them through the loading procedure. He positioned himself in the classic firing stance, sighted on the warden's chest, and pulled the trigger. The pistol made a satisfactory whacking sound. They heard the faint thud of impact and saw a white splash bloom on Household's coat.

"Take a turn," Williamson instructed.

Peter stepped up, leveled his gun, and fired, missing the target. It plopped into the trees. The others laughed and jeered. They were like schoolchildren on an outing. Peter reloaded, fired, and hit the target.

Dan sauntered up, told Household to get down off his horse and draw. He shot the warden with blue dye.

Georgie showed a trace of nervousness at her turn. She fiddled with the gun, squinted down the barrel. "I'm scared it might turn out to be real."

"Imagine it's someone you hate," Bob said.

She pulled the trigger, watched the pellet explode. "Ah," she said, smiling.

Bob was last up. He leaped out, taking up an American-cop-show stance, yelled, "Freeze, buddy!" and fired. This time, the dye was high up, just under the warden's jaw. Color splattered the man's face. Bob saw him curse.

He got back in line with the others. Just then, he thought he heard something. It was far off, so indistinct that he took it for the sea pounding on the rocks.

"Well, Mr. Goldman," Williamson said, "considering there's only the four of you, how would you like to play the game?"

Dan clapped his hands. "I'll tell you. We split into two teams. Me and Bobby boy, Peter and Georgie."

"Won't take very long," Bob murmured, aiming at the wall.

Georgie sneered. "Says you."

Dan waved them down. "In which case, there are how many wardens on the island?"

"Seven, including myself," Williamson said.

"You play referee. The other six form an attack force. They come out three hours after the game starts, with orders to wipe out all four of us."

"So we'll be fighting on two fronts?" Bob thought about it. "That's more like it."

"It's more of a test that way."

"Very well," Williamson said. "Shall we begin?" He went over and spoke in a low voice to Household, then took out his red beret and put it on. "I'll be with you to start with, show the main landmarks and the objective for the day. If you'd like to follow me . . ."

Bob saluted smartly behind his back. "I've got to pick up some film."

"More pictures?" Dan asked.

"He can catch up," Williamson said. He strode off across the clearing, climbed a path into the plantation. "This way," he called.

Georgie turned to Dan. "Colonel Goldman, sir."

"Lead on, Corporal."

They were into the trees when Bob came whooping up the path, carrying his own gun.

"Better not let the captain see it," Peter advised.

"I paid a fortune for this." Bob checked whether the pellets would load. "I expect to use it. You'd better watch out."

"It'll take more than you to bring me down, sonny."

"Your killer instinct's coming out." He smacked Peter on the shoulder. "You try to kill me; I'll do the same for you. May the best man win."

Peter watched him sprinting ahead to join the others.

"I'd prefer it if I did," he said.

20

He watched the body rise to the surface after it fell over the side. The old man's eyes were open wide, as if he could not believe that anyone would dare to kill him. As he rolled in the swell, the open mouth was full of water.

It was one less fool to deal with, the watcher thought, grabbing the throttle and pointing the boat into Silver Cove. Logan had been a miserable, evil-minded bastard all his life and no one would miss him very much. Now he was going to feed the fish in the dark, sweeping currents down the coast. It would be weeks before anyone found him, and by that time, everyone would know what had happened to him. They would all know.

He holstered the pistol, picked the rucksack off the slopping floor of the boat, checked the shore for witnesses. It was desolate. The boat scraped rock as it glided the last few feet to the beach, then the prow pushed deep in the sand.

Silver Cove. That was not the name on any map but, as far as he knew, it had no other. Fifteen feet of gray sand, backed by a craggy overhang three times that height.

He moved forward with the rucksack, jumped out of the boat. His boots splashed in icy water. It took half a minute to drag the craft up the beach, out of sight of the clifftop. After he had dealt with it he leaned back, sweating. He felt confident. Dangerous so early in the day, but he had made it. He was on the island, had made the first kill, and none of Goldman's scum knew it. It was like finding ants' nests when he was a kid. His father used to try all sorts of stuff to keep them down, but nothing finished them off until he tracked them to the nests and burned them out. He would find the entrances and exits, dig a little to reveal the minute corridors, then pour petrol on them. He watched them running in panic from the attack. Sometimes, fascinated by the action, he would sit there, lighting match after match that burned down in his fingers. Then, when he grew bored, he would touch flame to the petrol.

That was how it was now. He had these people under his thumb. They scuttled around, not knowing how much trouble they were in. They would soon find out, because he was ready to set a match to the petrol. They would find out very fast then.

He pulled the straps of the rucksack that was his makeshift Bergen over his shoulders, settled it on his back, and started to climb Silver Cove. He hoisted himself off the sand, getting the first lift from a jagged hollow chipped out years before. Hands reached for grips as they had been trained to. It was as much a memory of body as of mind. No matter how bad things had been over the last few years, he remembered everything. And he knew the island. If it could belong to any human being, it was his now. He had covered every inch of it, knew every crest, crag, and wrinkle of it.

"Terrain," his old boss, Major Enwright, used to say. He would smile at them with a gleam in his eyes. "Experience will show you that in-depth knowledge of the terrain is the greatest advantage. Take Vietnam—the Yanks go in, thinking it'll be easy meat. Well equipped, well trained, some pretty fair tactical minds. But they discovered the truth soon enough. Against indigenous population, people who know the ground, strangers never win. The enemy always knows of one more place to hide, one more good spot for an attack. If you want to start with a real advantage, get to know the terrain as if you were a boy there."

—Well, he thought, I start with an advantage, sir. I know every bloody inch.

21

BOB, WALKING SLIGHTLY AWAY FROM THE OTHERS, ALSO knew the terrain. At least, as well as anyone could, coming to the place for the first time. He had studied large-scale maps of the island for hours, working out distances, trying to visualize exactly what the contour lines would mean when translated into rock and earth.

It was difficult, though. As he tried to orientate himself, they came out of the small plantation. Before them, stubbled with gorse and bracken, was the moor. It was much larger than his imagination had made it. Some brown bird sailed overhead, crying. Far off, magnified in the haze, was the great hill, and half a mile away was the stream that fell from near the summit. It formed a pool at the foot, then drizzled through the moors to the south. They trekked over to it. Bob wandered off among the dips and slopes.

"Breolf's Burn," Williamson said when they reached the stream. "Fresh water, quite drinkable." He pointed south. "A half mile or so over the rise is Airigh A Cruidh, the biggest loch on the island. Really no more than a pool. Any stretch of water up here bigger than a puddle, and the locals call it a loch." He switched to a mound of gray stones where the burn curved away. "That's all that remains of the fourteenth laird's shrine."

"Shrine to what?" Georgie asked.

"The laird's religious beliefs included the idea that God was one with water, earth, and air." He searched his pockets for postcards of what the shrine had been. "Very elemental chap, to all intents and purposes. Family eventually locked him up to stop him spending any more of the fortune— Ah, here we are." He passed a card with an engraving on it of stone benches surrounding a statue of Aphrodite.

"Looks like a little Stonehenge," she said.

"Built to the greater glory of Water. There was also a cavern. Island's riddled with caves at sea level, but this was a big one halfway up the western cliffs. He tunneled down to it and made it a 'temple for the worship of the Earth.' That's collapsed now, I'm afraid. However, you'll be seeing the remains of his tribute to Air shortly."

Georgie ran down to the rubble of the shrine. She picked up a small piece and put it in her jacket.

Bob prowled up, hand on his gun.

"Will you stick with us?" Dan said. "Having you on my flank all the time makes me nervous."

"Are we in this to win or not?"

"When the game begins, you can play John Wayne all you like."

"John Wayne?" Bob crowed. "You're as bad as Pete." He set off after Georgie, yelling *Sands of Iwo Jima*. Georgie crouched behind the shrine, started a gun battle, refusing to be killed.

"Kids." Dan shrugged at Williamson. "This is what you find behind every sober-sided executive."

They came to the foot of the hill. It was tougher going than it looked. Breolf's Burn fell out of the trees here, crashing into foam. On either side the ground rose sharply.

"May as well go up from here," Williamson said.

Peter watched them jump and scramble. He hoped to go last, unobserved. But there was Bob, hanging back in exaggerated politeness. A sweeping gesture and a smile.

"After you, master."

Master. That was the joky title he had given Peter when he was a new face, picking up all the knowledge and experience going. He hardly ever used it now.

Peter was not unfit. He had kept himself in trim long before the health boom. He played squash regularly, swam as often as his schedule permitted, and jogged a few miles every morning when he was at home. Lately, though, he always seemed to be on business somewhere. And perhaps he had let the squash go a little, but that was because his usual partner was Bob. Bob got on his nerves too much these days.

—He also beat you solidly the last five times you played, didn't he?

—What does that prove? Is it surprising that you're run down, the way you've been overworking? It didn't used to be this bad, but there's no end to the work anymore.

—Is it that there's more work, or just that you're slowing down?

Thinking all this and trying not to, he took a run-up and jumped the rock. He grasped a branch to lift himself. He was making it easily, after all. No problem.

Then he felt Bob's hand under his backside, giving a helpful shove.

Somehow, it was worse than if he had needed it.

"Will you get your hands off me," he snarled, yanking himself up sharply.

Bob stood below. His face was innocent goodwill itself.

"What?" he asked.

Peter calmed down almost immediately. What the devil was wrong with him?

"Got a problem?" Dan called down from the trees.

Bob gazed at Peter. His smile seemed to say everything. That he knew all about Peter's fears, that he was only biding his time, waiting for his opportunity. Also that Peter was making a fool of himself. Then it was gone and Peter felt worse for making so much of it.

"Nothing," Bob yelled back. "Pete's giving me a hand." He sprang past without another word.

Peter leaned against the tree trunk, breathing hard. He took out his watch and stroked the smooth old metal. Nine thirty. Assuming he had the weekend free, he wouldn't be out of bed yet. He'd be lying next to Vickie, waiting for Liz to perform the Saturday morning tea ceremony. He wished he were at home. The day was running at half speed. His feet hurt.

—Oh, get up, you sniveling idiot. Show them what you're made of.

He got to his feet and went after the others. The problem with that idea, he was thinking, was that he sometimes had doubts, these days, about what exactly he was made of.

"Come on, Peter," Dan jeered. "You don't wanna get lost here. The natives're hostile."

—So are some of the visitors. He panted up the hill. So are some of the visitors.

22

DOWN AT THE LODGE, SOMEONE SUGGESTED THAT SINCE there was nothing to do for a couple of hours they might as well brew up again. Ellis put the kettle on and got the teabags out. Richardson, the English gamekeeper, washed the beakers while expanding further on the decline of the great English estates.

"It's the foreign money, see," he said. "What I reckon is, over here, we've got what you'd call a natural aristocracy. People with bloodlines that stretch back hundreds of years."

"Turn the record over, man," Ellis said, putting one teabag in the pot for each person. He noticed that Logan was still absent, off in his boat somewhere, and MacNeice had not returned from his birdwatching.

"These aristocrats," Richardson went on, "they have their faults, no one says they haven't. But also what they've got is blood."

"Aristocrats have blood, lads," Ellis declared, hunting for the sugar tin. "Old Richardson's full of these pearls."

"Blood that's connected to the land by centuries of ownership. Their forefathers had to do something to get it in the first place, you know? Win a battle or perform a special service for the monarch."

"I get a special service," Household said. "Every Saturday night from the wife."

"This is a serious matter," Richardson insisted. "All I'm saying is, you never heard of any unemployment problem back in the old days. And it's got to be better than being sold up, piece by piece, to foreigners."

"'Selling England by the Pound'," said Ellis, who knew his seventies rock. "Whatever that's worth these days." He could not find the sugar. It occurred to him that Richardson had left it in Williamson's office. He went along the corridor, peeped in. The tin was there. He picked it up, sneaking a look at the papers on Williamson's desk.

If he had raised his head at that moment, glanced to his right through the window, he would have seen the watcher come down the hill above the jetty. As he turned the page of a letter from the Edinville, the watcher went into a crouch beside the generator shed, flipped the control of his rifle to automatic fire, and took a fast look round the shed to see what was happening.

Ellis, reading a complaint from some resident of Baldrick about the wardens' rowdy behavior one night last week, shook his head and laughed.

The watcher's quick eyes spotted the movement. He ducked out of sight, waiting.

Ellis put the papers back in order, remembered to take the sugar, and left the office.

The watcher's face appeared again. He saw the way was safe.

It was fifteen paces to the lodge's front door. As he covered the ground, he would be visible from the office window at the side and the arrow-slit opening by the door. He could not hide the rifle, but in combat fatigues, he looked very much like a warden himself. He hoped this would give him a moment of surprise to work with.

He leaned his head against the wall of the generator shed. —Breathe right, he thought. Draw breath, hold it, keep it down in your lungs, then let it go slowly. He was cold inside, which was good. There was fear—because the lodge was red brick and the other house had been red too; only painted that color, but the memory was there. He had to get the fear in its proper place. They might have some real guns in the lodge, he could end up splattered over the walls. Thinking the right way was essential. Not to consider why he was doing this, not to get into bad memories of the red house. Cutting off from the past and future was how you did it.

"In battle," the Boss once said, "you should behave as if your life begins with the command to go, and lasts only until the end of the attack." Thinking of anything beyond that—wife, kids, parents—could be a fatal distraction.

—Life is only as long as the next attack.

He stood up, unslung the rifle from his shoulder, and stepped out in the open. He started the fifteen paces.

Cloud was clearing fast. The sun had burned through and gray masses of rain pushing by the rising hills were like polished blue steel. The breeze, less chill now, was redolent of the ocean. He took the air gratefully, feeling clean and electric inside.

He reached the door. It was heavy oak. The bearded faces of old-young men smiled down from the carved arch above. He put his fingers to the weighty iron ring and turned it carefully, heard the bar inside coming smoothly out of the latch. The door moved half an inch. The smell of burnt toast wafted out. Music playing softly. Also voices.

He pushed against the door. It swung easily. He kept the rifle leveled on the widening gap, holding it one-handed down at the waist. He saw the long hallway straight through to the back door. On the left was Williamson's office, right a storeroom, then the canteen. Its door was slightly ajar.

He stepped inside, shut the door, moved silently to the chief warden's office. No one was there, no radio either. He had to be sure of where the transmitter was, because it must not be damaged yet. If it was the one he could hear playing in the canteen, his task would be more difficult. He left the office and went on, touched the locked storeroom door. He saw that beyond the canteen were a bathroom and W. C. where fastidious players could clean up after a game. Opposite was the guest restroom. All were empty, but the radio transmitter was in the guest room. So the canteen was the important one, and every second spent loitering in the corridor risked the loss of surprise.

Voices in the canteen rose in laughter. Another protested unhappily that hardly any of Britain was owned by the British anymore. He had time to think that this was very true—especially of Scorba—before he nudged the door open with his rifle barrel (two-handed grip now) and stepped into the canteen.

It was all very fast, but slow in his head, as if he had speeded up or they had slowed down to a point where nothing could hope to deal with him as an equal.

The faces turned to look his way, everything else halted. One man standing, holding a kettle over a teapot; another with a fistful of beakers in either hand; three sitting down, one with his feet on a packing case. His mouth dropped open, cigarette falling gently into his lap.

An intake of breath—a kind of silent gasp. Eyes swiveled from his face to the rifle, then back to his face, trying to understand whether this was really a threat. His expression left them no doubt. Some of them even seemed to recognize him a little.

He felt ice and iron in the air.

Ellis began to scream.

He lifted the rifle and started firing.

23

"WHAT A VIEW," BOB SAID, CLIMBING THE STEPS AT THE tower's base. He had to shout to make himself heard above the blustering wind.

Dan surveyed his kingdom. —Maybe one day, he thought, when I'm old, I *could* retire up here.

They were at the top of Cruach Scorba, in the clearing at the summit. Spread out below, skirted by the ocean, the island was beautiful as a seam of new-dug coal can be. Nothing soft or gentle. Even the ocean looked as if it would cut and tear. The hills of Jora rose in the south, the mainland was a long, low smudge in the east.

They were surrounded by the trees that clung to the hill. The fourteenth laird's "Watchtower for the Lord" loomed over them. A triangular cylinder of red brick more than eighty feet tall, with arrow slits all the way up to the ruined top. At the base was a small locked door.

"Not very pretty, is it?" Peter said.

"The laird was after functional, not ornamental," Dan said. "Before they locked him up, he'd go up the stairs and sit in the room at the top and look at the world."

"It must have been pretty cold in the winter." Georgie stepped up to the tower and ran her fingers over words newly carved in the lichened brickwork. " 'The Swiftset Marauders were here—August,' " she read.

"What?" Dan snorted ostentatiously. He threw away his cigar and squinted at the graffiti. "Sons of bitches."

"Never mind," Peter said. "It's hardly a monument to the architectural heritage of the Highlands."

"So, you're an art historian. Let me tell you, before the top fell down, people used to hire boats to see this."

"Well, if it doesn't qualify for inclusion as a folly, I don't know what does."

"Quite so," Williamson said. "Disrespectfully known round these parts as 'Andy's Folly.' The fourteenth laird's Christian name was Andrew."

Peter nodded. "It's a tremendous view, though."

"If this was mine," Bob said, snapping away with the camera, "I'd live on it."

"A little far from town for a cosmopolitan like you," Dan said. "But you like it?"

"It's tremendous. Couple of years, they'll be coming from New York to play here."

It was no wonder, Georgie thought, that the laird had wanted the island for a retreat. Standing so high above the greens, grays, and blacks of the empty Highland coast, it was hard to believe that Edinburgh was only one hundred and twenty miles away, that people were rushing around, making money, crashing cars, all that sort of thing. It was not exactly her idea of paradise—she liked the city too much for that—but it was like stepping back to another age.

—And in a minute, we're going to be trampling all over it like a crowd of football hooligans.

"Is there any chance of getting lost?" she asked.

Williamson smiled a patronizing smile. "Well, you might get a little confused, Miss Lawrence. Three miles across doesn't sound a great deal of country, but it's bigger than you think on foot. Particularly with the hills and the forest. However, if you go astray, I'll be about to look after you."

"Thank you so much." She went down to where Bob was standing, apart from the rest.

"The tower," Williamson announced, "is your objective for the day. We play our game along the lines of the American version. In a few moments, we'll go down the hill again. I'll give each team instructions to make for locations on opposite sides of the island. At a given time—we'll synchronize watches—you will begin to move in. The object is to come up the hill and take the tower, to avoid getting shot, and to neutralize as many of the enemy as possible. You'll proclaim your success by two blasts on the air horns each team carries. If you are shot, you're out of the game. You can return to the lodge, or join me as a spectator. All clear?"

"I think we've got it," Dan said.

"You mean we have to climb this hill again?" Peter groaned.

"Precisely," Williamson said. "Only this time you'll be facing an enemy who will 'kill' you to get to the tower first. If you're neutralized, stay where you fall, and I'll pick you up."

"And when the wardens join in, we'll really start cooking," Dan said.

"I still think you have unfair advantages," Georgie said.

"Such as?"

"You were in Vietnam, and Bob's an expert."

"Twenty years ago, I was in Vietnam. I figure that balances pretty nicely with Peter's war experiences."

"Salisbury Plain," Bob cooed.

"North Wales," Peter insisted.

"Bob's still an expert, and I've never played the game," Georgie said.

Dan shrugged. "You know what they say. The female of the species is more deadly than the male."

"If it was hand to hand, maybe."

"Just give me the chance." Bob grinned.

"We have equal division here. One experienced old hand, one new guy. I'm being as fair as I can." In fact, the reason he had divided the teams like that was because (a) he did not want Georgie with Bob, (b) he did not want Peter with Bob, (c) he wanted Peter against Bob for business reasons, and (d) he did not wish to look desperate by having Georgie with him. Looking at it that way, it was an emotional minefield, and it made him wonder why he had thought of this trip in the first place.

"Just one more sight I think your guests might appreciate, Mr. Goldman," Williamson said.

"The cliffs?" Dan said. "Yeah, I think the cliffs would be a nice way to round off the tour."

They went past the folly, through a gap in the trees that opened out on the wide span of the ocean. It seemed like the sudden end of the island. The ground sloped gradually away for fifty feet, then disappeared.

Georgie crept close to the edge. "What's that noise?"

"Birds," Williamson said, as each went as near to the edge as he dared.

"Good God!" Peter said. "You can hardly see the cliff face for them."

The wind off the sea came blasting up the sheer drop, almost pushing them back. Birds were perched on every available ledge. Thousands of them.

"Kittiwakes," Peter said, recalling the names from boyhood. "Auks, fulmars, puffins."

"Also brown guillemot, black razorbill, a couple of peregrine falcons, and a kestrel," Dan added.

"I didn't know you were interested in birds."

"I like to see what I've got in stock," he said. He was lying again. The first time he had seen the birds like this, he had been filled with a need to know what each was called, where they came from, how they lived. But to mention it would have been like confessing that he wrote poetry. It did not fit with his hard-nosed image. Once upon a time this would not have bothered him, but lately he had been wondering a good deal about the difference between people's idea of him and what he felt inside. There were all kinds of things he wanted to tell someone. The someone was probably Georgie.

Bob's camera clacked like the birds spread out below them.

"Must be three hundred feet."

"Four," Williamson corrected.

"Never mind the feet," Peter said. "You're about six inches from imminent demise. Step back a bit before I have my first heart attack."

"All right, keep your hair on." Bob turned and photographed the path that snaked off to right and left along the cliff. "Amazing," he said. "They used to have a tradition in these islands. Once a year, they came out, tied ropes round their waists, and jumped over the side to collect eggs."

"Rather them than us," Peter said.

"Reminds me of something my old man made us do when we were kids. We had this cliff near the place where we lived—nothing like this, but fair enough when you're only four feet tall—and every boy in the family was supposed to climb it by the time he was eleven. Big tradition. If you didn't want to do it, he made you feel like a total fairy. Day I was eleven, I still hadn't made it. He had me up and down those rocks till I could hardly think."

"Did you do it?" Georgie asked.

"Yeah. Never been scared of heights since."

"Sounds like torture to me," Peter said.

"Oh, he's a bit of a psychopath, my old man."

They returned to the folly, slightly breathless with fear and excitement. Williamson got them together and sorted the teams out. Dan and Bob took the blue pellets, Peter and Georgie the yellow. Williamson handed each of them matching neckerchiefs to wear for identification purposes.

"Anyone for camouflage?" he asked, offering sticks of greasepaint.

"May as well do it right if we're going to do it," Georgie said, and began daubing the greenish muck over her face. The others followed suit. The atmosphere became like the countdown to a team game at school. Greasepaint ended up all over the place.

Williamson checked his watch. "Right, we'll synchronize now. I make it half a minute to ten thirty."

They marked at ten thirty precisely. Williamson led the way down another path to the northeast.

"This is going to be tremendous," Bob said, touching the butt of his holstered gun for luck.

The watcher slammed through the remaining rooms of the lodge. Something was wrong: he had seen six wardens go onto the island. Williamson was out there with the VIPs. But there were only five bodies in the canteen. One warden was absent.

He kicked into the storeroom, sweeping the AK47 over the narrow gap between shelves. No one. He ran down the corridor, out the back door, scanned the clearing for a retreating uniform. Nothing.

He started to swear. This meant that Williamson and another were loose on the island. It was not that he feared any real trouble from them, but picking off two wardens would take extra time.

He moved back into the lodge, still covering the angles. He went to the guest room, sat down at the table where the radio gear was set up, and picked up the handset. He put out a call.

After a minute or so, a girl's voice came on. She sounded unsure of the equipment. "Hello, this is the Edinville Hotel."

The watcher closed his eyes, trying to keep his voice steady. He was speaking to someone who worked at the hotel—some local girl, probably, who was glad of the job.

"Edinville," he said. "This is Scorba here. I'm Mr. Goldman's pilot. I have a message from Mr. Goldman. Would you take it down, please?"

"Just a minute." He heard her fumbling for pencil and paper. "Right, go ahead."

"It's as follows." He smiled despite the tension. "Mr. Goldman's party will spend the night on the island. The staff will remain here also. What you have to do is contact all the families of the staff, and get in touch with Mr. Goldman's office in London to let them know he'll be out of contact till tomorrow some time."

"What's all that for?" the girl asked.

"Och, the man's got some idea about playing the game at night. And you know the boss always gets his way. Now, will you do all that for me, love?"

"He's going to go about shooting in the dark?" The girl giggled. "That's loony."

"Never mind that. Just do what I asked, will you?"

"All right." Her tone softened. "Is David there?"

"David?"

"David Richardson."

He swallowed hard. "No. He's out with Mr. Goldman's party. Everybody is."

"That's a shame. I wanted to talk to him."

"Got a message, have you?"

"Not the sort I'll give to a stranger."

"Never mind, aye? Speak to him tomorrow, when he's earned all that overtime."

She started to say something more, but he cut her off because the effort of being pleasant was getting too much for him.

Thinking too much again. He closed off thought and tried to push it out with the artillery fire in his head. You could not operate effectively with your mind on other things, so you had to get cool. Cold inside. Like the moment when you confronted the wardens in the canteen. Think about the plan, that's the way to do it. Plan and execute, keep moving. It was ten forty-three, and there was much to do.

He went out across the clearing, climbed into the small plantation. He wondered which of them was left out there. The wardens all looked much the same to him. Which one would it be? There were no guns on the island; he had made sure of that in the lodge. But even some half-assed warden could be dangerous if he had time to realize what was going on.

He cleared the strand of trees, could see no one on the moors. The burn plashed over rocks to the south. It was peaceful. It was good fighting country. He lifted his field glasses, caught a sun reflection from the forest to the west. Two figures moving along the tree line, going south. Williamson was not there. He tracked right, searching for the others. Down at the water shrine, a kestrel perched on the old stones. He saw its head turn slowly. It spotted something—a smaller bird, perhaps. Wings beat the air and it soared up from the burn.

—You and me, the watcher thought, moving out for the big plantation. You and me, old friend.

24

GEORGIE STOPPED.

"Feet hurting?"

"A shade," Peter said, pulling up.

"Mine too." She sat down and eased her toes. "I don't know where Dan got these boots. I think mine were designed for a platoon of dwarfs."

He took out his watch. "We only have ten minutes before battle commences. Where's that map?"

She passed it to him. He turned it this way and that until it was right way up. "These Gaelic place names look the same either way. We're supposed to be at some peasant cottage. I can't even see one."

"Do you think Williamson's watching us?"

"He's had an eye on you all morning." Peter glanced back at the big plantation. There were so many bumps and hollows to the moor that they could be surrounded by a tank regiment and not know it. "I imagine he's keeping close to Dan. Don't want the boss falling down a pothole, do we?" He took out a bar of chocolate and offered it to her. She broke off a square and popped it in her mouth. He lit a cigarette and puffed on it hungrily.

"You know, I'm a little nervous of all this."

"So was I." She nodded. "I didn't want to get shot at, even in fun. But it's okay now. I must be getting the spirit."

"Williamson's right, you know. Those pellets could blind you."

"That's why we have to remember to put the goggles on at zero hour."

He hung his head, looking at the ground.

"You'd rather be at home in bed, wouldn't you?" she said.

"Spot on, my child. I was thinking about morning tea and reading the papers. Even the falling pound would amuse me this morning."

"Why on earth did you come? I more or less forced Dan into letting me, but you didn't have to."

He did not answer, blew a stream of smoke that whipped away on the breeze.

"And what is it between you and Bob?"

He raised an eyebrow. "Bob and me? Nothing, nothing at all."

"You're joking, Peter. The atmosphere between you two's been prickly ever since Edinburgh. Have you argued about something?"

"Listen, Georgie," he said, stepping back behind the wall of seniority, "you may have access to Bob's intimate thoughts, but it's hardly the business of a personal assistant to know what's going on at executive level."

She had been thinking of ways to tell him how glad she was that they were teamed together. Stung by his coldness, she got up. "Okay, we'd better move on."

He listened to her walking away, not looking. He felt bad. It was like telling off Liz.

"Well, Bobby boy, how shall we play this one?"

Bob shook his head. "You tell me, General. You're the one with experience."

"Will you lay off my 'experience,' for God's sake."

"But you're the only one of us who knows what it's really like, you know . . ."

"To kill someone?"

"Well, yeah."

"It's not like killing, not with a uniform on, through the sights of a rifle. It doesn't feel like murder."

"I always wanted to ask you about it, but—" Bob almost looked awkward.

"Lately, there hasn't been the time, I know."

They paused on the edge of saying more.

"What rank were you, anyway?" Bob asked quickly.

The moment passed. Dan shrugged.

"I was what they called a D.A.K."

"What's that?"

"Dumb-Ass Kid. That was after I was an F.N.G."

"F.N.G.?"

"Fucking New Guy."

"You're putting me on."

"No, I'm not. I thought you read all those war books."

"Not so much on Vietnam. That one was just a mess."

"Ain't it d' truth?"

"Now, something nice and clean and simple like the Falklands: straight in, kill a few baddies, that's my meat."

"You don't say? —Watch that rock."

They went up a rise. Bob looked back.

"There's Williamson."

"Where?"

"In the trees there, by the stream."

"He's taken off his beret. He'll get shot at."

"I'll shoot him. Was he S.A.S.?"

"You freaks think everyone in uniform's S.A.S. or Green Beret. Captain Williamson was in the Essex Regiment. He saw duty in Northern Ireland, so get off his case."

"Northern Ireland. We should nuke Belfast."

"Are you serious?"

"What d'you think? It's the sort of thing my old dad used to say to annoy Mother. I tell you, though, some of the head cases I went to school with meant it. And most of them went in the army."

"That's a pleasing thought. Come on, we have work to do."

"It'll be more fun when the wardens join in. Can't see it taking long to get Peter and Georgie, can you?"

"Never write Peter off until the last shot's fired. He sticks at it till he gets results."

Bob thought: —He used to, but let it go.

They came within sight of the ocean and the island of Langa across the narrow channel to the north.

"Lend me your glasses," Dan said. He directed his gaze to Langa, the torn black face beneath smooth green where gulls nested. Bob tried to read from the map the Gaelic name for the channel.

"Bealach a'Choin Ghluis."

"Lousy. You British're all the same. Go abroad, never try to learn the language."

"All right, how *do* you pronounce it?"

"Don't ask me. I'm a stranger here myself."

Bob sprinted the few hundred yards to the cliffs. A smell of seaweed and ozone came off the rocks below. He snapped pictures of a seal basking on a flat rock, then returned. "Rough," he said. "Windsurfing weather."

Dan was drinking in the glory of it. "God, what a place. Can't you see what the fourteenth laird was getting at when you stand here and look at all this?"

"Crazed old coot," Bob said. "Rains too much for paradise."

"You don't have a spiritual side, do you?"

Bob laughed. "You'd last about five minutes without the stock reports. It's not your style."

"I don't know so much. I think I understand him. The peace here—maybe you can't feel it without you were raised in a place where nature came in windowboxes. Can't you see it? . . . I never knew the name of a bird before this island. It's so big, so . . ." He glanced at Bob, who had covered his face by now. These were the things he wanted to tell Georgie. How come he ended up saying them to smart-ass Bobby? "Okay, punk. Do something useful once in your life and tell me the time."

"Two minutes to go. What say we start now and get the jump on them?"

"With Williamson prowling around? He'd court-martial us and throw us over the cliffs. We wait, my bucko. And keep your hands off the firepower."

"Okay." Bob took a turn at studying the view. "I know one thing. It's a lot different, looking at a map and being in the field . . . Hello."

"What now?"

"Peter's decided to go early. I saw him on that ridge by the stream. Least, I think it was him."

"Don't forget Williamson's out there, and the guy we didn't meet."

"No matter. No one's taking that hill before me."

Dan took out his gun and loaded it. He slipped the goggles on, stared at Bob, who had done the same. They both broke up.

"Do I look as fucking stupid as you?" Bob asked.

"Short-sighted mercenaries," Dan said.

He counted off the last seconds.

"Twenty."

Peter squinted behind his goggles. Georgie stood in the doorway of the derelict cottage, scrutinizing her gun. She raised it, pointed it at the wall.

"Any master plan?"

He shook his head.

"You're the one with the national service. I thought you—"

"Look, Georgie, I apologize. I'm tired."

"I know." She bestowed a smile on him. It was very gracious and beautiful, and Peter understood why Dan continued to play the fool over her. He flicked the cover on his watch.

Ten.

Near Breolf's Burn on the lower slopes of the big plantation, Williamson sat and lit a cigarette. He supposed this was a pretty cushy way to make a living—but for all that, he wished he could get in on the action. Even a little paint shooting.

He puffed slowly. Perhaps he could get one of the lads to adjudicate when they came out. Why not? He fancied shooting a few members of Joe Public today.

He checked the time.
Five seconds.

The watcher settled down to see what happened next.

—Oh, Mr. Fucking Goldman, I've got a surprise for you. You wait until you find out what it is.

—You never hear the one with your name on it. That's what people who know nothing say, even if practice proves it's not true. Well, you'll hear all the others. Believe me, you're going to know why, Mr. Goldman. Better believe it.

No seconds.

25

THE MOMENT OF BEGINNING WAS STRANGE FOR GEORGIE. She had been reluctant about the shooting, wondered if she had made a mistake by insisting on coming. But the morning flight in the old aircraft, the sense of leaving ordinary life behind, the hard trek across moor and through forest had psyched her up to the point where she couldn't wait to move.

She winked at Peter and sprang up, racing toward an outcrop that provided cover. In a moment, she was wriggling over the top on her belly, peering at the country below the big plantation.

Peter scrambled up next to her.

"You caught the spirit of the thing all of a sudden, didn't you?"

"Keep your head down. We don't know they didn't follow us."

"That's against the rules."

"Dan only sticks to rules when he likes them. I wouldn't put it past him or Bob to be out there now, waiting to zap us when we go past."

He put a finger under his goggles to rub his eyes. "Sure you've never done this before? You're General Patton's daughter, aren't you?"

"I don't like being beaten. We stand a good chance if we're careful. Bob thinks he knows it all—he knows the terrain, so he thinks anyone who doesn't will make the obvious approaches—that makes him overconfident. He won't think about the unpredictable. Dan's one for jumping in like a hero. He likes to make a splash. So he's careless about keeping his flanks covered."

"Upon what do you base all this stunning character analysis?"

"The way they do business."

He thought about it. Of course, she was right. Dan was forever pulling off stunning coups at tremendous risk; the WonderBar deal was proof of that. And Bob prided himself on knowing every detail of a possible transaction before he went into the room.

"What degree did you take?" he asked. "Psychology?"

She shaded her eyes, gazing into the black line of the forest. "We should've brought binoculars. Can't see anyone, though. Shall we move on?"

"Whatever you say." He threw away his cigarette. "For the moment, I'm content to rest in your hands. Just don't pull a Gallipoli on me."

"We've got to get somewhere defensible, so we can plan our attack. I bet that's what they're doing."

"Lead on, MacDuff."

She got up, ran quickly down the ridge to a patch of heather. He followed, sweating.

Williamson coughed quietly, turned his head to spit on the ground. He held the cigarette out and grimaced at it.

—Have to give it up, old boy. The demon weed's coming to get you.

A footstep crackled behind him. He leaned over and spied past the tree trunk.

"MacNeice, that you?"

No answer, no sign of life. Apparently a branch falling. Still, MacNeice was about somewhere.

Williamson stood, yawning. The problem with this job, apart from the idiotic Cowboys and Indians of the guests, was getting up so bloody early. He hadn't had one decent night's kip for months. He stretched his arms up, seemingly relaxed. Then he lunged into cover, rolling easily into the ferns that were starting to die with the end of autumn. He peeped out of hiding, searching for movement.

It was just like the lads to spring something on him in a situation like this, the boss present and all. Often enough, when he was on duty, they would try a surprise attack on him to see how good his reflexes were. There were some odd types among the wardens. The ex-army ones were always chipping away at him, seeing if he still had bottle. So this was probably MacNeice, the teacher, on his way back from loitering with the damn birds, deciding to put him on a bit.

—Well, we'll see about that, won't we? There was no evidence, but someone was there all right.

"MacNeice, you idiot," he whispered rather happily, "I'm going to hang you out to dry. You'll be washing dye out of your hair when I've finished with you."

The watcher scurried into cover higher up in the trees. He breathed fast because of the close call with Williamson. He had been coming in from the high ground when he all but stumbled into the warden's lap.

—Christ, sharpen up. You were almost on top of the bastard . . . I'm rusty. Three years out of circulation, when did I get a chance to keep in shape?

—Bullshit. It's all in your mind. You were brilliant back at the lodge. The Boss would have been proud of you. Just sharpen up.

He stayed put until his heart slowed; then he skirted Williamson's position, listening. He went down the slope until he reached the edge of the forest. No one was close. The long, shallow bowl of land with clumps of gorse and a shattered dry stone wall running through it was empty.

Movement on a ridge. He lifted the rifle, homing in on the girl's head as she trotted along the rise. That was stupid, if she expected to last long in their pathetic game. But she thought she was facing guns with a range of less than fifty yards. She wasn't to know that he was here, tracking her with a rifle that was accurate enough to blow her brains all over the landscape.

He switched over to Peter, studying the face. The man was a little long in the tooth for stuff like this. His expression showed the strain. He was limping badly now. These people had all the money they could use, but they were amateurs at looking after themselves. He decided to call the older man "the limper" from now on. At least until he was dead.

He went back to the girl. She was talking over her shoulder to the limper. She was really enjoying herself, jumping around like some cadet on a weekend exercise. He leaned forward, getting balance and sighting her carefully with the rifle.

Oh, she was lovely. Lovelier than the photograph. The sun was on her hair, her skin was honey. She looked so alive.

He lowered the rifle. He felt powerful. He could hold the girl's life in his hands for minutes at a time and, instead of taking it away, let her keep it for a little while. And she did not know. He was powerful, more powerful than any American millionaire with his seaplanes and real estate and companies. Whoever said power grew out of the barrel of a gun was right. On Scorba, surrounded by these influential people with their money and credit cards, he was top man.

He waited until they dipped out of sight, then moved higher up the slope to a ledge that gave vantage across the length of the moors. There was Goldman, crouching by a broken wall on the north moor. The young one, bright boy, was checking the terrain with field glasses, but the watcher was safe behind trees before bright boy had turned his way.

He felt like God. It was tremendous to be in this position of absolute life and death. He could have taken them all out now if he wanted, but it was the buildup that counted, to make Goldman and his people realize what was happening to them. They would see their well-heeled world collapse slowly around them until there was nothing left but the death.

The watcher checked back on Williamson. The "chief warden" had to be removed first.

He picked up the rifle, checked the mechanism, flicked the safety catch off, and went down the hill toward Williamson's last position. Williamson was in there, smoking, taking a breather. It was time for him to learn what the other wardens already knew: that the survival game on Scorba had suddenly turned from a bit of fun for businessmen into something serious.

Deadly serious.

Bob ran to the burn, lay flat beside the flashing water.

There was enough drop to the stream's jagged bed to lie in, unseen by the casual passer-by.

Time? They had been out an hour and he was separated from Dan as they worked in toward the big plantation. They were taking it slowly because Dan insisted that Peter was not easily fooled. Bob thought the caution misplaced. He was willing to bet that they could have established themselves on the hill by now, ready to pot the opponents as they blundered up.

He rolled on his back and dabbled a hand in the burn. It was shockingly cold—like putting your hand in glass. When he lifted his palm from it, his fingers were numb. He sniffed the water, drank a mouthful.

He raised his eyes to the irregular heath south of his position, saw movement a long way off. A camouflage-colored flicker. Had to be Peter, he supposed, since Dan was working up the cliff path to the northwest. If it was old Pete, he was way outside where he should be by now. Whoever it was, he was too far off to chase. He scooped another handful of water. It tasted of earth and iron, but okay. Probably good in a fine malt whisky.

The watcher hit cover as Williamson came through the gloomy undergrowth. Pine needles prickled under his hands, a sweet smell. He was close enough to see the veins in Williamson's face and the stitching on his collar. For the last hour the Captain had been doing all his tactical tricks; going to ground, doubling back. He was enjoying himself.

None of the tricks threw the watcher. Williamson was an officer who had gone to seed. All his remembered moves showed the rust of unuse. The watcher had only waited so long because he wanted to get his man a good distance away from the rest before he struck.

He rose, following Williamson's tracks over the broken hollows and hills below the cruach. It was difficult going because the forest and ferns disguised hard drops and sudden rises. He had the target in view, but not close enough for a clear shot. Besides, he enjoyed this: trailing this man who thought he knew all the dodges. He might be good enough to impress civvy-street executives but there was no way he would survive long on a real battlefield. It was all learned, and learned hard. As the Boss used to say: "There are learned soldiers and natural soldiers. The naturals survive longer—unless they're also reckless."

The kestrel hovered over its prey in the big plantation.

Williamson paused, went down on his haunches, listening. He caught the low sound of footsteps in the forest. He nudged a branch to one side and peered through, saw a figure creeping past not thirty yards away. He had time to note that there was no identifying armband, but the figure was gone before he could be sure it was MacNeice. Perhaps the others had come out early too. Maybe they were all hunting him. He cursed the lot of them, but one thing was sure—he would not be taken easily. This shadowy figure was about to receive his comeuppance.

He checked his gun. The white pellets he carried were loaded in. By the time he was finished, MacNeice would look as if the sea gulls had been using him for a latrine. He began moving parallel to MacNeice's course, aware of the man without being able to see him. The trouble with these pellet guns was that you had to be close and very careful not to have even a branch in the way. The pellets broke up easily, and you would be left with painted leaves and your opponent firing back at you while you fumbled to reload.

The ground dropped. Williamson smiled, remembering that the trees gave way to a clearing farther on. That was where he would go for the kill. And MacNeice, the ex-teacher, could eat all his rubbish about army training being a waste of time.

He moved ahead to get the drop on his man. There was a moment to steady the arm. He drew a bead on the opening of the path where MacNeice would come out.

A branch shivered. Williamson aimed. The opponent came out, half-turned from him. He saw the head and shoulders, waited for the torso to be in plain sight. Shadows and light.

"Okay, my friend," he muttered to himself, and fired.

The soft plop of the pellet smacking home on the opponent's jacket was loud in the stillness. Williamson started to get up, jeering the enemy.

Then he saw it was not MacNeice, and he saw the staring eyes flick to him, the rifle swinging up almost as fast as the eyes, and he saw the flash, heard the explosion even as he sprawled back in the dirt. It was like the end of the world. He lay stunned on the ground and watched a tree trunk above his head shatter in a hundred splinters that rained down on him. A piece of the soft inner pulp fell on his lips; he tasted the resin of the fir tree.

There was no time to be surprised, nor to think about it. He scrambled back, propelling himself as fast as he could until he managed to turn and get on his feet. He clawed up the rise. His brain ticked frantically over each shred of knowledge it had gained—each second filled to bursting with the race of perceptions and reactions. Is the ground ahead clear? Don't call out for help, he'll locate you by the sound. Am I showing up on the horizon? Is there cover between me and the enemy? And there was panic. He had never personally been shot at before. Oh, yes, some of the impersonal kind, in Belfast; scattered fire that was meant for anyone in the way. But never this.

He got over the slope. One moment's pause against a tree, head swiveling, eyes bulging, trying to locate the enemy.

Who was this man? How did he come to be on the island with an AK47? It was like some bad dream.

—Keep moving, you fool. He's after you.

He set off again, breath pumping in his chest until it burned. He had to reach the guests, warn them, get them out. They must have heard the shot, but they weren't to know. It was his duty to get them safely back to the lodge, radio for help.

He was going up the path out of the plantation, heading for daylight. Bloody stupid thing to do, he thought, outlining himself against the brightness. Get off the path into the trees again. Left or right? Right was a mass of ferns and branches; make a hell of a noise going through that. He swerved left.

Something sharp and tight snagged his legs. He went down hard, striking the earth with his face.

The watcher came up behind him as he tried to untangle his feet from the wire stretched between two trees. The watcher smiled down at him. The rifle barrel was expressionless.

Williamson did not scream. He fought.

The watcher shot him once in the chest.

His jerking movements became more frantic for five seconds. The watcher saw him struggle with horror, the realization that a fist-sized hole in his back was leaking his body's essence into the muck. Then Williamson choked a gobbet of blood onto his shirt, and the aorta burst in a sudden crimson surge.

Williamson gave up the fight. He relaxed back on the ground, the last breath bubbling out and fading.

The watcher frowned. Gingerly, he kicked the entangled boot that rested on the wire. Williamson was gone.

He knelt, face wrinkling with disgust, tried to bring himself to touch the body. He decided he could not. He used the rifle barrel to jog Williamson's boot, untied the wire and spooled it in his pocket. He got up, looking at Williamson's distracted eyes. Blood oozed steadily from the wound. He did not mind looking, and it was not death that made him loathe to touch. It was simply that touching anyone was too much for him.

He reached in a pocket of his tunic and took out a box of Tic Tacs. He flipped the box and shot one into his mouth, sucked on it to get the flavor going.

He had to move on before someone came looking for the cause of the shots. It had taken two to get rid of Williamson, but the rest would be easier. There was one warden left, then the four civvies.

Leaving the body where it fell, he went out of the trees, looking for high ground to start the next phase of the operation. He was not sure who would die next, except that it must not be Goldman. As far as that went, he was spoiled for choice.

26

DAN LISTENED FOR FIVE MINUTES, WAITING FOR AN
explanation of the shots. He was well aware of the no-guns
rule, but if those weren't rifle shots, what the hell were they?
They were far off; he could not accurately judge the direction from his resting place behind a wall on the north moor.
It was pretty obvious that someone was playing cowboy.
Maybe the warden or Bob. He might have brought some
firecrackers along to put the frights on the others. Someone,
he decided, would have to be reprimanded for this.

He bobbed up from behind the wall, without considering
himself as a target, and marched down the moor toward the
big plantation. He would soon deal with this.

Georgie was in the trees. She had been moving in short
bursts, then hiding up for minutes at a stretch to see if anyone appeared. Her adrenaline was already pumping at a tremendous rate before the shots came. She was beginning to
understand how Bob could be so hooked on a game like this
one. She was scared all the time because she might be discovered any minute and feel the sting of a pellet across her
back. She felt five hundred percent alive because of the fear.

Bob said, when she asked him about the game's appeal:
"It's a tremendous thing. You get all the thrill of hunting and
being hunted without the risk."

Everything around her had a brightness and a crystal
hardness that she could not remember seeing since she was
a child. She could actually *taste* the air. The greasepaint on
her face smelled heavy and waxy, but it did not matter. She

had been crawling on her stomach through the dirt, whipping her gun round to aim at the slightest noise. It was fun.

And now these shots. What did they mean? She knew so little about the way they played the game here that it could be part of the routine. Maybe it was a signal to the wardens. Two shots meant: "Come in, Captain Williamson, you're wanted on the radio."

She heard nothing from anyone else. Peter had disappeared some time ago to circle the hill in the hope of taking Dan or Bob by surprise.

She turned slowly. The gun did not feel so heavy now. She was itching for a good excuse to fire it. Sooner or later she had to come across one of them. She only hoped she would get the first shot in. Her real ambition for the day—not that she would have admitted it to anyone else—was to beat Bob at his own game. It would, finally, put a dent in his confidence and, perhaps, serve notice that they also were opponents in business. It was not her intention to be a personal assistant all her life. She was already looking for openings in the departments, and if it took fighting with Bob to get somewhere, she would do it.

She picked a fir cone off the ground and lobbed it into the undergrowth, waited for reaction, saw there was none. She stepped out in the open. Which way was north? She checked the tiny compass Dan had provided with the combat fatigues, looked at the map of Scorba. Which way was she facing? In all the old westerns Bob had on videotape, Clint Eastwood and John Wayne could tell where they were, what time it was, and how many Indians were over the hill just by looking at the sun. No use at the moment, though: no sun. She pushed the hair back off her face. Usually, she had a wonderful sense of direction, but that was in central London.

She put the map away and took what it said was an easterly direction. Getting out of the trees would help her find out where she was, and maybe what the shots meant.

He hardly breathed. Peter was creeping over the open ground below him, with no idea he was being watched. Bob shifted to keep him in view. Suddenly Peter darted left; then he drew the gun and made pow-pow noises. Bob almost laughed out loud. After all the bellyaching this morning, the old sod was getting into it at last.

It didn't really matter, although it would be more fun to blow him away now that he was trying. Like a bullfight, the survival game was only truly exciting if the bull put his heart into it.

Bob waited until Peter was going away from him, then followed. He kept back just beyond the ridge, imitating Peter's course on the high ground. This was the part he liked best: when the prey was under his thumb and did not know it. The tension began to build from this point to what he once heard an American player call "the best high there is." Maybe that was so. His heart rate was up, his muscles thrummed with suppressed power. At times like this, he knew why all the best-intentioned pacifists would never stamp war out of the world. Hunting and killing was a rush. And he couldn't help wondering sometimes how much greater the feeling would be if it were for real.

He stopped to get the trembling of his hands under control. A look over the rise told him that Peter was still ambling along unawares.

—How can he be so insensitive? If it was me, my alarm system'd be going off all over the place. The guy's got no antennae, no sixth sense. Fatal when you're fighting a war.

Just then, Peter halted. He took out cigarettes and lighter, lit up with a hand cupped against the wind. Bob shook his head. Peter's trouble was that he came from a generation that found out how harmful fags and bad food could be too late. He'd smoked since school, spent most of his life drinking too much, eating all the wrong foods. No wonder he was beginning to run down. Whose fault was it? Bob felt sorry for him, but in the way he pitied the unemployed and poverty-stricken in television documentaries; it changed nothing.

He observed Peter take out his watch and flick the cover. Clock watching again—bad news when your mind was supposed to be on the game. He scuffed on his belly along the rise to check the country ahead for good points of attack. It was all moorland where Peter was heading, with the big plantation off to the left. A gully lay a few hundred yards beyond, with a ruined crofter's hut at the end of it. The rise closed in above the gully, and he would be able to get in close enough to Peter there for a clean shot. The only risk was that they would both be visible from the big plantation, but it was better than two hundred yards to the nearest concealment in the trees. The pellet guns could not shoot that, and no one would be able to creep up on him.

So, it was time to put Peter out of his misery at last.

Peter sank his watch in his pocket and considered his choices. Increasingly this reminded him of national service. He'd spent a week on training exercises in the Welsh mountains then. Similar country, same hollow moan of wind over the hills and in the trees, same bleak skies. On that occasion he was leader of a team. Naturally he got them all lost. They ended up sitting by a lake with sheep for company until a search party found them. They never saw the enemy then, but spent the whole time worrying about an encounter. Just so now.

He peered at the gully and the hut at the end of it. It looked like a nice place to hide, so long as no one was there already. He could finish his cigarette in peace and, perhaps, wait for someone to come to him. The wardens would be out soon. He went forward, smoking thriftily, wondering where Georgie had got to. What if she was shot? How would he know? Maybe that was what the gunfire had meant, although he recalled no mention of this earlier.

The land narrowed down toward the gully. It was a bottleneck with the hut as cork. No movement there. It was safe.

Bob sprinted ahead, circling the rise above the gully. He came back to the edge at the point where it fell away to the hut. When Peter came out of the bottleneck he would be an easy shot less than twenty yards below. Bob raised a finger to the wind, checked for the speed. Even gentle gusts could drift the pellets off course if you did not choose your moment. He bit his lip excitedly, trying to keep quiet. He dropped to one knee, settled the pistol over his forearm as he sighted into the gully.

—Come on, Peter. Show yourself.

Georgie rubbed her forehead. Greasepaint came off on her hand. She turned three hundred and sixty degrees, swearing under her breath.

—Where am I, for God's sake?

She glanced at the compass again, thinking that she would never live it down if Williamson stepped in to give her directions.

—All right, the answer's simple: start walking and go in a straight line until you get out of the trees. It's not the Amazon jungle, after all.

She pushed by some overhanging branches in the gloom. Her foot went down, searching for ground that wasn't there. She teetered forward, lost her balance, and tumbled down a steep incline. Branches whacked her face as she went.

The earth she fetched up on was not soft. Groaning, she rolled over and struggled to her knees. Her gun had fallen into the boll of a tree farther down. The compass was nearby, little glass face shattered. To make it worse, bright daylight glowed through on her left. She had been that close. Well, that was it, as far as she was concerned. She would quit all the guerrilla-style prowling and get out where the ground was clear. If someone shot her, so much hard luck.

She reached to pick up the gun. In doing so, she had a direct view down through the trees to a patch of flat ground.

In the center of that ground was Williamson.

There was a moment of incomprehension, when she asked herself why he was lying that way, with his red beret on his chest, why the soil under him was dark and wet. Then she saw that the red was not a beret.

She fell over. She was aware of her legs giving way, and she fell on her hands and knees.

She said, "Oh, Christ," quietly, several times. But she stopped herself from being sick. She even managed to move closer, while a thin string of saliva trickled from her mouth. All she could hear was her own shivering breath. She touched the warden's tunic with one fingertip. His eyes were open and clouded. Steam rose faintly from the mess of blood on his chest.

She convinced herself that saying "Oh, Christ" all the time was getting her nowhere, and she stopped saying it. She pushed the goggles off her face to see better. She was quite certain he was dead. But his face seemed so ordinary.

Like her father. That afternoon the police came. How they said he was found in his car, far back in the woods, with a length of garden hose leading from exhaust pipe to passenger window. Mother turned hysterical. She attacked Georgie, who was then fourteen, screaming: "It's her doing. It's her fault." A policeman held her back until she broke down, crying. She said: "I'm sorry," in a pathetic voice; then a doctor came to sedate her. Georgie heard the police wondering who would identify the body for them. She asked if she could do it, to be helpful. They stared at her: the dead man's daughter. She mirrored their gaze calmly. They did not realize how young she was. They took her in a police car. On the way there, one of the policemen smiled a lot and told her everything would be all right and kept glancing surreptitiously at her legs and her breasts. Then the mortuary, and she leaned over to get a closer look at her father's face. It was shiny and the color of cherries, but the same face. She had always imagined that people "looked" dead, as if something had gone out of their bodies that you could label. Here was the man she used to call Daddy, and except for the color, he might have sat up and said hello. Later, the police asked questions, the mother and the daughter. Did they have any idea why he killed himself? Of course they had ideas, but the mother refused to tell. And so, in the end, did Georgie. She never told anyone.

She realized she was whimpering in the back of her throat, which was worse than saying "Oh, Christ" all the time. She stopped that also, wiped the spittle from her mouth.

She had no idea what this meant—accident or murder—but she had to find Peter and the others.

She rose, shaking her head. Williamson's face was her father's. She turned away, making for the light, beginning to run.

The cry flickered past him on the wind. He thought it was a bird. His attention shifted for a second. Then he forgot it and gave full concentration to Peter, who would emerge from cover any second now.

A spine of gorse irritated his knee. As he moved the half inch that eased it, Peter came out of the gully. It was a surprise; he was nowhere close to where Bob had expected, and he was zigzagging low to the ground.

—He must have sussed me out. Or he's just being careful. The bastard.

Peter bobbed and weaved across the stretch leading to the hut, never taking a straight course or stopping in one place long enough to allow careful aim. In another ten seconds he would be into the safety of the hut, and that would give him tremendous advantage. Bob shuffled round quickly, drawing a bead on his target again. Taking them on the wing was always the most difficult. He squinted down the long barrel of the Magnum, swung a couple of degrees ahead. It all depended on guessing which way Peter would jump next, and Bob fell back on instinct. He let it flow into his hand and gun, aiming for the spot where he knew Peter would be in half a second.

He squeezed the trigger, felt the hard snap of the gun firing.

Blue dye splattered over Peter's right shoulder, stinging his face. He was so startled by the impact that he missed his footing and went down like a felled tree.

Bob leapt up. His grin was wider than London Bridge. He raised his arms triumphantly, whooping and laughing at what he had done.

"First blood to our side."

Peter tore at the goggles, smeared the dye off his cheek. He looked bitterly at the hill, where Bob was doing some kind of victory dance. He wanted to lie down and weep. If he had to get shot, couldn't it at least have been Dan? He watched Bob caught up in the excitement of the "kill." He was beating his chest now, still laughing. He was so alive it was unbearable.

"How's that, you old bugger?"

"You were lucky," Peter called back.

"Lucky? Why, you sore loser." He shook his gun high in the air, yelling: "The winner and still fucking champion!"

Peter heard another report somewhere far off, like the shots before. He opened his mouth to ask what it could be.

The top of Bob's head exploded. A pink corona blossomed around him, like the suddenly released spray from a beer can, and the whole body arched back. His face twisted for an instant. He gazed wildly at Peter, a child asking why. It could only have been a reflex. The next moment, he came forward over the crest of the hill and fell. He rolled like a bag of meat, making terrible, meaningless noises through slack lips. He came to rest three yards away.

Peter stared at the pieces of blood and brain on the grass where the body had rolled.

Georgie tried to guess where the shot had come from. Northeast was all she could be certain of. She took off her jacket and threw it aside. She was sweating heavily and the coat was dead weight. She called out again, knowing how stupid it was if someone was out there with a gun, but she did not want to be alone anymore. The island was too big, too cold, too dark.

A man appeared, running from the direction of the burn. She dived flat, waited until certain it was Dan. Her fingers clenched the earth under her hands. The soil was hard. She could smell its sour odor.

"What the fuck's going on?" he demanded, when he was in shouting distance.

She clambered up. "Don't stay in the open. Don't stand still."

He half-paused, surprised and annoyed, then resumed running, jumping a chattering thread of water.

"What is it? What's going on?"

Her head shook mechanically. "Don't know," she said. "The warden's dead. Someone shot him."

Dan saw the glaze of shock in her eyes. He caught her by the arm and dragged her toward the stream. He pushed her into the channel it cut. The water hurried over smooth black stone. She knelt beside it as he checked that they were alone.

"Williamson's been shot. Is that right?"

"I told you," she said.

"Was it an accident? Did it look like an accident?"

"He didn't do it himself. There wasn't any gun. Only his stupid bloody pellet thing." She leaned over the water, head drooping. She covered her eyes, pulling at her face as if re-molding it. "There was a hole in his chest."

Dan peeked over the channel's edge again. Everything was clear. He had been walking in to find Williamson when the last shot came. He had started running then, not knowing why. But something about the sound of it, not so far away, struck a note in his head. He tried to remember what it was.

Georgie rocked slightly. He put a hand down to touch her, but chickened out.

"Georgie, where is he? I have to see for myself."

"He won't be able to help you."

"No, Georgie. Where is he?"

She pointed to the trees behind. "By the path."

"Okay. Look, you stay here. I'll be back in a while, all right?"

She went on rocking.

He took another look round, then sprang up and made for the trees. Georgie was safe where she was, if there was truly anything to be afraid of. Personally, he wondered if there had been some kind of dumb accident. He could not believe anything bad was happening on his island. Until that was certain, though, he would take no chances.

He lunged into the trees fast, breaking through the smaller branches on the way up to the path. It took a few minutes to find the body, but there it was, just as Georgie had said. No wonder she was in shock; the wound was a real mess. It took him back twenty years—

—Hey, that's it.

He bent over the body, closing off his mind to the sick smell of bleeding meat. The wound came from something high-powered. Rifle, not handgun. And the shots he heard, the familiarity of them. Back in Vietnam, Charlie used AK47 rifles. Charlie was what they called the Vietcong, and AK47s had a distinctive sound to them even when firing single shot.

There was nothing useful around the body. He got up and retraced his steps. He noticed that he was having difficulty breathing. This was the only physical sign of reaction to death. After twenty years, no matter how cool he had been about it back then, he had to expect something.

Having seen the evidence for himself, he was more careful about recrossing the distance to the burn. He recalled the way they used to do it, on the few occasions when there was clear ground not loaded with Bouncing Bettys and booby-trapped artillery rounds and M-14s. He got back to her.

"Did you find him?" she asked, as if he had been looking for a friend.

He sat, panting for breath, nodded. "I think we should find the others."

"It's not my fault," she said.

The oddness of the words jarred on him. "I know. Don't worry about it."

"I think I know why." She leaned toward him urgently. "It's Williamson. One of the other wardens doesn't like him, maybe he's always bullying them. So they shot him. It's murder."

"Maybe you're right, baby. Let's find the others and head back to the lodge. However you see it, this is police business. Where's Peter?"

"He was going to skirt round to the north and come in behind you."

And Bob, he knew, was doing the same thing in reverse.

With luck, they had found each other somewhere to the east of the big plantation.

"We take it easy," he said. "Maybe we're not in danger, but we keep our heads down until we know for sure. You okay to move?"

"Yes."

"We'll go through the small plantation, okay? If someone's out there, he'll be in the trees, but we'll have cover too." He tried to help her up, but she yanked her arm from his grasp.

"Stop treating me like an idiot child, will you? I'm fine."

"Okay, you're fine," he said. "Listen, when we cross the open ground, don't stick to me. Zigzag all you like and keep your distance."

She nodded. "Colonel," she said softly.

They moved together. He went first, although he would have liked to stay close to her. All the way to the safety of the trees, which was better than half a mile, he dodged less than she did. Somewhere in the back of his mind was the thought that any sniper out there would prefer him for a target, so Georgie would get away. He tried to guess where any fire would come from, struggling to revive antennae developed many years ago, but it was no good. All that stuff was long-buried. He had made sure of that. And he wasn't taking it seriously yet. Accident, the evidence said. Some freaky bastard warden who got his kicks following the action with real hardware. Back in 1967, he'd known a guy from the Marine Corps who relaxed on leave by sticking a gun out of the hotel window and leading passersby, finger on the trigger the whole time. So, Williamson had come across one of his wardens indulging in the same happy shit and, maybe in surprise or argument, the guy had let off a shot.

It seemed more likely than the other theory, anyhow: that someone was after them. Hardly anyone was supposed to know where he was, for one thing. And for another, if some rival or psychopath had taken out a contract on him, why knock over Williamson? A pro does the job he's paid for and leaves it at that. The accident theory held more water.

They reached the trees. Dan turned, hushing Georgie as

he checked out the darkness. In truth, there was nothing to see, but he thought she would feel better to see him looking.

"Go northeast," he said.

"That's where the last shot came from."

"I know, but that's where Bobby and Peter are. We got to team up again, make sure everyone's okay, then get back to the lodge."

They moved through the gentler rise and fall of the small plantation. Dan smelled the sappy, sweet fragrance of the trees. He listened for more shooting or for voices. Nothing, though. All was normal; he could hear the background rush and pull of the ocean to the east. There were few places on the island you could get away from that sound. It was one of the things he had loved about it from the start.

They encountered no one on their way to the upper end of the small plantation. Birds fluttered in the thick branches overhead and they were both scared by some small animal disturbed by their passing. It was ridiculous, like they had been left alone on the island. But Dan knew that an entire battalion could be hidden in country like this.

They rested at the edge of the trees, looking northwest across bare heath.

"There's nowhere to hide," Georgie said.

"We'll take it down that fold in the hills. If you see anything, anything at all, hit the ground and find yourself some nice, thick gorse."

She followed his instructions listlessly. He could not tell if she were all right or not. It was the first time he had ever seen her look vulnerable, but she would not let him help.

The sky was an iron lid. It gave an impression of being exposed in the open and closed in at the same time. They ran beneath it toward the sea, until Georgie stopped dead and pointed.

"Over there."

He looked. Saw Peter limping toward them through the heather. He was carrying something. A weight that was too much for him. He saw them waving at him, and the tears that were mixed with blood ran down his face. He stumbled, dropping the burden. Dan lunged for Georgie, to stop her seeing what he had already seen. She shrugged him off, fell down beside the body.

Peter knelt opposite her with his head pressed against the ground, crying. They looked as if they were worshiping the damaged carcass.

Dan stared. He felt everything slipping into the dark.

3

Real War

27

IT WAS A WIDE, FLAT TRAIL, BUT IT CURVED IN SNAKY SWEEPS and was flanked by thick brush and big-leaved, sickly-looking trees. This would not have been so bad if the two squads were in the positions they were supposed to be, moving through the tangle on either side of the trail to protect the flanks from ambush. As it was, the squads had dropped way back, or his squad had moved forward too fast. They had come up the trail without protection and now six of them were pinned down by snipers.

"Jesus Lord," Smitty said, hand over his helmet, face in the dirt. "Those dinks must be shitting themselves over this."

Dan lay next to him in a hollow that looked as if it had been a shell crater last year. "Why?"

"We walked into it like guests at a wedding. That fucking Connor." Connor was the platoon leader. A Green Beret. He had taken the five of them out ahead with him. Him and his tiger-striped shotgun. He was the first to go down, arm blown completely from the shoulder. "Fucking Connor," Smitty said again.

"Fucking army," Dan, who was Daniel then, said.

"Fucking everyone," Smitty said. "Oh, shit!"

The explosions came close together, one of them going directly into a hole where Six Pack was hiding with the radio. As soon as the roar of the mortars died, they could hear Six Pack screaming over and over with the machine-gun fire.

"There goes the fucking radio," Marty yelled across to them. Marty had been walking around all day with a cool look on his face, saying: "I dropped some acid, man. You wanna try some?" Now he was acting as if the ambush were a tea party.

Daniel lifted his face out of the dirt and watched Marty get up from cover like there was nothing to be afraid of. He dodged over to Six Pack. A stream of fire kicked dust at his feet. He looked like a dancer. Just as he reached the hole with smoke coming out of it, Six Pack stopped screaming. Daniel waited; then, through the rattling fire, they heard Marty saying, "Radio's all screwed up."

"Same goes for Six Pack," Smitty said. His brown hand clenched on his helmet as the mortar fire started again. Daniel gritted his teeth, closing his eyes as if being in the dark would make him safe.

"Where's the others?" he asked, realizing his voice was somewhere near being a screech. He gulped back on it, trying to stop the hot tremble of fear in his belly from burning out like that again.

"See what's happening to us?" Smitty said. "Well, those other guys got some of the same back there. Connor should've kept us together. Charlie's going to take us to pieces." His rich drawl sounded scratchy. "Don't see no help from behind for a long time."

Daniel shivered on the ground, feet scrabbling at the earth every time a shot came close.

"How long do we have to stay here?"

Smitty raised up to spit. "Who's the senior guy here?" He called it loud to everyone left alive. "Who's senior?"

"That's you," Marty said.

"Right," the Griffin said. Daniel saw his wide yellow eyes blinking over the edge of the trail.

"We make Smitty captain." Marty began to laugh. "Or colonel maybe. How'd you like being general, Smitty?"

Smitty was the oldest of the four guys left. He was twenty-three.

"Thank you kindly for the honor, gentlemen," he said. "But my daddy always told me to keep out of the gold braid."

"Shit, Smitty, what do we do?" the Griffin said.

Smitty closed one eye, screwing his face up as bullets pinged off the ground around them. "Well, Griffin, it's like this. You roll yourself up nice and tight on the ground."

"Yeah?" the Griffin said.

"Then you stick your head between your legs."

"Yeah?" the Griffin said.

"Then you kiss your black ass good-bye."

"Oh, shit."

Daniel saw the V.C. come out of the trees close behind the Griffin.

It all took so little time. The Griffin twisted over, lifting his gun, face stretched out of shape with fear. Then the V.C. was letting him have it with the AK47, and the Griffin smacked back on the ground with a red fountain starting from his groin. Daniel started to aim at the V.C., but he was too scared and too slow. The jerking of the Griffin's rifle finally found a target, and the V.C. went down like a balloon collapsing.

The Griffin began to scream. Not like Six Pack had done, but in words, screaming: "Mama, Mama, oh Mama, it hurts, Jesus Christ, Jesus Christ."

"Can't we do something?" Daniel asked.

Smitty was breathing as if he had run a mile in three. "You make that crossing," he pointed at the ten feet of trail that separated them, "and you can do whatever you like."

The Griffin went on screaming, and once more, Daniel saw the blood pumping out of him.

He began to wish that someone would put another bullet in the Griff to end it. How could they stand listening to it, even from an enemy?

The mortars started again, blowing up part of the undergrowth on the edge of the trail. Marty fired at random from where he was, and then he joined in with the Griffin's screams.

"Shut up," Daniel yelled at him, not knowing whether he meant just Marty or the Griffin as well. "Shut up, you fucking pervert."

"Community singing." Marty laughed. He popped away at the trees, aiming at nothing, screaming again.

"You stop that," Smitty bawled. "Or I'll ram that rifle up your fucking asshole." He subsided, shaking.

It did no good.

Bam—Bam—Screaming.

The Griffin's cries got hoarse, the words fell apart. He sounded like a man with bubble gum clogging his throat.

It was too much. Daniel squirmed around to Smitty, tugging at his jacket. Smitty was crying, the sobs coming up from deep in his chest, and the worst thing was that Daniel could not hear them for the gunfire: the quick, staccato sounds of the AK47s and the mortars, and the Griffin and Marty.

Flies swarmed in the air above them. Tears streamed down Smitty's face; dirt stuck to his face. Daniel stared at him, not believing it. Smitty was always cool. Smitty stayed sane and helped all the others to keep their heads through all the shit. To see him lose control was worse than losing it himself.

He formed Smitty's name, and his expression gave him away. Smitty touched at the tear streaks, began to rub at them as if he were trying to wipe away all the days and nights of fear and the terrible things he had seen over and over again until they were carved inside his eyes.

"I can't take it no more, Danny boy," he said. "I can't."

Daniel almost hit him. He had always relied on Smitty to see him through this fucking war.

Marty stopped screaming.

"Hey, Danny. Whadda we do?"

Daniel clenched a handful of Smitty's jacket. "I don't know," he snapped. "Let me think."

Marty gave a jackass laugh. "This is very metaphysical," he said.

Then it all started again.

"Dan?"

He snapped out of it. He was cold. He squatted against the remaining complete wall of the hut. Peter stared at him.

Bob's body lay on the old stone floor, the shattered head and upper body covered with the jacket he had been wearing. One hand stuck out from under the coat, palm down on the ground, strangely alive-looking. Dan's eyes flicked to it, expecting it to twitch or something. He knew that Bobby was dead—half the kid's brains had been blown away—but he could not accept it as he had Williamson's death. The hand lay like a crab on the floor.

"What is it?" he said.

"What're we going to do?"

There it was again. The question first asked of him all those years ago. On that day, he did not know what to do. He had to think for himself for the first time in his life, not just slide easily along and allow some other sucker to take the shit. What had he been thinking about Vietnam? All that high-minded stuff about getting away from it and leaving it behind. He had never been troubled by those days, had he? Nothing bothered him.

—It shaped your whole life, you schmuck.

It had made him realize that you would always be in trouble as long as you let someone else give the orders, and he had come back swearing never to let it happen again. His climb to all the money and the power started then, didn't it? If there was any one explanation of where he was today, it was that time. He had sworn he would always have an answer when they said: What do we do? Yet he was paralyzed now, like the kid who complied with his draft papers mainly because he could not decide to do otherwise. It had been Peter who decided to backtrack to the hut when he realized they were a target from the tree line.

"Williamson's dead too," he said, hearing the words roll out like the beginning of a casualty list.

"The warden?" Peter said. "How?"

Dan told him. Saying that Georgie found the body made him look at her.

She sat opposite him, huddled down by the wall, as far from the body as the cover provided by the ruined hut allowed. She did not move. She had said nothing when she saw Bob. She looked over the ragged stonework, eyes wide open, staring away from the gully to the sea. There were no tears, no collapse. Nothing.

"What's happening?" Peter said. "Who's doing this?"

Dan gnawed at the thick skin along his thumbnail, biting

through to the flesh without realizing it. What to do, what to do? He had to think clearly, but he felt as if someone had crept up and filled his head with concrete. Every physical sense was tuned up to an unbearable level, the brain was frozen. Just like the old days. Going out on night maneuvers, the medics used to hand them Dexedrine and all kinds of uppers, but he never took them because any kind of action would send him so high that any more would have blown his mind out. His middle-aged body was no longer accustomed to feeling like this. Every movement of the breeze like a blade on his skin, the stench of his own fear-sweat and Peter's, the grating of the stone under their boots. He wondered how he could have got through a year of feeling like this all the time.

"Roland Ashe," Peter said.

"What?"

"He threatened to get you, didn't he? Why shouldn't he carry out the threat?"

He took hold of Peter's jacket to pull him close. "If it was someone after me personally, why shoot the other two?"

"Practice."

"Don't be stupid, Peter. Makes no sense."

"What makes sense to you?" Peter's voice broke. He was still trembling. "Tell me what makes sense to you."

"I don't kn— Has to be some kind of accident."

"Two of them in one morning. You like your coincidences cut thick, don't you?"

"Will you get a grip."

"Someone's trying to kill us."

"It's a psycho. It must be."

"What's a psychopath doing on this godforsaken rock? We're a hundred miles from the nearest city. They don't ship them out here, do they?"

"Will you shut up and let me think."

"Fine." Peter's voice rose to hysteria. "You sit and deliberate while whoever it is moves in."

"Drop it, Peter."

The warning was there. Peter sank back miserably.

Dan tried to think. But it was difficult, because this was the same thing as before, and that idea stuck in his mind and started going round and round. One minute, walking around thinking everything was okay; the next, looking at carcasses that used to be friends.

Peter took out his watch and flipped the cover. He lingered over the inscriptions a long time before saying: "Ten past two. Where are the others?"

"Others?"

"The wardens. The wondrous wardens who look after the gullible public here. They should be out and about by now. They were meant to be here by twelve."

Dan shrugged, not really listening.

"Unless it's them," Peter said.

"All of them?"

"I'm just considering the possibilities."

"If it was the wardens, they could've taken us all out when we stepped off the boat."

"Maybe they're coming now. They may've realized what's happening and stayed under cover. Perhaps someone's gone back to the lodge already to radio for help. After all, there're no guns on the island, are there?"

"Only one," Dan said.

"So, they wouldn't try to tackle it themselves. They'd call for help."

It was hard to let the hope die, but Dan could not meet Peter's eye.

After a while, Peter turned away and stared at Bob's body. "Vickie was right. She said there was something sick about playing murders like this. She told me we'd all get a shock if it suddenly turned out to be real. Bob got a shock, didn't he? . . . He looked so surprised when it happened." He stroked the worn gold of his watch. "I shouldn't have come."

"Next time, refuse the invitation."

Tears came into Peter's eyes again. "I was so afraid of him. Scared to death that I'd walk into my office one day and find him behind my desk."

"Peter."

"That was all it took? One bullet? It was so easy."

"Peter, for God's sake."

"What're we going to do?"

Dan's nostrils flared at the smell of the body.

"Georgie?"

She closed her eyes. "Yes."

"You okay?"

"I'm all right, thanks."

He scuttled over the floor to her. "Try not to think about it," he said quietly.

"I'm not thinking about anything." Her voice was so ordinary. She turned to him and she was smiling her usual flippant, beautiful smile. "There's nothing to worry about."

Something in him twisted with pain at the sight of her. He reached to touch her.

"Don't," she said. The smile was still there, but all the light was out and for a second she looked as dead as Bob.

"Georgie, let me help you."

"Keep your hands off me."

"You're in shock, kid—"

"Just don't touch me." Her voice was something near a shriek.

Peter grabbed him. "For God's sake, leave her alone."

He struck the hand off, determined to snap her out of it. But she was turning from him, going back to the view down the hill to the sea. Her shoulders were drawn up. She tensed.

"You're really in control of yourself, aren't you?" Peter said. "The Vietnam veteran, the man with all the experience. Why don't you lay a booby trap, or make a bow and arrow out of your belt and a couple of sticks? That's what you people do, isn't it?"

"Lay off, Peter. You're over the line."

"Well, start acting like the boss. You're forever telling your junior employees that the world's a battleground. Let's see some proof."

"I'm warning you—"

"If I want to be threatened I can stand up and let our own personal hit man take shots at me. We're all going to get killed because someone doesn't like your business methods."

"Shut up."

"Your past's catching up with you. You'll get all of us—"

A chunk of the wall exploded in tiny fragments. Dan heard the whine of the ricochet as the gunshot echoed from somewhere up the gully. Splinters of the wall struck his cheek. Peter yelped as shards embedded themselves in his hand. Georgie fell back and the gun rang out again, chipping at the wall above Dan's head.

There was nowhere much to hide. The sniper had moved up on the rise to a place where he could see in through the door of the hut. By hunching into the corners on either side of the door they could just keep out of the firing line, but it was tight. Georgie lay on one side, face against the cold floor, staring fixedly at the rabbit droppings strewn around. Dan was squashed up to the corner with Peter almost hugging him to take up less space.

"All right," Dan said, raising his voice every time the gun blasted another piece of the wall. "It's okay. One guy out there, no more."

"One's enough," Peter groaned.

"One guy with a pop gun," Dan said, remembering how Smitty used to laugh whenever they came across an abandoned AK47. "Well, look what we have here." He'd grin, tossing the rifle with its curved magazine high in the air. "Someone out there thinks he's playing soldier boy." But it paid to remember that the AK47 could kill people just the same as any rifle.

"He'll lay off in a second," he said, smelling the damp earth against his face, different from the fetid stink of the Vietnamese soil where others had died.

"How d'you know?"

"If he wanted to kill us, he could've taken us out just now. I was sloppy, he could've had me. This is just to scare the shit out of us."

"Effective, isn't it?" Peter said, shivering each time a bullet whacked home.

Dan looked to Georgie. She was in the same position, never flinching or showing any sign that she was bothered by what was happening.

"It's okay," he said to her, though she did not seem to hear. "He'll use up the magazine any time now, then I figure he pulls back." He had been counting the shots. AK47s took a thirty-round box. The sniper started off with single shots and had moved over to automatic. He was nearly empty.

"Georgie, snap out of it. When we get the chance, we run like crazy, you understand?"

"Just tell me when."

Why an AK47? he was thinking. Lousy little gun for long-range shooting. What did it matter? He wasn't shooting long range.

A bullet struck the floor six inches from his head. He noticed the smears of blood on the floor where the splinters had gouged him.

Then the shooting stopped. He lifted up a fraction and peeped over the wall. It was far enough to see and far enough to get his head blown off if he was wrong. As he scanned the gully, he saw the hunched shape of the sniper running along the top of the rise.

"Okay, let's go!"

"What about Bob?" Peter asked.

"Forget him. Georgie, go."

She got up, looking curiously at the gully.

"Go on. Head for the small plantation. Peter, take her."

They went together, Georgie shrugging off Peter's guiding hand. Dan looked back at the rise and the sniper was not there. He noticed then that Georgie was not wearing her jacket anymore. The way weather conditions were going, she would freeze in no time. He snatched up the blood-splattered coat that covered Bob and carried it with him. The last he saw of Bob was the one eye that was still in his head staring crookedly off at an angle, like Robert Kennedy's in that famous photograph at the Ambassador Hotel.

He ran after them, never staying in a straight line, yelling at them to do the same. But Peter was doing all he could just to move, limping in those damn boots. Georgie kept going, but looked back too much.

"Keep going," he said. "Into the trees."

They were already out of the firing line (he hoped). They

reached the trees ten yards ahead of him. He crashed through the low branches and fell hard on the needled floor.

Peter lay with his back against a trunk, breathing heavily. Georgie checked back to see if they were followed. Dan dragged himself to a sitting position, panting.

Peter shook his head. "Dan, I'm sorry."

"Forget it, man. The first time I ever saw someone killed, I couldn't eat or sleep for a week. It doesn't get easier."

"There he is," Georgie hissed.

"What?"

"The killer. There, by the hut."

Dan looked for himself. The sniper was going up the gully away from the hut. He was too far away to make out clearly.

"Who is he?" he muttered. "Who the fuck is he?"

"What was he doing there?" Georgie said.

"Checking on his handiwork," Peter said.

"We can't stay here. It's too close to the open. Let's move on and find somewhere defensible. Georgie, put this on." He took off his own jacket and held it out to her.

"What about the other one?" she asked, gazing at it.

"It was Bob's."

"Let me have it."

"It's . . . it's dirty."

"I know. Give it to me."

Peter frowned as Dan handed Bob's jacket to her. She held it by the collar, studying the congealing mess across one shoulder. She put it on the ground and started rubbing it hard in the dirt. She held it up, shook the loose muck off, and put it on. She looked at the two men, who were watching her with something like horror in their eyes.

"Are we going?" she said, getting up.

They followed her, going up the gentle slope into the dense part of the small plantation.

Georgie grabbed a thin, whippy branch to help her up the slope. She saw the mud on her sleeve, reddish-black where she had wiped it on the ground to remove the blood and bone and gray tissue.

—Is that all it is? She tried to reach inside herself to find the emotions the others had shown. She felt nothing at all, except a vague loathing. At first she was not even sure of that, but when they tried to touch her, she knew. There were the two men—Peter cried like a child, Dan was pale and shaken. And she could only think that this blood and bone and brain matter had been part of a man who slept with her last night. It did not bother her. She was interested in a technical way, as she had been at school in biology lessons. How could a mass of water and minerals make a human being? How could there be nothing more to Bob than a big lump of cells that looked like a gray walnut? When she was a girl, she would stand naked in front of the bathroom mirror at home, looking at her body. She would think of the way men stared at her, and imagine all the bones under her skin, the skull beneath her face, the blood pumping from the wet muscle of the heart, the foul juices swirling in her stomach, breaking food down into a mess of puke, the shit and the piss. She wondered how anyone could ever face touching another human being when they knew these things.

Bob with his head broken open, Williamson with a great hole in his body.

She saw Peter overtaking her. She knew his body was sweating, churning out odors and nauseous fluids, just as hers was. —We're all carcasses, she thought.

—Why don't I feel anything? I looked on his face and it was ruined, destroyed, but I felt nothing. I should, shouldn't I?

Her father's calm face on the stainless-steel table.

—I'm not best placed to feel anything very much.

Dan stopped below her, checking again to see that they were not followed. A black stubble was already showing on his jaw. He looked as though he had been fighting all his life. He turned and caught her watching him, managed a smile. She thought she ought to smile back.

She reached in a pocket of the jacket, felt Bob's knife and the map folded there.

"This is okay," Dan said, turning a circle. "Well covered, but we can see any bastard making an approach."

Georgie lifted her face to the light filtering down through the trees. High overhead was a tiny shred of gray-blue sky. She thought about Bob lying down there on that cold stone floor.

They sat on the ground. Peter dug in his pocket and took out the chocolate. He offered it round and was surprised when they took some.

—How can we be eating when a friend's just died?

—Because we're hungry. We'd better eat, hadn't we, otherwise we won't be sharp enough to deal with this.

Dan's face had a sharpened look about it. His eyes were bright and hard and he seemed to be covering every inch of ground all the time as he spoke.

"Take off those scarves. We're conspicuous enough as it is." They removed the neckerchiefs Williamson had given them. Dan scuffed a hole in the earth and buried them.

"Right, what do we know? We've got two dead for certain."

"What about the other wardens?" Georgie said, chewing.

"I guess they're locked up in the lodge."

"Not dead?"

"They can't be," Peter said. "There were five of them and that engineer down there the last we saw. Even if no one was armed, it couldn't be easy to kill all of them with one rifle."

"They're dead," Georgie said. "They could've got out by now, but they're dead."

"Okay, we can guess on that all day," Dan said. "Let's leave it that they're out of action. Who else is left?"

"The old man with the boat."

"Anyone seen the boat?"

"Hang on." Peter tapped his forehead. "What about the other warden? Williamson said he was out alone somewhere."

"And we don't know what he looks like," Georgie said.

"Maybe it's him." Peter took out his watch and stroked the cover with his thumb again.

"Why him?" Dan asked.

"Why anyone?"

"Do *you* know what he looks like, Dan?"

"I saw photographs of the staff when they were hired. I can't remember."

"Why should he want to kill us?" Georgie persisted.

"Ex-army?" Peter said. "Perhaps he's gone mad. Remember that fellow in California who machine-gunned the local McDonalds? Perhaps he couldn't stand civilian life anymore."

"MacNeice was a teacher of physical education," Dan said.

"That sort of kills that idea, doesn't it?" Peter said. Suddenly he grinned at Dan, who smiled back. They both felt guilty at the same moment and turned serious again.

"Say MacNeice isn't the sniper. That means he's out there somewhere, and perhaps the sniper doesn't know."

"He'll be armed with what we're carrying." Dan tapped the pellet gun at his side.

"At least there's an element of surprise."

"This guy, whoever he is, knows his way around. I figure he's studied the terrain. He's a fair shot too. He wasted Bobby from something like three hundred yards. Not easy with a pop gun like that. And normal people don't get to use an AK47 every day of the week, not in this country anyhow."

"Then it's a professional?"

"Williamson was regular army. Saw time in Northern Ireland. He should've been hard to take."

Georgie unfolded her map and spread it on the ground. The island, scaled at two inches to the mile, lay in its trap of ocean. Jora was south, the tiny bare rock of Rheisa Mhio Rhoidan southeast. Above was Langa, and across the sound was Laing and the little marker for Kinlosch Ferry.

They were all conscious of the map being Bob's, not island property. A small stain on it looked like blood. They gathered round it, began studying the details.

"We're here," Dan said, pointing to a small circle of contour lines to the northeast. "Half a mile from the sea in the east, mile and a half from the lodge. The killer must have been somewhere here, along the northeast tree line of the big plantation when he shot Bob. Williamson's body's about here, a mile southwest of the water shrine."

"He gets around, doesn't he?" Peter said.

"He was last seen by us over here by the crofter's shack. He headed west to the big plantation again."

"Which isn't to say that's where he went."

"He's not close."

"How can you be sure?"

"I'd have seen him."

Georgie took another square of chocolate. She seemed almost bored.

"What we have to do is think in terms of how to get out of this, where to go, what to do."

"Why not stay put?" Peter asked. "You said this was a good place."

"Not that good. If our friend finds us, he doesn't have to come close."

"Then what d'you suggest?"

"I'm thinking."

"Come on. You're the one with the war experience."

Dan finally yanked the plastic goggles over his head and threw them on the ground.

"Look, why don't we get this straight? Yes, I was in fucking Vietnam. Infantry. One year, just like hundreds of thousands of other guys. I got shot at, I got through it, but it was mainly luck, not judgment. The difference between me and the ones with their names on that wall in Washington is I kept my eyes open all the time and lucked my way through. A Green Beret I never was. Understand?"

"All right."

"Just stop thinking I can make guerrilla fighters out of you in three easy lessons."

"Why don't we swim for it?" Georgie said.

"Remember what the old man said?" Peter's thumb rubbed hard at the pheasant on the cover of his watch. "It's a good mile and a quarter across the sound."

"Not there." She pointed to the southern tip of the island, separated from Langa by no more than half a mile.

"No good," Dan said. "We'd make a hundred feet in those seas on a day like this."

"Get something, then. A log, maybe. We could use it to keep afloat, then we might drift close enough to some other island to swim for it."

"This ain't the Mediterranean in July. It's October, and the water temperature out there'd kill us in a few hours. You see any boats around this morning? Neither did I. We can't risk it unless everything else fails."

"That's a point," Peter said. "If the killer isn't MacNeice, how did he get onto the island?"

"Two possibilities. He hijacked Logan, or he has a boat of his own."

"So we'd better look for it if we want to get off this rock," Georgie said. "He must have some way of getting off."

"Correct. That's item two."

"What's item one?"

"Get to the lodge, see what's happened there, and get on the radio, if it's okay."

"Can't we just barricade ourselves inside?" Peter asked. "It's pretty solid. We could sit tight and wait for help to come."

"We could, if our friend lets us get that close."

"Cheer me up some more."

"I figure we'll get more done if we go for both items at once."

"How?"

"You two go looking for a boat, while I check out the lodge."

"What?" Peter and Georgie said it together.

"The longer we're here, the more chance there is someone else dies. Being together makes it easy for one man on his own. If we split, he can't follow all of us."

"This island is three miles across," Peter said. "That's a lot of coastline to cover on foot."

"Look at the map. The high cliffs all along the west side mean no one puts in there—the climb takes too long. If he took the lodge first, he didn't come in from the mainland

side. So that leaves us the northern shore: the current's fast,
there's maybe one place for a small boat to come in safe. Or
it's in the south." He pointed at the channel separating them
from Jora, thumbed a stretch of the southeast. "Plenty coves,
good-size cliffs, nothing hard to climb. I have to guess, I'd say
somewhere down there."

"That's the other side of the island," Peter said. "How do
we get there?"

"It's mostly forest. And, with a little luck, the sniper follows me because he wants to stop us taking the lodge."

"It's dangerous, Dan."

"Sitting still here looks to be pretty precarious, my man.
I'll dig up everything they pounded into us back in Chu Lai
and slither the distance on my belly if necessary. All you
have to do is go very carefully when you hit the open ground.
We set schedules. When you establish the situation, make
your way back to me. One of you have a compass?"

Georgie showed the good compass that Bob had brought.
Then they pooled their equipment to see what use could be
made of it. There were Bob's hunting knife, two compasses,
the large map and two smaller ones, three bars of chocolate,
Peter's cigarettes and lighter and, of course, the pellet guns.
Two from the island's stock and Bob's .44 Magnum. Georgie
had taken it and left her own. Dan picked the guns up and
peered hard at them.

"What is it?" Peter said. "Can we convert them to shoot
something solid?"

"Don't get your hopes up. Better keep them anyway.
Maybe there's something in the lodge we can use."

They checked the time, agreed it was two thirty.

"Look at it this way." Dan tried for a smile. "If we stay
healthy till dark, someone'll get curious at the hotel and try
to contact us. Then we'll be fine."

"Fine," Georgie said.

They collected the gear together. Dan listened for a while,
heard nothing but wind rushing in the treetops.

"Okay," he said. "Follow me, but don't stay too close." He
realized this was old habit coming back. When you were

going through territory that the gooks had literally peppered with mines, you found yourself trying to step light, walking in a braced, unnatural way, and if you got really nervous, then you tried to step where the guy ahead of you put his feet, until he got pissed off with having you for a shadow. If you persisted with it, then any Bouncing Betty or frag mine that he happened to trip would waste you as well as him. Therefore, don't cling to my heels. Even if it was twenty-year-old advice, it was still good. If they huddled up, the sniper could waste two for the price of one.

He glanced back as he broke out of secure cover, saw Peter and Georgie moving with that same uneasy gait. They were all conscious of walking with dark weight on their shoulders.

—I've got to get them out, he thought, as they moved into the dangerous light. I've got to do it right this time.

28

THE WATCHER CLIMBED PART OF THE WAY UP TO THE FOLLY. He rested on a small plateau over a steep drop, from which a large part of the island was visible. It was a beautiful day now. Beyond the point of Ard Laing Saraba Hill was a stretch of scarred velvet like the rough, humped back of an old whale. He took out the field glasses and swept a few degrees south to pick up the stunted tower of Craignash Castle. The one thing he hoped he would not see was a boat in the sound. The way the weather had turned, it was possible that someone might put out from Baldrick.

Headache. It should have been gone but there it was, pounding away in his skull again. When he saw his last shot strike the target he felt it go out of him sweet and clean as before, but now it was back. He popped another Tic Tac in his mouth.

—Why isn't it colder? Cold like Darwin. Then they'd suffer for real. They'd get hungry and start shivering in those joke fatigues they're wearing.

He picked up a stone and threw it into the trees below. The enemy was in the small plantation, most of which he could see. He was prepared to wait until they gave indication of what they were thinking; then he would go after them and carry on killing them. The simplicity of it was wonderful.

Peter noticed his feet were hurting again. He had given them no thought in all the panic and action. Only now, as some sense of normality returned, did he once more become conscious of the pain.

It was the same when he was a kid. He used to fall over, cut himself, get bruises the size of tea plates when he played. He never noticed at the time. And once, in the countryside near Bath where they lived for a time, his dog was chasing sticks and went after one that landed in the next field. As she slithered under the fence she ripped a two-inch gash in her haunch, but she never flinched. She was too busy with physical exertion. Only started moaning later, when they reached home. He had been scared and shocked, forgotten everything mundane. Now he had time to think and feel. Too much time.

The sniper could be right behind them now, aiming carefully.

He raised a hand and cupped the back of his head self-consciously. The useless comfort he once gained by hiding under the covers when trying to sleep in the scary dark. If Frankenstein's monster came in the night, the bedclothes would protect him.

He let his hand drop.

They came out of the plantation. Dan went ahead to check the ground, then beckoned them out. He lifted Bob's binoculars and scanned quickly, tracking up toward the folly.

They went on across the rough grass they had covered not long before.

"Try to keep below the horizon," Dan said. "Don't make yourself a target on the skyline."

The faint, metallic rustle of the burn to the west faded. The land descended gently and broke up into rocky shore. They picked their way as close to the water as they could. Georgie looked out across the sound. Laing hunched in the sea.

"It's so close," she said. "If someone was over there, we could signal to them."

"Langa's even closer when we reach the point," Dan said, "but there won't be anyone. No one goes to them."

They jogged along the shoreline to make it harder for the sniper. The wind sideswiped them and the air was full of spray. Then the grass humped up thirty feet or so and the rocks climbed out of the foam. They dodged along the point, running out so near to the northern tip of the island that the sea closed in on either side. Strong currents ground through the channel, breaking into salt rain on the rocks.

Eyes almost screwed shut, Peter gazed at Langa. It was close. He could see the jagged textures of stone, hear birds screeching over the battering sea.

"Christ, Dan, can't we swim that? It's no more than half a mile."

Georgie, who had put her goggles on to protect her eyes from the spray, took a bright yellow package of film from a top flap of Bob's jacket. She drew back and threw the package high and long out over the sea. It struck the water, bobbing crazily. Most of the time they couldn't see it for the choppy violence of the water, but when it appeared it was sailing fast away from them as if under power.

"It was just an idea," Peter said.

Dan used the binoculars again, checking all the shore they could see to the west. There were some fair-sized cliffs leading to the sheer faces of the northwest. Nearby a white cascade showed where the burn emptied into the ocean.

"Pretty safe to say our guy never moored along here," he said.

"Unless he had a friend," Georgie countered.

"Now, wait—"

"We're talking as if it's one man all by himself." Her eyes looked even deader behind the rain-flecked goggles. "But if this is a contract killing—"

Dan started to laugh it off. "Contracts only happen in the movies, Georgie."

"No, they don't. You know that better than we do. Just say it was a contract, someone hired to kill you. Why should he be working alone?"

"We've heard the same gun every time."

"So, the other man brought him over, now he's waiting there," she pointed to Langa, "in a quiet cove."

"Or he could be at the lodge, guarding the other wardens," Peter said. "If it's kidnapping, they could already be on the radio."

"I hate to interrupt the debate," Dan said. "But we're in a nice little corner here. He *or they* start shooting, we've got nowhere to go. Let's discuss it back in cover."

Taking a last look at the mound of spires that Langa made in the sea, they turned and started inland again.

"It doesn't make sense," Dan said, as they worked their way through the plantation.

"We can't assume it's one man," Georgie persisted.

"We assume nothing if we want to stay healthy. But think about it. Someone decides kidnaping me is a good idea. They have to believe I can raise a couple of million dollars, which I couldn't. But say they think I can, so they try it. You hijack an entire island, you're not talking amateur night. They must know when I'm coming, how the place is organized. They know we have seven men plus a boatman, plus you three—" The slip hurt all of them a little. "You two. That means they need a raiding party. And they don't wait until we're scattered all over the island. They grab us when we're taking a cup of coffee and warming our feet in the lodge."

"They were late," Peter said. "I've heard of some terrible blunders in kidnaping cases."

"Yeah, think about Lindbergh. But that's two guys on a get-rich-quick jag. Taking this place is a military operation. And there's one more thing about this idea."

"Which is?"

"If we're hostages, why is he shooting to kill?"

Georgie's face wrinkled in disgust. She dug in her pocket and took out some more chocolate.

The gloom swallowed light from above. It was like moving through a green sea. They were slow because Dan told them to be. Peter mentioned a theory that said if you ran very fast no one would be able to hit you for all the trees. Dan laughed silently and said that the idea was fine if the ground was even and clear and if you had no more than a few hundred yards to cover.

"You and me," he whispered, "we don't want to get into a three-mile sprint, do we?"

Then he silenced all talk because the noise was one more thing to make them a target.

Dan started looking for good straight branches.

"What for?" Georgie asked.

"Sharpen them to a point," he said.

"Very useful against a gun," she said.

"Call it psychological comfort."

"So, when he starts again, we just run at him with our nice, pointed sticks, yelling our heads off to scare him?"

"You know the old saying."

"Which one?"

"Flee a knife, charge a gun."

"Very intelligent. Where did you pick that up? In those mean streets?"

He did not lose his temper. "I read it somewhere. Anyhow, I'll feel better with something more than this knife."

Peter trudged on, ignoring them, lost in thought. His eyes were strained from the dark and from trying to look everywhere at once.

Dan found a branch that was relatively straight, got the knife out and sawed quietly through it near the trunk. He picked up a handful of earth and smeared it into the fresh, yellow-white cut on the tree.

The country rose suddenly to a long outcrop of scrub grass and heather like an upturned boat. There were no trees on it. They circled quickly, cutting deeper into the forest. They saw a worn pathway going up the side of the hummock. Dan went up the path, stood on top gazing around. He came down again.

"Three hundred and sixty degrees of nothing," he said. "I could see the water from Laing Sound to that castle on the mainland. There isn't a thing on it but foam."

"Whose brilliant idea was it to make a survival game so far from civilization?" Georgie asked.

"Seemed like a good idea at the time," Dan said, not wishing to mention that Bob had suggested it.

"Glasgow's no more than seventy miles away," Peter said. "Edinburgh's a hundred. We were in warm, comfortable beds this morning, in the middle of a busy city. How can this be happening?" He looked at his watch. At home, lunch was over. Vickie would be in town with Sarah. Liz would probably stay behind, playing the sensitive adolescent with some terribly deep book. He could see her there, sprawled on her stomach on the bed, *The Catcher in the Rye* or *The Heart Is a Lonely Hunter* open before her. Did they still read those old things? He would ask her when he got home. The word *if* occurred to him, but he put it away at the back of his mind, listening to Sarah's voice instead. At breakfast on Friday morning she had grinned at him over her bowl of Start and taunted him about the weekend.

"You're not really going, are you? I wish I could see it. It must be the first geriatric adventure game in the country."

At first he allowed the jibes, sniped back at her with doubts about her own physical fitness. But she went on giggling with Liz, improvising on the theme of middle-aged S.A.S. men until he finally snapped at them to shut up and get off to school and college. He knew he had overreacted by the change in their faces and the look of surprise Vickie gave him. Kindly, funny old Dad lost his temper.

—I left them thinking of me like that. A quick, subdued good-bye and a halfhearted kiss on the cheek from both. Vickie probably told them how I was under a strain at the moment, and they probably gave me the benefit of the doubt. But they'll remember how we parted, and that's all wrong. When I get home from this—when, not if—I'll tell them I'm sorry. I'll pick them up and hug them so tight they won't be able to breathe. Big as they are, I'll hug the life out of them.

The forest was hard going toward the east. It got more sheltered and the undergrowth was thick with bracken and dead wood that closed around their feet.

Dan stayed a little ahead so he might spot any trouble before they ran into it. He had the knife in his right hand and the sharpened stick in his left.

Georgie kept referring to Bob's compass, seeing that they were going too far east. The daylight from the sea down there began to show through the trees.

"We're nearly there," Dan said. They paused at the rim of a deep reentrant where the trees leaned down a slope that flattened into a deep shovel. "The lodge should be over the next rise."

They started down. Dan went quickly, swinging from one slender trunk to the next, feet scuffing easily in the dirt. He had a sort of grace that made Georgie think he was enjoying it all. Peter slithered down more or less on his backside, using his hands to keep moving, while she took it carefully, afraid of twisting her ankle and being left immobilized.

She looked to where Dan was reaching the floor of the reentrant.

She wondered how he could feel the way he did about her. Bob had known how worthless she was, had kept things in perspective. How was it that Dan could not?

She remembered Bob lying under the jacket she now wore, and wanted to throw it off.

Then the shooting started.

29

SHE SAW THE EARTH FLY IN LITTLE SPITTING EXPLOSIONS near his feet. The shots came from somewhere up on their right, four or five in the space of ten seconds. Dan was caught by surprise. He leapt back, fell, and twisted over on his belly. He scrabbled away from the spot. The firing followed him with a steady stitching of the earth.

"Get back up the slope," he yelled, scrambling to his feet. Peter swung round and started climbing. The shots struck wood from the trees around him. Some bird that had been nesting in an upper branch took flight near Georgie, scaring her off and making her slide back down the slope. She heard the rifle cracking away and got a grip again to stop her slipping into the gunman's line of fire. Dan came up behind her, grabbed her arm, and yanked her with him to the cover of the trees. She fell at the rim of the reentrant, and Peter came up last, breathing heavily. He slumped down next to her.

"Oh, shit," Dan whispered, as the firing stopped and they were left with the sound of their own breathing in the flat silence. "That was so stupid."

"I'm glad you were first down there," Peter said.

Dan rolled on his back, sucking at the air. "We should never have gone down there at all. We got to skirt round the edges, like we should've done to begin with."

"He might wait for us."

"He might. I think he'll move again. He's still playing with us. None of this is for real yet. Boy, he's really enjoying himself."

"Maybe he's just a lousy shot," Georgie said.

"If I keep doing dumb things, we'll have plenty of chances to find out."

"Don't be so hard on yourself," Peter said. "We're in no situation to think coolly about anything."

"We'd better try harder. It's the only way we stay alive." He got up, still breathing hard to quell the sense of panic. "Oh, that bastard. He's really loving this." He lifted a branch and peered across the reentrant. "He was over there some- where. Must've figured what we were trying. Better hold tight a while. Maybe he'll give us some clues. Anyhow, he's close, and we don't want to stumble into him."

They stayed in the shadows on the edge of the slope. They did not speak or move. Their breath came back. There was no sign of action from the other side.

"I'm going over," Dan said finally.

"Is that a good idea?" Peter said.

"The best I can manage."

"I'll come with you."

"Oh no, you don't. I don't want you crashing around the undergrowth, giving me away."

Peter looked to see if there was criticism. There was noth- ing but faint good humor again.

"I'll be five minutes is all," Dan said. "I go out, see what's cooking, and come back."

"Just don't get shot, will you."

"Peter, my man. I intend to get all of us off this island and back drinking a hot toddy by the fire this evening. We're going to be okay."

He buttoned up his jacket and crawled into the gloom. Pe- ter watched him parting the ferns until there was no more sign of him. He sat back and stared blankly at Georgie.

"What if he gets killed?"

"He won't," Georgie said. "He's the man who can avoid photographers from the *Sun, Mirror,* and *Star.* One little sniper's no problem." She smiled crookedly after the words, as if she could not work out where they had come from. She took the map out and studied it again. "We'll have to check all this stretch on the south side, won't we?"

"I'm afraid so," he said. "I can think of better things to do with a Saturday afternoon."

"So can I."

"Georgie?"

"What?"

"I'm sorry about Bob."

"So am I. He was fun, wasn't he?" She felt the words go out of her without really connecting them to Bob at all.

"I don't suppose you remember when he took up skiing for the first time. Before your time, wasn't it?"

"No, I remember."

"We went to the Alps in the middle of the season. He tried to get me on skis, but it never did work. He was skimming all over the slopes and I was lucky to be able to slide gently down to the bottom for a drink."

"He was enthusiastic about things," Georgie said, recalling how they raced downhill in the middle of a blizzard once to reach the hotel before dark. Stupid thing to do, but he was speeding ahead, laughing like a maniac, and it seemed like nothing more than crazy fun.

"The way he tried to make me proficient," Peter said. His eyes glittered. "He was a tear-away. How he could be a good businessman too, I'll never know." A tear dropped and splashed on the back of his hand. "He once said he'd have my job in five years . . . Oh, you know, joking, of course. He always said things like that with a smile. But I knew he meant it."

"Never mind."

"He was ambitious the way I used to be." Peter stirred the tears on his hand.

She wanted to turn away. He was breaking down in front of her and she could not face touching him to give a little comfort. It was like seeing someone in pain behind a high fence. She could see him and knew that he needed some words or contact, but she could not get past the fence. She was locked out, and all the grief she should have been feeling for Bob was on the other side with Peter and Dan.

The undergrowth rustled. She reached and took hold of Dan's stick, raised it to strike.

Dan came out of the dark, flicked a nervous glance at her. She put the stick down.

"He's gone," Dan said, squatting on his haunches, ignoring Peter's attempts to conceal his crying. "Found a couple of cartridge cases and some footprints but that's all, folks. Our friend, whoever he is, wears good army boots. Better than ours. He'll be dancing the tango when we're lying down with foot rot."

"Why doesn't he stay in one place?" Georgie said.

"Because he knows better. When he lost us down there, he knew we could figure his position. We might have come up behind him for all he knew. Anyhow, it's more fun this way."

"You keep talking like that—"

"That's the way he's thinking. Believe me, he's making as much fun out of this as he can. It's his idea of good times."

"He knows we're trying to reach the lodge."

"Certainly."

"He's got all the advantages," Peter said.

"Not all. For one thing, when we're deep in the trees like this, he's as blind as we are. For another, one guy—"

"One guy," Georgie sneered.

"Let's assume he is, since we got no evidence for parties. He's alone out there, and there's three of us. He won't know if we split, and when he finds out, he can't follow everyone."

"So we split up now?"

"Right. You and Peter work your way in and strike south when it's clear. I'll keep our friend with me by kicking up some noise while you get going."

"I don't like it," Peter said. "You're taking all the risks."

"No way. I'll be so careful, he'll think I'm a mouse."

"What happens when we've checked the shore?"

"If there's a boat, great. Either way, we rendezvous back

on the high rise south of the lodge in three hours. That ought
to be long enough. If I stay lucky, I'll be in the lodge, and
all our troubles could be over."

Peter took Dan's hand. It was not quite a handshake.

"Ah, come on, Peter. Don't get sentimental."

"Be careful."

"You too. Georgie?"

She looked up.

"Don't be a heroine, okay? If you see the guy, if you hit
trouble, just head back to that rise. If I'm not around, assume I've struck out, and find somewhere safe until dark."

She shook her head. "There isn't anywhere safe here," she
said.

Dan watched them move off to the west. He saw Georgie
turn and look at him, and Peter's hand come up in a
halfhearted wave.

—Stupid, he thought. Don't attract attention like that.

They were lost to view. He went down on one knee. His
stomach twinged with hunger. He took out the last three
squares of chocolate and gobbled them down. His energy
was low, he knew that. The cold was seeping into his clothes
so that he wanted to button up tighter. But there was nothing else, and the flak jacket would be warm enough when he
was moving again.

—Won't stop you being scared, he thought, touching the
knife in his pocket. —Nothing stops that until the danger
goes away. That's fine, though. Smitty always said you got dead
when you stopped shitting yourself with fear.

"Great concentrator, fear," he once said. "It's like those
actors in the movies. I heard one of 'em tell Johnny Carson
if he didn't get all churned up before he went on, the performance would be nothing. I figure we have the same thing
with fear out here. Lose that and you get sloppy."

"How about grace under pressure?" Dan asked.

"Never met the girl," Smitty said. He never really looked
frightened, though. Until you got to know him, you could be

forgiven for thinking he was very cool about the whole deal. Dan made that mistake until that day on the wide trail in Vietnam. After that, he realized that Smitty had lost control of the fear. He had been using it, channeling it into his every move in battle, until finally it grew too much to control.

—The time has come, gentlemen. Let's get to it.

He began to gather stalks from the ferns, leaves and lichen, moss, heather, whatever was available. He smeared his face with dirt to improve on the makeup. He reached in the neck of his jacket, found the drawstring and yanked it out. He used it for a headband, knotting it as tight as comfort allowed. He took some of the ferns and stuck them under the cord. More of the leaves were fixed in the shoulder flaps and pockets. Yes, it would look pretty stupid—like Lear, he thought, not because he knew Shakespeare but because he remembered Olivier dressed up in weeds on the TV. But the idea was not to be seen. In the jungle, what they looked for was a man-shaped outline, so you broke the outline with leaves and twigs and made it hard for them.

When he was finished he felt like an out-of-season Christmas tree. He sniffed the air. If he was to attract the sniper's attention without getting shot, he would have to be better than careful, but anything was better than having Peter and Georgie on his mind.

He went off through the trees. The knife was out; he was ready to kill if it was needed. He had not thought it would be so easy to get that feeling back, but the numb stupidity was gone and replaced by anger. The knife was like a natural extension of his hand. God help the sniper if he should get careless and allow a hand-to-hand attack.

—And God help you, you old bum. Since when did you start on the tough-guy stuff?

He thought about Georgie going with Peter, and there being no guarantee of what might happen. He would have kept her by his side if it were possible, but what about Peter then? Anyhow, she was safer where she was.

Except—

—Except, what if our friend follows them instead of me?

He realized he was thinking too much, not noticing where he was going. He told himself to shape up. Daydreaming was fine for a country stroll, not for this. Charlie was out in the forest, and maybe he was following Georgie, maybe not.

So he went on, with the doubt growing in him as he tried to empty his mind of everything but survival. Round and round: Bob lying in a pool of his own brains, Georgie's hating eyes, Peter crying, Smitty sobbing like a baby, Six Pack screaming, Marty saying: "Cosmic, man." The smell of sweat and the stench of other mens' guts.

He tripped, caught his forehead on a sharp branch. Blood dropleted on his fingers when he touched the spot. He straightened up, wondering if Charlie could scent his blood. They used to tell stories back in Nam about gooks who could sniff you out like dogs. The momentary pain concentrated his mind, and that opened his senses to everything outside him again. No matter how he felt about letting Georgie go, he had to put it on hold for now.

He tracked down the reentrant, sticking to cover. He wanted to get as close to the shore as he could.

Then at least he could dive in the sea if things got too hairy.

The watcher scowled. Something he did not understand was going on. He had spotted movement in the trees and followed. They were no longer heading for the lodge. He had meant to scare them, but not that much. Now he rested up on the uneven ground on the plantation's edge, overlooking the burn. He could see the country to the south if they came out.

A twisting curtain of misty rain whipped over the moor. It was fine and cold and he watched it patiently, wondering what their game was now. He stroked the rifle close to his chest, waiting.

—One man by the plantation's edge, with a gun. A real gun, and I've never seen him before. What on earth's going on?

MacNeice, flat on his belly in the prickly grass, observed the watcher through his binoculars. He was trembling all over, had not been able to stop since he found Williamson's body in the big plantation. His face was white. He had been sick three times.

Up on the high cliffs to see how the razorbills were doing, he had lost track of the time, only looked at his watch when he began to shiver from the cold. Cursing mildly, he had slipped his notebook away and started the precarious climb back up the cliffs.

Of course, he had missed the arrival of the VIPs, and he bet himself that Williamson would give him a hard time for it, but it had been worth it to check on the razorbills.

He reached the clifftop a little after twelve forty-five. At one fifteen, as he walked along the south shore, he heard shots. That made him curious, because he knew as well as anyone that guns were taboo on the island. It occurred to him that Mr. Goldman's party might have decided to do some real shooting before they got down to the game. But what were they shooting at? The shots came from the big plantation. They were shooting near the cliffs then, banging away at all his lovely birds.

Angry, he turned toward the hill and started the climb. Damn it, didn't they know that the birds had made their home on the cliffs for centuries? This was more their place than any man's.

He reached the burn where it sprang out of the hillside. More shots, this time from the north. He searched the north moors with the binoculars, saw a huddle of people going down a gully, carrying something.

More shooting.

He got very confused. The three people looked like strangers, had to be the VIPs. But where were the other wardens? It was usually Williamson who climbed to the folly to oversee fair play. There was no sign of him.

MacNeice had a bad, sour feeling in the pit of his stomach even before he found Williamson's body lying in the dirt with a sticky black hole in its chest. After being sick, he ran across the safe low ground of the south moor until he fell, sure that he was suffering a heart attack.

After a while the pain subsided. He dragged himself to the edge of the loch and drank greedily to get rid of the taste of vomit. Then he crept up to the higher ground where a thread of water began and looked north.

—Terrible, he kept thinking, seeing Williamson's face with all the meaty color going out of it. Dead eyes gazing at the treetops in placid contemplation. MacNeice had seen his mother dead, but only after the undertakers were through with her. Williamson was horrible.

He wondered about the stranger with the gun. Fair bet this one was dangerous, since he had the rifle. But what to do about it? No one seemed to be around. He suddenly had the awful idea that everyone else had got off the island, that he was the only one left to face a gun-toting loony.

He scuffled back downhill and kept out of the stranger's sight as he hefted his well-fed bulk across the moor to the small plantation.

Georgie lifted her head, listening. She raised a hand to stop Peter.

"What?" he asked.

"Shh."

They stiffened. Both heard it clearly at the same moment. Footsteps crashing through the undergrowth.

"Oh, Christ," Peter said. He started to tremble.

Georgie stood immobilized. Fear came up and swatted her so hard that she stopped thinking.

"Hide, for God's sake," Peter snapped.

They threw themselves into a patch of ferns. Georgie felt sharp stone rip her hand. She glanced at Peter, took some comfort from the fact that he was scared too, but no longer self-pitying. His lips drew back over his teeth as the footsteps came closer.

—He must be charging us with bayonet fixed, she thought. What's he playing at?

Peter grabbed her arm, pointed to a clear space between

the trees. A man stood there, panting for breath. He looked
more frightened than they were. Goggles were round his
neck and a pellet gun was at his side. He carried no rifle.

Georgie slithered through the undergrowth to the stranger's right. Peter rose slowly, setting himself on one knee,
head down, back creaking. He looked for Georgie, could not
tell where she was. The man was standing as before, hands
on thighs, bent over and wheezing for breath.

A branch snapped somewhere behind Peter. He glanced
back nervously before realizing it was Georgie. The man
heard it too. He jerked upright, staring fearfully, then came
forward, striking branches aside. Peter thought this was stupid behavior, whether the man was the killer or not. Big man,
though, would not be easy to bring down.

—And when did you last do any all-in wrestling? Never
mind, there's an old saying: the situation shall provide the
strength. It had better.

The man came by, as close as he would ever be. Peter
waited until he had his back turned. There was no point in
being gentlemanly about it. He sprang off the ground, hitting the man squarely between the shoulder blades with his
shoulder. The man's breath went out with a whoosh. He
staggered and fell heavily. Georgie popped up from the ferns,
throwing herself on him. Peter got astride him as he struggled over, throwing her off. He got hold of the windmilling
arms and did something he had not done since school. He
knelt on the man's upper arms, bearing down hard until
movement stopped.

"All right, who the hell are you?"

"Get off, will you. Get off!"

"Name," Peter insisted, getting the man by the throat,
clinging on hard. He was so frightened he wanted to smash
the man's face in. "Name."

"Look at my lapel, you daft bastard."

Georgie scrubbed dirt off the label on the man's jacket.

"MacNeice," she said.

"Aye," he said. "Bloody MacNeice. I'm a warden. Will you
get off before you break my arms?"

"Not yet." Peter held on. "We don't know what you've been up to, do we?"

"Hiding," MacNeice groaned. "Who're you, anyway?"

"Part of Mr. Goldman's group."

"Call us targets," Georgie said, searching the pockets of MacNeice's coat. "Nothing here." She flicked through the notebook. "No bullets."

"Bullets?" he said. "Look, I heard the shooting, I found Captain Williamson in the big plantation. I don't know anything about it."

"Where've you been all day? We can't move without getting shot at. You've been wandering at liberty."

"I was watching the birds. Always do when things are quiet. First I knew about it was when I heard the shooting. How do I know you're not the ones doing it?"

"I'm Peter Bailey. This is Georgina Lawrence. We're with Mr. Goldman."

"What's happening?"

"I was hoping you might have an idea. Have you seen anyone else?"

"Not a soul. Except some chap with a rifle."

"What did he look like? Did you know him?"

"Never saw him before. I thought he was one of you. He was all dressed up in uniform."

"So even if we saw him we might think he was one of the wardens. Christ."

"Will you get off, please!" MacNeice said urgently.

Peter released him, watching him carefully. He wasn't entirely convinced.

"Look, the only gun I ever fired was an air rifle. I couldn't hit a water tank at ten feet without taking careful aim. Where's Mr. Goldman? I thought you said he was with you?"

"He's at the lodge, trying to work his way in and find out what happened to your workmates."

MacNeice sat up, rubbing his arms. "This is terrible."

"That's one word for it."

"Are they after Goldman? Is that it?"

"We don't know."

"Don't know? Someone's gunning for him, and we all suffer for it."

"Keep your thoughts to yourself."

"Where're you going, anyway?"

"Looking for a boat."

"That feller I saw. He was near the lodge path."

"Mr. Goldman knows what he's doing. You'd better stay with us."

"Oh, no." MacNeice gulped at the bile rising in his throat. "I've got to go to the lodge. If the boys are locked up in there—"

"It's dangerous."

"Maybe I can get the jump on this chap. I know what Goldman looks like. Maybe I can help."

Peter studied him. "All right."

"What about the rendezvous?" Georgie whispered to him.

Peter shook his head. "Go carefully," he said to MacNeice.

"I'll do that." MacNeice turned to Georgie. "Miss, you ought to sit down. You look awful."

"You haven't got any food, have you?" she said.

He shrugged. He began to walk away from them, and Peter watched him go. When they were alone, he closed his eyes.

"I don't know," he said. "Was he all right, or did he fool us?"

"He could've shot us," Georgie said. "I think he was genuine."

"I was so scared."

"Never mind."

They started for the moor. "I think I dislocated my shoulder knocking him down."

"You did it well."

They came out of the trees. The moor, rough and barren, sloped down to the sea. It was quiet, and the drizzling mist swept the spiky hills.

"Remember to zigzag," Peter said. "And keep away from

me. If he's watching, perhaps he won't be able to decide between us."

"You're welcome to go first."

"I think we'll let good manners pass this time."

"We'd better hurry. Time's short."

She hoisted her trousers and notched her belt tighter. Her fingernails were ruined. She wondered how she could think about manicures at a time like this.

"Ready?" he asked.

"When you are."

He counted it off on his fingers, storing breath for the run to the hills. She noticed the length of his hands. The creased skin of his palms, the little scratches.

"Go," he mouthed. They went off fast.

Sunlight had gone. Through the dense cover it was possible only to see gray cloud.

—Good, Dan thought. The blacker it was up there, the better it was below, as long as the rain held off. Rain would make it very unpleasant indeed, since most of this operation had to be performed on the belly, nose a couple of inches from the soil. The sky was turning evil, though. The bad, bruised color that meant rain, lots of it.

In this place rain would be wonderful. Their clothes were waterproofed up to a point, but he knew from past experience that if you were out in the field for half an hour in a heavy downpour, you would be swimming at the end of it. In this climate, you would also be cold as hell. Hypothermia-type cold. Not to mention slopping up to your eyes in mud.

He elbowed his way forward, silent and, he prayed, invisible. His watch showed ten of four. Peter and Georgie would be down on the shore now, checking for transport. He already had the feeling that none would be there; maybe that was just his bad attitude.

But he had such a lousy feeling about this guy. The other two could chitchat all they liked about kidnapers and parties of mercenaries storming the island, but he knew it was one guy. One bad ass with a gun and a thing for spreading people's insides all over the landscape.

Worse than that, he felt as if the enemy were also something not really human. He had tried to put a face on the guy, the way he always did with Charlie back in the old days. Then, it was just a dead-looking Oriental face, because that was how they usually looked, dead or alive. That flat-eyed, sullen look that covered hatred and resentment of the American invaders.

With the sniper, Dan had no image of a face. It was worse that way, like one of those late-night horror movies where the bogeyman's face is never seen until the shock revelation in the last reel. You spent the time getting worked up over what would eventually appear. There was a dark man out in the trees, toting a gun, grinning down the barrel, eyes yellow and shiny. Mad as hell, bang, bang, bang.

—Hell of a way to think, as Poppa used to say.

He inched forward. Getting close to the lodge, the ground was rough. Rock stuck through the earth. It was covered with lichens, so he did not see it until he scraped skin off.

He thought of the lodge. The inconvenient fact that there was open space all around it. You were relatively safe until it came to the final approach. The front was open down to the rocks and the jetty. Both sides were flanked by rising ground that was perfect for a sniper to rest up on. Behind was the semicircular yard where they had paraded for Williamson only a few hours ago. It was unavoidable—to reach the lodge, you had to go out in the open.

—When we get out of this, he thought, when we're all safe and sound back in someplace civilized—New York, maybe— and when Georgie's over Bob, I'm going to marry her. Everyone should have a life ambition. I'll marry the girl if I have to abduct her. Tell Mamma she's related to Princess Diana or something. I don't care about kids or any of that stuff, just so long as we have a couple of dozen. And we'll live in the city, where you never see a wild animal or a tree ever. After this I also give up trying to be Robert Redford.

This kind of action I don't need anymore. I'll have kids and a dog and sell everything and get fat like Poppa.

He crawled over a steep ridge that was mostly rock, scuttled down the other side into the shadows of young, slender trees. The chimneys of the lodge, ornate spirals of red brick, showed above the tree line below. The tip of the jetty was farther off to the left. He saw the waters of the sound scudding by, shook his head slowly. He could see the ferry, the cars parked nearby, the road going up over the hills to Baldrick and the hotel. A mile and a half across the water, that was all.

He felt lonelier than he had ever done in his life.

The watcher moved along on the north side of the lodge. Something was going on now. He had watched the plantation until he saw the enemy emerge, two of them. Why hadn't he expected them to split up? He had been overconfident, that was the truth. He had believed they would huddle together, refusing to be alone. It had been difficult enough to get them moving. Now one of the men was wandering by himself.

—I know which one.

He ran for the lodge, careless about maintaining silence because he was angry. They were not playing it right anymore. If Goldman was by himself, how could he witness his people being plucked away one by one? The tension could not build properly if they scattered all over the island.

He forced himself to calm down by stopping to reload. Knelt by a muddy trough where a burn formed in the winter months. Breathing regular and unlabored, pulse not too high. The few birds in the trees jabbered at him. He wished they would shut up, let him hear what was going on. The pulpy, rotten smell of the forest came to him in clammy gusts.

No fucking trees to obscure things where he'd been. Just miles of green and brown scrub, gorse, marshes, and bog. The forest gave better cover, but it also gave the enemy chances they should not have had in a straight fight in open terrain.

He carried on, slow and silent now, eyes directed to the ground, looking for tracks. He went down the stream bed and worked round the lodge in a wide curve. Finally, in a place where the gloom made a patch of bare earth, he saw telltale signs of the enemy. Small scuffs in the dirt, a broken fern.

His smile returned. He began to feel all right. His fingers clenched on the rifle.

MacNeice came up in the tracks of the watcher. He carried a stout branch now, heavy end down, swinging it like a club to work the rhythm into his arm.

He did not really know what he was doing. He was a former physical-education teacher, not a soldier. The largest thing he had ever killed was a fly—even spiders were flushed down the toilet with a guilty conscience. He always enjoyed the physical effort of sport, though, and did not think exercise for its own sake was much of an idea. He liked rugby because it was played rough. He could throw his big frame about with the best of them, and never felt better than when he brought a good run to a halt by tackling the other man with a long, flying leap.

He was no hero, but if someone was trying to kill them all, he was prepared to do his bit.

He moved with surprising grace for such a big man. The skill had developed when he first took up birdwatching seriously. He could get within a few yards of anything in feathers, and if you could do that, you had no problem moving in on a human being . . . At least, he hoped so.

He stopped. Gently, adjusting his balance all the while, he sank into the undergrowth.

Ten yards ahead, crossing his path, was the man he had seen in his binoculars a little while before. He was carrying the rifle, intently following some trail.

MacNeice felt sick again, though there was nothing solid left in his stomach. He held the retching sounds in his throat, eyes watering. Suddenly found himself repeating the prayers from morning assembly at school. Very personal now, a hotline to the Lord.

—Please God, let him not see me. Please God, please . . .

Remembered to breathe, very slow, torturing his lungs.

The man with the gun went on. He flickered in and out of sight as the camouflage of his jacket merged with the background. It seemed that he was appearing and disappearing at will. MacNeice, a superstitious man always, felt his belly knot in fear. At first, when he tried to move, nothing happened. The sight of the gunman fading into the shadows made him do it. He cut off to the right, wanting to put a little distance between them; then he went on a parallel course, up toward the ridges above the lodge. He knew the gunman was also trailing someone. Maybe he could stop another person getting killed.

30

"IT'S HOPELESS," PETER SAID. "HALF THOSE LITTLE BEACHES we can't see from up here, and it'd take all day to climb down and check them."

"You know what we need?" Georgie said.

"What do we need?"

"A boat."

He grimaced. "Very funny. What the hell're we doing this for? We should be back with Dan before he gets himself shot on our behalf."

"There's only a bit more to do. Come on."

They trekked along the southern cliffs and the rocky shore in the gathering shadow of rain clouds. The sea was marble and the tiny spearheads of two islands stuck up two miles away. They looked barely large enough to stand on, but Georgie would have given everything she had to be safe on the big one—Reisa Mhio Rhoidan, according to her map—until someone came to help. Behind them was the long sweep of the southern shore. Masses of striated limestone and sudden drops. The hills of Jora were agonizingly close across the turgid waters of the Whirlpool of Corravreckon. They had one last hill to climb before they were back at the small plantation.

"I don't think I can manage it," Peter said. "My feet are killing me."

"You'd better." She smiled. "I'm not carrying you."

"If only we could find one good hiding place here. One place where we could sit tight."

"We'll be all right," she said.

He took out his watch. He saw her staring at it.

"Sarah's going to university, isn't she?"

"Yes, thank God. She's bright enough, and she wants to do it."

"You never went, did you?"

"My mother and father worked themselves to death getting me through grammar school. They couldn't afford any more. It wasn't so bad in my day. You could work yourself into a company without a degree. Look at Dan. I don't think he ever read a textbook in his life, but he's a millionaire. We were the last generation who could make it in business without solid qualifications—not to mention a sound knowledge of computers. You know how I learned the intricacies of the electronic age?"

"You went on a course, didn't you?"

"Oh, yes. And I came back none the wiser. It took Sarah to get me proficient with a keyboard. I don't envy you the world we've made. It changes so fast, you have to be a chameleon if you want to keep up."

"It's better than that."

"Is it? I wonder what's going to become of everyone. What sort of life for my daughters, for you—more and more traffic, less and less space. Eyes glued to a video terminal display all day and the television screen all night."

She gazed at his long, kind face while he was unaware of it. She bet he had photographs of Vickie, Sarah, and Liz in his pocket. She imagined him picking the girls up when they were small, swinging them high in the air, laughing with their laughter. He still liked to try it now they were too heavy. Why couldn't her father have been like that?

"You all right?" he asked.

She nodded. "I'm fine."

—Stop thinking about that. This isn't the time or place.

But it never really went away from her. The farthest it could be pushed was the back of her mind—never all the way out. She had heard that time healed all wounds—her mother used to say it a lot—but she did not believe it. A lot probably depended on the nature of the wound and whether you could get help for it. Some injuries you could not reveal. You tried to heal them yourself, and maybe you botched the job, and maybe it was too much to deal with alone.

She saw that the hill was flattening out. She walked to the edge of the cliff. The grass dropped steeply to it.

"Wait a minute," Peter said, coming after her.

She reached the lip, clinging to handfuls of grass, poised high over the water.

"Christ Almighty," Peter said, groping along the slope.

"Look on the bright side," she said. "We're not targets on the skyline anymore."

"Very reassuring."

"Hang on." She stiffened. "Look."

"I can't. My eyes are closed."

"Open them."

He did so, wishing he hadn't. Georgie pointed down and to the left where the cliff sank to a reasonable height.

"What is it?"

He bit his lip. "Piece of driftwood?"

"Beyond that crag. See it, in the cove there."

Now he saw it too. The stern of the old fishing boat, pulled high up on the sand.

"Logan's boat," he said.

"I thought so."

He turned back to her, started as if he were going to hug her, then remembered where they were. "One bloody miracle. That's all it needs."

She was already clambering back to the crest of the cliff. He followed, and they ran toward the cove. She kept clenching her fists and shaking them at the sky, her face bright and hard with triumph.

"We're going to get away," she said.

"Where is it?"

"We can't see it from up here. Too much overhang."

"Right, let's get back to the lodge, find MacNeice and Dan, then get out of here."

"Wait a minute. We've got to see whether it's all in working order."

He studied the rocks. "I'll go."

"You stay here. I'll just go down and take a look."

His eyes changed. She saw this and smiled.

"You checked the last one. It's my turn."

"I'll keep watch."

"Haven't got a decent length of rope anywhere, have you?"

"You can't play the hero *and* have it easy."

She shrugged and went along the cliff, searching for an easy start. The boat was pushed up right under the cliff, impossible to see without going all the way down.

She was glad Peter had been persuaded to let her do it. She wanted to get down and back quickly, not sit on the cliff worrying about him. He was gamer than he had been at the start, but she noticed how tired he looked.

She started out going down some gentle rocks on her backside, using her feet to brace the descent. Then it dropped away and she turned to face the rocks, using her hands too, working her fingers into clefts and cracks in the ancient stone. She began to get the sensation of clinging to a vertical wall. She looked up and saw Peter watching her. She had to stop herself from hanging on so hard. Breathing deep, she arched her body away from the rocks. She found a ledge and got one foot to it. She wished she could do this barefoot: the boots made her feel numb to the surface of the cliff.

—Come on. I spent years doing this when I was a kid. Climbed every rotten tree in the park. Even the big oak that no one else dared. That was before she stopped trying to be the boy her father wanted. Said he wanted.

She reached around with her foot for another hold. She saw her hand gripping the pocked skin of the cliff. It was white and tensed. The wind blasted at her from below.

—Remember *A Pair of Blue Eyes*? That cliff where the updraft was so powerful it blew the girl's hat up in the air?

—Shut up, you idiot. It's not Thomas Hardy I need here, it's Chris Bonington.

Another foothold. She got a toe into it and let her weight go. She saw a good ledge, wide enough to stand up straight on. It might be far enough down to see the boat.

She swung out from the rock one-handed and pushed off hard for the ledge. The sea yawned beneath her as she flew, making her realize how stupid it was to hurry.

She struck the ledge awkwardly. Her body whumped solidly against the face, all her breath hissed out. If instinct had not cut in, she would have fallen. Her fingers scraped at the rock, found purchase, clung on. She hung her head back, wheezing to breathe, and saw the blood left on the lichened stone.

Peter's voice came down from far off: "Georgie?"

She couldn't speak.

"For God's sake, don't do anything like that again." He was somewhere right above her now. She could not see him.

"Come on up," he yelled. "We know the boat's down there. Let's get the others."

She had control of herself. Her arms and legs had stopped shaking. She carried on. It was lucky that the next stage was not difficult. She lowered herself to another tiny ledge, found more to grip. She swung, one foot stretching for purchase. Now she was fifteen feet up, and the spray off the rocks was all around her like mist from an atomizer.

—I must be mad. Next time Peter volunteers for something, he can have it.

The colorless sand was below her, sea lapping up to the tidal line. She reached down, fingers surveying, found a crease. She put her weight over on the hand, discovered too late that it was slippery with bird shit.

She fell the last twelve feet.

Twelve feet does not sound like much. But as she lost her grip and started her fall, she thought that twelve feet was the height of two tall men. Long way.

She managed to twist, realizing that falling on her back was not a wonderful idea, saw the ground coming up to meet her fast. Well, that was okay, because sand was nice and soft.

Not this sand. It was a few inches of grit over a rock shelf, and as far as she was concerned, it might just as well have been the rock. She hit it, trying to strike with both feet, more or less succeeded, but staggered. The impact went right through her, cracking her neck. She fell in the sea.

"Get out," Peter was shouting, somewhere above. "Get out of the water."

—Good idea, she thought, wishing he would fall off the damn cliff too. She started to get up, palms smarting. The water rose and knocked her down again. She got up, lifting the weight of her sodden clothes. She did a few steps to the sand, stood up properly. Nothing appeared to be broken. The waves lapped at her. She kicked out at them, raising spray that flew back at her.

"Bastard," she said.

"Are you all right?" Peter asked. She saw his face at the top. It was very high when you looked at it from down here.

"Yes. Stop making so much noise."

He stood waiting. She looked at her hands. They were really a mess now, and she was going to have some magnificent bruises on hip and shoulder later. She limped across the tiny cove toward the boat. The engine looked okay, from what she could see. It was going to be fine. She went into the shallow cave, checking the boat's hull.

On top of the cliff, Peter heard her cry out. The scream was not of pain or fear. It was rage.

She knelt in the boat, folded up with head on knees. Her hands beat at the planks where they had been smashed all the way through to the sand underneath. The anchor that had been used as a pickax lay behind her, one of its points still buried in the wood.

She stopped beating at the planks, mouth quivering with frustration. The damage was so bad that they couldn't hope to float the craft, and there was nothing they could repair it with.

She pushed herself to her feet, lost her temper again, and lashed out at the seat, snapping it in half with her boot. She saw the ropes and nets stashed under the seat. She took the longest rope and coiled it over one shoulder. She could not see what use it would be, but it was all she could find.

She stepped out of the dank shadows. Peter gazed down at her. Nothing needed to be said.

She started the climb up.

Dan wiped the sweat off his face. Cold day, but he was sweating plenty.

He had made it to within a hundred yards north of the lodge. He was side-on to it, able to see a little of the rear entrance. The yard was wide and empty. On the other side was the ridge where he planned to meet Peter and Georgie in a while. He had gone over every inch with the binoculars and seen no indications of enemy presence. The lodge was silent and still; the forest around the yard held no one.

—Of course, this doesn't mean he ain't there. He may just be a whiz at hiding.

He sucked in the air, picked up a fallen pine needle, and chewed the hard flesh until the bittersweet oils came out. The taste was horrible, but he was tired of being dry-mouthed.

The problem was that he had been in position for well over ten minutes and still had not moved. There were a hundred yards between him and the safe cover of the lodge: a skid out of the trees down a rough slope, then a straight sprint across relatively even ground. Nothing to hide behind, open to fire on all sides. If Charlie was out there, it would be good-bye and good luck from Dan Goldman, businessman, playboy, and TV chef.

So it was risky, and he could not get the enthusiasm together to actually make a start. Frozen like he had been the first time he faced enemy fire. The Cong pouring rockets and machine-gun fire into the camp, and the only thing that got him into gear was Smitty kicking him, yelling above the noise: "Wake up, you son of a bitch, and watch your own ass."

No Smitty here. Just him, with no idea where Charlie was, because Charlie only fired when he felt like it.

—If I still smoked, this'd be the time for it.

He knew he must get moving. There was the lodge, quiet and open. The wardens might be locked up in there. The radio might be in working condition. At least the place had thick walls and was easy to shore up against attack. Once the three of them were inside, it would be easy.

The problem? What if Charlie had worked out the moves? What if he was sitting in the lodge, facing the door, with that evil little rifle aimed at belly level?

Nice question. Naturally, there was only one way to be sure.

He checked his watch, chewed the pine needle, thought about Georgie's empty eyes. He found himself wishing he knew everything about her, because he knew nothing. Her file had the usual details: age, birthplace, education. She was born in Manningtree; he always remembered that, although he had never been there. The only strange thing was that there was no name in the "Next of kin" box. He had never asked her about it. She did not talk any further back than university days.

The thought hung there in front of him while his eyes passed again and again over the terrain below. Having some abrupt insight into Georgie's character was no use at all here and now. A large injection of guts was what this moment required.

—Think about saving her life. There's a great motive for you. Concentrate on bringing her out of this in one piece.

He was really scared. He knew that because of all the thinking he was doing. Generally, he ticked over without making too much effort. This entire weekend had been heavy with meditation. It had to stop.

He took one last look at the short sprint across easy ground that could turn out to be his own personal killing field. It would be less than ten seconds once he reached the flat stuff. Ten seconds was nothing much to run, just a long time to be in Charlie's sniper scope.

—Go on, for God's sake.

The watcher stood on the hill above the yard. Easy and relaxed with the rifle up and ready. There was the slight smile turning up the corners of his mouth. It did not touch his eyes. Through the rifle sight he focused on a small portion of the slope north of the lodge. He lifted his face from the sight, watched the long, rock-studded bank. He knew the American was in there, under the trees. Goldman had tried to be clever, sending the others off as decoys. He had been very good, moving through the forest. Pretty good for a civvy, pretty sly. But the watcher knew what he was trying to do, and when he knew, all he had to do was move to a good vantage point and wait.

The sign had come two minutes ago. No more than a pebble rattling down the bank. No one else would have seen it, but the watcher was sharp-eyed, brother to the falcon that wheeled over the forest.

He was still angry. Goldman had thought to fool him. He would teach Mr. Goldman a lesson—not kill him, not until the others were gone. Maybe just wound him, slow him up so all he could do was watch the rest of it.

The watcher licked his lips. He had always known this day would be fun, but he had not realized how good it would be.

—You move now, Goldman. You come out and show yourself.

He saw movement, a shade to the left of where he had expected. The Yank was coming down, ready to chance his arm.

The watcher lifted his rifle. It fitted to his grip perfectly. Range perhaps a hundred yards. Allow for the speed the American would run. Oh, it would be beautiful to see him go down.

His finger tightened on the trigger. Goldman edged down out of the trees. His face was a study in fear and watchfulness. A rabbit, scared out of its mind.

Fire at will.

Branches cracked behind him. For a moment he could not believe it. No one would dare. Then he was swinging, the rifle dropped from firing position, and he knew the attack was coming from behind, from the rocks above him. He could not get the gun up fast enough.

He saw MacNeice plunging down on him from the rocks, the stick raised high over his head. MacNeice was scared too, but dangerously scared and coming down fast.

He had forgotten about MacNeice.

31

"WHAT WAS THAT?" GEORGIE SAID.

Peter hauled her up the last couple of feet and took the rope from her shoulder. He said nothing, but she read his face.

"Gunfire, wasn't it?"

"We'd better get back," he said. ". . . No, you stay here. Your clothes're soaked."

"It won't do any good to sit still. I can't light a fire, can I? And I'm not staying here alone."

"You'll catch your death."

"I could catch that anyway. The cold's not the most dangerous thing anymore."

"All right."

She tugged at his arm. He seemed frozen. "Peter, come on."

"Yes . . ."

"Come on."

Dan hit the dirt, arms over his head. Despite his old certainty that he was going to live forever, he was sure in that second that he would feel the bullets tearing into him, clubbing him down. He saw a picture of himself twitching as blood spurted from him, fade-out, end of show.

When he realized the shots had missed him, he was up and running for his life before thought had a chance to take over. His senses got him up and he pounded across the wide, wide emptiness that separated him from safety.

He ran expecting the next shot to kick dirt at his feet and the next to blow away his guts. How fast was the firing on an AK47 switched to single shot? It was a purely academic matter now, because there was no more shooting, only a screaming shout from a throat he did not recognize; then he was onto the lodge's neatly mowed lawn, sweeping round the back, past the narrow windows and smashing through the door, falling into the corridor, kicking the door shut to protect his back.

He had made it. Great God above, he had, after all, made it.

He couldn't stop the laugh rising; he let it go. Tried to keep it quiet but it bubbled out of him, and he lay on the cold floor of the corridor, laughing like a fool.

The sound of being alive.

After a minute he got up and tried to lock the door. There were no latches and no key, so he made do with propping a chair against it so he would have time to react if Charlie attacked.

He turned back to the corridor, nose wrinkling, smelling something familiar. He called hello, no longer expecting a reply. If anyone were in here, they would have heard his entrance. He saw the doors were open all down the corridor, some of the locks snapped out of the frames. He stopped breathing through his nose because the stink was too strong. He went down the corridor, glancing through the doorways. He came to the staff canteen.

They were all there, except the boatman and MacNeice. The room was daubed with their gore.

Even to a man who had seen some horrors, there were a lot of bodies. One had sprawled over the electric fire and his chest was scorching where it touched the bars with a scent like roasting pork.

Dan picked his way over them, turned the fire off. He stepped in half-congealed puddles of blood. Everything looked as if it had been under a scarlet rain. Ellis lay propped up against the wall, a stupefied expression on his face. Two of the others lay in each other's arms. It was an accident they had fallen that way, but Dan could not stand to look at them. He saw the bullet holes in the walls. Charlie had made certain of things here. Poor Household was almost cut in two.

He toed a couple of cartridge cases on the floor. He walked out of the room and closed the door. Nobody should have to suffer the indignity of being seen when they had died that way.

With little hope, he checked the other rooms. The store was filled with stuff, none of it any use as a weapon. Petrol, though, which might be useful. He blinked at it, wondering why his mind refused to function again. He stared at his hand and saw the blood on it. He rubbed it against a pack of toilet rolls, smearing the paper.

What was next? The radio. Where did they keep it? He left the store, walked back to the guest room.

That scream he heard as he ran for the lodge. What did it mean? What had happened to stop Charlie taking his best shot?

The radio had been hacked to pieces. Even if he were an expert with the things, he doubted it could be made to work. He rubbed his eyes wearily. That put the lid on the whole deal really. He had come to find out what had happened to the wardens and to see if the radio was any good. Negative on both counts. He had expected it but it was a bitter cup to swallow after all the risk.

He glanced out of the window, realized he was in view. No one was there. He picked up the broken microphone, thinking that Charlie had touched this a few hours ago. Charlie, whoever he was, had been here, killed and smashed, and left his smell mingled with the stench of their death. Dan stared at the microphone's glossy surface, saw fingerprints on it. Charlie's fingers? He wished even more that he knew what the guy looked like. This whole thing was preying on his nerves. He could smell the guy but couldn't put a face on him.

He threw the microphone aside, went out of the room toward Williamson's office. If there was any booze around, the

Captain wouldn't mind him taking a couple of measures for medicinal purposes.

He was, perhaps, three paces from the office, right in the corridor's center, when the chair holding the door shattered into fragments. The door crashed open, swinging solidly against the wall.

And Dan forgot everything he should ever have remembered. He did not make a dive for Williamson's office, he did not hit the floor. He whipped around, totally shocked, knowing that if he had to check out now, he would at least have seen the face of his killer before it happened.

32

HE STOOD IN THE DOORWAY, A FIGURE MADE OF SHADOW. The AK47 pointed down the corridor, but it did not fire. He came into the lodge, clutching his forehead. Blood trickled between the scarred fingers.

"Goldman?" he said.

Dan tried to speak. Nothing worked.

"I'm MacNeice." Following the other's petrified gaze, he looked down at the rifle, then back at Dan. He pulled the trigger. Nothing happened. "Bloody thing's jammed." He glared at Dan again, lowered the rifle. "Don't worry," he said. "It's not what you think."

"I don't know what I think," Dan whispered. "I gave it up."

MacNeice put the rifle down and spread his hands. One of them dripped blood on the floor. "I'm not the one you think I am, understand? I'm not the owner of the gun."

"Then how come—?"

"I took it away from him. I was tracking him and I saw he was getting ready to shoot you. Not that I give a shit for you, but I thought I'd better jump him."

Dan wanted to move but was afraid his bowels would let go. He slumped against the wall. He saw MacNeice's jacket with the name sewn on.

"Bastard did me a bit of damage," MacNeice said, "but I managed to get the gun away from him."

"I think I owe you," Dan said.

"You don't owe me anything. I just did your dirty work for you."

Dan could not think of anything to say.

MacNeice touched the gash on his forehead. "I've got to get something for this," he said. He glanced through the canteen door. "Christ."

Dan found it possible to stand again. He recalled the first-aid kit in Williamson's office. He fetched it, reached to take MacNeice's arm.

"Get away, will you!" The eyes were burning.

Dan took a deep breath. "I'm . . . sorry."

"Sorry?"

"About the others. About all of this."

"If it weren't for you, none of it would've happened." MacNeice snatched the kit and delved inside for antiseptic and bandages. As he cleaned the wound, he said: "This is your fault, *Mr.* Goldman. You think about it."

"Look, what happened out there? Where is he?"

"Maybe he's dead. I tied him up, but I think he's dead."

"Did you know him? You ever see him before?"

"No."

"What does he look like?" This was important. He leaned closer to MacNeice, who shuffled back.

"Ordinary. That's all. What d'you care? He's not shooting at you anymore, that's the important thing." He wrapped a crepe bandage over the gauze covering his wound. He pinned it at the back.

Dan glanced out of the open door. It was almost like night out there. The trees were bending over in the damp wind that brought rain in its wake.

"Looks like you were an ace in the hole, my friend."

"That's fine." MacNeice picked up the rifle and started fiddling with the firing mechanism.

"Better leave it for the cops."

"Just a minute." He stared at Dan, and Dan felt cold all over. The guy really did think he was the biggest shit in the world. But with his buddies splattered all over the walls in there, maybe he had just cause.

"You sure the guy's out of it?"

"I told you. I tied him to a tree up there. He won't get out. But likely he's dead anyway." He smacked the rifle with the heel of his hand, tried the trigger again.

"I want to see him."

"Should you not get your friends in out of the cold? Rain's coming."

"Yeah, you're right. I'm not thinking too good. I thought my hour had come back there."

"Well, you're all right now, aren't you?"

"I'm fine."

"See anything?"

"It's all quiet. Nothing going on."

Peter checked the time. "Where the hell is he?"

"Not so loud." Georgie slid back from the rocks that formed the only cover on the hill south of the lodge. "He'll be here in a minute," she said. "With a helicopter and champagne, knowing him."

"Maybe, maybe." Peter frowned. "Where's MacNeice?"

"Give it time. They'll both turn up."

"Everyone's gone home." He gazed at the folly on Cruach Scorba. It was shrouded with mist now. The sea was being ripped by the wind, jagged white showing on black silk. "You're shivering."

"I do that when I'm freezing."

"We have to get you dry clothes. You can't wear them."

"Never mind now," she said. He could hear her teeth chattering. "We'll give him a few minutes more."

Dan kicked the broken chair away and opened the door wide. MacNeice was still messing with the rifle. He just hoped it would not go off.

He stepped out in the open, searching the south ridge for

the others. As soon as they were down and safe, he would go into the trees and check that the sniper was out of the game. There they were, up on the rocks. He waved to them.

"It's okay, everything's fine."

"He shouldn't be out in the open like that," Peter said. "What did he say?"

Georgie stood up. "Wait a minute."

Dan's voice came up to them from the yard again. "It's all right. MacNeice is with me. We've got the bastard."

Peter stood too. "You're joking," he called.

"No kidding, my friend. Georgie, you okay?"

"Soaked, but fine."

"Okay, come on down here, both of you."

Peter glanced at her. She shrugged and they started to climb over the ridge.

Dan couldn't wait. He came across the yard, walking quickly at first, then breaking into a run. "We're going home."

"I buy the first round," Peter laughed, as MacNeice came out of the lodge.

Only it wasn't MacNeice.

Peter's mouth dropped open. His stomach seemed to fall away. He looked up at Georgie, and her face had gone fish white. She screamed down the hill: "Dan, it's not Mac-Neice. It's not him!"

Peter switched from the killer. Dan's eyes widened and he faltered in his run.

The watcher leveled the rifle, raised his head to give them a smile, and Georgie was screaming at Dan to get out of the way, Peter was yelling too, and Dan was half turning, desperately looking for somewhere to hide.

—Asshole, he thought. Fucking asshole. He could not believe he had been so dumb. MacNeice had been far too young, and too small for the jacket he wore. What a lousy, stupid thing to go for. After all the years, after coming back in one piece from Nam. All the years telling himself he could not be fooled. To fall for a trick like that.

But it was worse than his mistake. He knew it as he started to run again. He had screwed up once more, failed to make the miracle happen, just like before.

He heard Georgie crying out his name, lifted his eyes and saw her up there with Peter. He wanted to tell her he was sorry, that he loved her, that it would be okay.

It was too late. Surely it was too late? —Can't be, he told himself, not like this. The monster had a face now, but he still did not know why this was happening. He had to stay alive to find out, couldn't just give up without knowing. He thought: —I don't stand a chance if I keep running away, nowhere to hide in this godforsaken shithole of a yard. I'm out here, I might as well do something. What the fuck is this, anyway? We've got years, I'm going to take out this guy, and Georgie and me, we'll get married and have ten kids, and *that's* how it'll be. No one's killing me this easy.

He tried sideslipping to the left, then fast to the right. With the screams of the other two ringing and ripping through him, he swept all the way round, started toward the watcher. If he could just get in before a fatal shot went home it would be okay. He could still take the game. It was born of desperation and being in a corner there was no other way out of, but he gave it his best shot. He lunged.

The watcher never looked as if he had a problem.

Gunfire. Loud like the ocean booming on jagged rocks. Three rounds. No misses.

Dan only heard the first two.

Rain.

4

The Terrible Rain

33

"STUPID THING TO DO," HE KEPT SAYING, TRYING TO PICK the slivers of rock out of his shoulder. "Stupid bloody thing. Shouldn't have done it." Fingers plucking at the holes in his flak jacket. Not even feeling the pain.

Georgie took her face out of her hands, rolled over onto her knees. "Let me do it," she said. He didn't hear. "Peter, stop it." She grabbed his hands and forced them down.

The rain fell forever. It was a river in the air, not like any normal rain they were used to. They huddled in the weak shelter of branches in pitch darkness.

She began to remove the splinters, pulling them from his flesh. He did not react at all, just shook his head and muttered furiously: "Stupid thing to do."

"He wasn't to know. How could he know?"

"Oh, God."

When Dan was shot down, he had actually stood up in full view of the sniper, shaking his fists, crying: "You bastard," at the distant, smiling face. As Georgie skidded and fell, he started to leap down the hill toward the lodge, so crazed that he forgot the rifle and the danger. A bullet struck the rocks behind him and sprayed fragments over him. He had fallen then, and some degree of sense came back. He grabbed Georgie and threw her over the ridge, ran with her down the reverse slope of the hill, stumbling, hurting himself. Now there was the rain and, imprinted on his eyes like a lightning flash, the sight of Dan striking the concrete of the yard, breaking like a scarecrow.

"Georgie?"

"What?"

"Maybe he was only hurt. Maybe he's still alive."

Raindrops splashed on the ground. Rain found its way through the branches, dripped on their heads.

"No, he isn't," she said.

"Might be," he insisted.

"No. He's dead." She sat back on her haunches. "Most of it's out now. Try moving your arm."

He lifted it slowly, winced. "That bastard."

"Quiet. You'll give us away."

He got up on his knees. The rain drove so thickly that it was impossible to see or hear anything more than a few feet away.

"We're safe enough," he said. "He won't move in this any more than we will. He's hiding in the lodge, keeping nice and dry."

"Don't count on it. Please, Peter, keep your head down."

"Stop telling me what to do."

"I just want us to stay alive, for Christ's sake!"

He subsided. "I'm sorry. It's just . . . Dan was the only one of us who knew something. He had experience. If he . . . if he couldn't do it . . ." He wrapped his arms round his body, shaking with cold.

She knelt there, smelling the sourness of their sweat, wondering how they would get out of this. Peter was right: Dan was the one who knew what it was like to be under fire. Bob had some experience of it, playing the game so often. They were the two liabilities, and they remained.

The watch came out of his pocket. He held it to his chest.

She pulled her collar up; a pointless gesture, since she was already sodden and numbed by the falling temperature. "It's night. Someone'll come looking now."

"We can't count on it anymore," Peter said. "The bastard was in the lodge. He probably worked out some trick . . ." He spat on the ground. "I wish we knew why. Why he's doing this, who he is."

She breathed out slowly. "I know."

The rain pattered in the undergrowth like a crowd on the run.

"I recognized him when he came out of the lodge. I know who he is."

He sat on the floor of the corridor, knees drawn up under his chin. His head was full of the noise. He rocked back and forth, moaning. His clenched hands rammed against his skull with the beat of the pain.

—Son of a bitch, fucking Goldman bastard. He ground his teeth together until his jaw ached. Making me kill him that way, out of order.

Not that the American did not deserve it, trying to fool him, trying to play the soldier. The bastard had camouflaged himself, gone rooting through the undergrowth on his belly.

And then to set the warden on him like that. It was the last bloody straw. He was being fair with them, fairer than they deserved, taking them one at a time. But they couldn't even fight for themselves; they sent in an employee to do their work for them.

It had been closer than he liked to think about. MacNeice jumped him with that great club of a branch. The first swing made a lucky contact, slashing his forehead.

He'd fired wild, missing the warden's bulk. The next blow jerked the rifle from his hands. He screamed then. MacNeice swung once more and he felt the club whistle past his face. He got his hands to it, gripped, twisting up and round. MacNeice was a powerful man, but he was a teacher, not a soldier. He cried out as his wrists bent, let go of the branch. The watcher grinned, then he turned it, getting in the initial, stunning blow before MacNeice could run. He used it economically after that, watching as the big man's face disintegrated.

He tightened the fists against his skull, remembering the impact traveling up the club into his arms. Nose and cheekbone breaking, blood spurting. The last attempt MacNeice made to cry out before he thrust the thick base of the branch into his mouth, smashing teeth.

He had not wanted to do that. He couldn't bear to think how close he had been to the man, how MacNeice had grappled with him before he died. Goldman made him do it, trying to be clever.

He managed to get the dead man's jacket off, was so mad that he forced himself to do it. His own had been ripped across the back by MacNeice's blows and would be useless against the weather now. He put it on.

Then he headed for the lodge, not realizing until he was there that the rifle had jammed. He intended killing Goldman by then, but it had not made him feel better. The look on Goldman's face as he thought he was going to die the first time, then the crawling slime of his relief when he thought he was safe. The second time, when he realized what was going on, was good. Letting him run far enough to be a target again, the gun unjammed, shooting him.

Then the pain returned. The anger was too much to hold. He had wasted the man who brought all the troubles, but too soon.

He rocked so hard that he struck the wall behind him. He didn't care. It was so difficult to think of anything but the pain. All he knew was that when the rain let up, he would see the old man and the girl squirming in the mud with the life pouring out of them. They would have to suffer in Goldman's place, and the island would be purged.

"You know him?" Peter said. "I don't understand. Are you saying all this is happening because some jilted boyfriend of yours took umbrage?"

"No, I'm not. Just listen, will you? How much do you know about Scorba and the Edinville before Dan took them over?"

"Next to nothing. I handled some of the paperwork, but this is my first visit."

"Well, you know how I met him. When I left university, I had a job lined up with an electronics company in the Midlands. But the job started in October and I wanted to do something different while I was waiting. So I looked through some copies of *The Lady*, and saw the advert: 'Young, enthusiastic person wanted to perform various duties in Highland hotel for the summer season.' The money wasn't great, but it was full board and I'd never been to the west coast. I took the next train up. The hotel was miles from the nearest railway station, and the old man drove to Glasgow to fetch me himself."

"Old man?"

"The manager, Mr. Waterhouse. He was English, but he'd gone to Scotland with his wife and son in the fifties to take over the hotel, and he never got away again. Nice man, really nice. He looked like some kind of ship's captain out of *Moby Dick*. You know, face like an apple from too much tippling. He drove me back to this little nowhere village on the coast called Baldrick. And that's how I came to the Edinville.

"It worked out quite well. The hotel must've been really grand at one time, but it was a bit faded and rundown. It ticked over nicely enough in the summer. I started as an assistant to the old man, organizing the staff day-to-day—there were about ten altogether—but after a while I was doing a bit of everything: keeping the books, reception, running the bar. It was just as well because old Waterhouse's idea of managing was to socialize with the customers and give them drinks. Oh, nothing sloppy or anything like that. But he was . . . relaxed, old-fashioned. He once told me that he'd spent the first thirty years of his life in the city, worrying himself sick and getting ulcers. Then he came to the Edinville and fell in love with the country, and wanted nothing more than to live out his days there. I was always going to him with ideas for streamlining and building up custom, and he'd wag his finger at me and say: 'Now, now, young lady, that sounds like progress to me. Can't be doing with progress here.' Then he'd ask me to sit with him on the first-floor balcony and have a glass of wine . . . 'Now, now, young lady . . .'

"I suppose he really got to like having me about the place. He said I was so efficient that he could leave all the routine stuff to me and get on with the important things. I never found out what they were, but it was a nice time at first. The weather stayed good, and I got tanned and didn't have to think about pressure for a while. The old man used to suggest occasionally that we could make the job a permanent thing. I knew there wasn't enough money in the hotel to warrant it, but it was fun to chat about it and pretend it might happen. I didn't think anyone took it seriously.

"Halfway through July, the old man's son came home on leave."

"Leave?" Peter said.

"He was in the army. I think he was a Para. Joined when he was eighteen because there wasn't any work in the town. He'd just done a tour in Northern Ireland and got badly shaken when he was blown up in Newry. He was in a Land Rover with his best friends. He walked away from it, but two of them died and another was paralyzed. He came home one night, walked all the way from Oban with a rucksack on his back. Funny kid, really—"

"Kid?"

"He was twenty-one but he seemed younger. Very shy of me. The old man was so pleased you wouldn't believe it. 'Now I've got my two children with me, let's open a bottle.' I was his honorary daughter." She smiled, but Peter couldn't see this in the gloom. "Harry wasn't in the mood, though. He went straight up to his room and slept round the clock. Woke up screaming his head off. Nightmares.

"He was all right most of the time. He took me out in the old man's car. We went all over the countryside, and there wasn't a thing he didn't know. Showed me places where villages were before the enclosures, the sites of battles. He was always saying he'd take me out to his island one day, but we never got round to it. He was distant with me, but that was mainly shyness. He was still in shock, I think. The old man did everything to make him forget about it. They were so close, maybe because Mrs. Waterhouse died when Harry was still a boy. We ended up like a sort of unofficial family.

"But then one evening—" She stopped. The rain splashed unceasingly around them. A look of pain and distaste crossed her face.

Peter said: "What happened?"

She was sad, huddling in the rain. "One evening, the old man had more to drink than usual. It'd been a quiet day and the three of us spent most of the afternoon on the balcony, watching things going on in the town. So we were drinking and telling jokes, and Harry went indoors for a minute, and I was sitting next to the old man on the swing seat, and he tried to kiss me."

She scratched a stick in the dirt.

"There we'd been all that time, him talking about me as his 'honorary daughter,' and then he—he put his hand on my leg and tried to kiss me."

Peter watched her hands digging at the ground. Through the fog of panic and the constant presence of fear, his mind latched on to all the things Vickie had said about Georgie, the things he had noticed about her.

She went on speaking, but he knew she had stopped telling him a simple story. Her voice was filled with disappointment. "He smelled of drink and his hand was red and bony and old. He whispered to me: 'C'mon love. Just a little kiss, just a little smooch for your old man.'

"I couldn't stand it. I must've hit him. By the time Harry came back, I was standing by the balcony and the old man started covering up, telling another joke."

The stick broke in her fingers. Peter waited until she gathered her thoughts again.

"He apologized later, said he was drunk and he was just a daft old fool who couldn't resist a pretty face. And after that it was more or less all right. I only had a month to go, so I didn't give notice or anything. Back to normal, except for Harry. I think he knew something happened, but not exactly what. He was never quite the same to me after that.

"Then Dan arrived."

"That was around the time he bought the island?"

"Correct. He turned up at the hotel one day with his current lady friend and asked for the best room in the place. The Edinville wasn't a millionaire's hotel in those days. The woman he was with—some society kiddie or other—looked as if someone had asked her to spend the weekend in a pig shed. But you know how Dan is. He took the grandest room we could manage and proceeded to play the American tourist to the hilt. Most of the staff thought he was wonderful, but he put some backs up, especially when they found out why he was there.

"Harry got annoyed when he found out. He used to play on this island when he was a kid. He said the coast was nobody's property. He wouldn't have anything to do with Dan, started sulking in the pub in town, trying to get up a petition. But then he had to go back to his regiment anyway, so he never had a chance to do much about it.

"I got to know Dan while he was at the hotel, especially after he had a massive row with the society kiddie and she insisted on going home. One lunchtime he quizzed me about what I'd be doing after the summer, what I'd done at university, that sort of thing. Next day he offered me a job."

"Which you accepted?"

"You must be kidding. Straight from university to personal assistant to a man you read about in the papers. Of course I took it."

"And left the old man to cope by himself?"

"I gave a week's notice."

"After what happened, it was probably the best thing anyway. Especially if the son was gone and you were going to be alone with him."

"I suppose that was part of it." She shrugged.

"I don't believe it," he said.

"What?"

"Well, beautiful you are, my dear, but I can't believe this boy is going to wait all this time and then start killing everyone in sight because you refused his father a kiss. Or even because he had a secret crush on you himself."

She snorted. "Oh, for God's sake, Peter. Think about it some more. Not me. Think about what became of the hotel after Dan decided to buy the island and make a survival game out of it."

He frowned. "We made an offer to the owners. Same family who sold the island. Twenty-first laird of something-or-other."

"And the hotel had to be completely renovated and converted, didn't it?"

"From the reports I saw, it needed it."

"What happened to the manager, Peter?"

"He had to go out with the rest of the junk. We brought in a management team of our own and set them to work."

"Do you know what happened to Mr. Waterhouse after that?"

He swallowed. "Oh, good God."

"He was nearly sixty. What chance does a sixty-year-old with a taste for his liquor have of getting another post these days?"

"We gave him a very generous golden handshake. Didn't have to, you know. But Dan said we'd keep things sweeter if we avoided offending the locals. The old chap went away with his pockets bulging."

"He got pushed out of his home, out of the place he loved. They both did."

"But that's the way it goes. If he'd been a better manager, perhaps his employers wouldn't have been so glad to get rid of the place."

"Forget about our side of it. Just think how he must have felt when he got the news. How Harry must've felt for him."

"Well, do *you* know what happened to him?"

"He wrote to me for a while after I left. I think he was upset that I didn't stay, but he dropped me the occasional line. The last time I heard from him was the summer of eighty-two. Harry's regiment had gone out to the Falklands. He was badly hurt. They were shipping him home for treatment."

"They had medical teams out there."

"Not that kind of wound. The old man said that psychiatric casualties in the Falklands war outnumbered physical ones five to one. I think Harry must've seen one horror too many after the thing in Northern Ireland.

"The old man's letter went on about how Harry was all right, but he needed a lot of rest. Just after that, Dan moved in to take over and the letters stopped."

Peter sat very still, thinking about it. The fingers of his right hand gripped tight on the watch.

"All I did was sign some papers," he said quietly.

She ran a hand through her sopping hair. "It was Harry. I'd know him anywhere."

"I don't believe it."

"He couldn't stand the idea of anyone messing around with 'his' island. Think what must've gone through his mind when he discovered we were ruining his father and his island at the same time. To a soldier, the survival game must look like the final insult. We brought it on ourselves."

"We? Dan, you mean. He's the boss."

"And we put his ideas into practice. I deserted, you and Bob did the groundwork for the takeover."

He didn't want to believe it. "I should be at home now, watching a western. I'm a businessman, not part of a wrecking crew."

"Oh, come on. You've signed plenty of agreements that sent people's jobs down the tubes."

"That's business," he said.

"And sometimes, it's somebody's world."

"It can't be," he said. "All this because some psychopathic ex-Para reckons we destroyed his father." He snorted. "I thought it was something big, millions of dollars . . . One nut case with a gun."

"He probably thinks he has good cause."

"When I get my hands on him he's going to wish he'd given up the ghost in the South Atlantic."

"If it keeps raining, maybe we'll be all right. Someone has to come soon."

"No. He's done something, fixed it somehow. If we rely on help arriving in the nick of time we'll go the same way as the others."

"What brilliant plan do you have in mind? We've got a length of rope, that's all."

"Dan had the knife. What else was in the boat?"

"The anchor and the engine, some kind of fishing net."

"Big one?"

"Of course a big one. Logan wasn't fishing for goldfish."

"Engine," he said. "What's in the engine that we could use?"

"Chop him to bits with the propeller."

"Tie him to it and send him speeding off across the sound." He snapped his fingers. "Petrol, there's petrol. If we find some bottles as well."

"What for?"

"Molotov cocktails. Petrol bombs. But we need bottles."

"Plenty in the lodge."

"Very funny."

"No, I mean it. When he leaves we can get in."

"Dan tried that, didn't he?"

"One of us would have to play decoy."

"Any volunteers? It's not much of an idea for the one who plays game for our friend with the rifle."

"I'll do it."

"No."

"Suggest a better idea. We can't attack until we're properly equipped. Besides, there're dry clothes and food in there. We need both."

"A signal fire too." He pulled at his nose thoughtfully. "Never mind the boat. There'd be petrol in there as well. We'd need it to start a fire after this rain."

"Come on, Peter. Say yes before I change my mind."

"What if he catches you?"

"He won't. Not if we move while it's still raining."

"He was in the Falklands. He'll be used to this."

"Peter, it's dark."

"He'd be used to that too."

"I'm not letting you run down there so he can pot you like a rabbit through the window."

"It would help," he said, nodding. "We won't get food anywhere else."

"So?"

"All right."

She started to get up.

"Hang on," he said. "We have to plan. If we walk off and just do it, we won't last five minutes. This chap knows what he's doing. He'll work out ways we'll go, things we'll do, because he's been trained to. If we think our way through we can surprise him, give ourselves an edge. Can you remember the way the island looks?—Don't get the map out, it'll be soaked. If you're to be the decoy—and that's our best bet, since I don't have your wind—plan a route. I want a good hour to go in, prepare things, and catch you up. If this Harry's busy with you, it might give me a chance to creep up on him."

"An hour?" She coughed. "That's a bit more than I had in mind."

He actually smiled. It was the kind of grin he used to flash when he was one of the sharks.

"Change of heart?"

"No. If it's going to bring him down."

"We'll bring him down. Now we know who he is and why. Up to now it's been like taking part in a race where no one tells you you're competing. Christ knows what he thinks he's accomplishing. He doesn't even have a way to get off the island."

"Maybe he doesn't care," she said.

Harry's fingers drummed on the floor. Rain continued, light had gone. He stood up and walked to the electrical box by the front door. Found switches for the exterior floodlights and flicked them on. Opened the front door and gazed out over the forecourt. The rain had turned to silver bars. It was impossible to see more than the first couple of feet of the jetty. The sea, invisible, thundered in the sound. The mainland, empty and silent, was lost in darkness. It was the end of the world here. How could anyone ever have stood in a place like this and had the nerve to think there were new continents over the western horizon?

Rain dripped from the arch above the door. The lights were a good idea. In the unlikely event that anyone came down to Kinlosch Ferry, they would see the lights and assume all was well. He stooped and brought up a handful of mud. He smeared it over the bandage. If this was to turn into night maneuvers, it would not do to run around with a white band glowing on his forehead.

He turned and shut the door. The lodge was depressing. It reminded him of the places they had put him in over the years. Fluorescent tubes on the ceilings, neutral paint on the walls, shiny floors. Easier to clean when the more difficult patients messed themselves or shed some blood. He had been that bad right at the beginning, after the red house.

It had still been dark when they finally took the house. The weather so overcast that dawn made no difference. Off to the southeast occasional flashes of enemy fire kept them aware that nothing was going to be easy. The other companies were working their way down toward Darwin, and the fire support from H.M.S. *Arrow* had ceased some time ago.

The Argies had surrendered moments before. Coming out with hands over their heads, a miserable, pathetic-looking bunch. Harry and the others could not believe that this was all the enemy was. Someone was jabbering in Spanish to the prisoners, asking if they were all out. Orders came down from the Boss to get into the house and check for booby traps or stragglers.

"All right, get in and clean her up," the sergeant ordered.

Harry and another two. Their names did not matter anymore. Good mates, both of them. One a Scot. They dodged across the gently sloping terrain before the house under the theatrical light of illuminating rounds. It had been their first taste of real combat, and the company had come through well. Not a man from their platoon lost.

They crashed into the house through the bullet-pocked doorway and began to work through quickly.

"Christ," one of them was saying, "did you ever see anything like it?"

"I nearly bought it," Harry said, turning over a pile of blankets with his boot.

"Fuck you," they jeered.

"I heard one go past me about six inches away."

"Hero of the week." The ground floor was clear. A nice little farmhouse kitchen wavered under their torch beams.

They started up the stairs, the constant thud of enemy stonking magnified by the walls.

"Listen to it."

"After this we take the fuckin' weight off."

"And tea, lots of hot, sweet tea."

"Grub. I could eat one of them sheep on the hillside."

Someone made a joke about General Galtieri. It was a good joke, but Harry could not remember how it went now. He only recalled that they laughed like mad about it as they took a room each on the first floor.

"Fancy living here?" someone said. "Right pisshole this is."

"Makes you wonder, dunnit?"

Nothing at all. Peace and quiet. Nice soft beds.

"Just this one and we're done."

They came together at the last room. All the torch beams congregated on the doorknob. Harry twisted it and ushered the other two in like a doorman.

"What do we have here?" one said. Torch beams separated again, flashed dully on a brass bedstead. Gray light from the window misted over a bed and a chair.

"I fancy a kip," someone said.

Harry was in the doorway now. He peered into the room. "What's that?" he muttered, seeing a strange shape in the corner beyond the chair. His question was lost in the chatter of the others.

He brought his torch up, caught the streaked animal face with its slick of fear and staring eyes.

"Jesus—!" someone said.

The hurried struggle for guns began, but Harry saw the little Argentinian's hands twitch around a Lee Enfield, and he threw his torch aside, diving sideways as the shooting started.

They never stood a chance. It was sheer fright from the enemy and they had relaxed too fast. Harry crashed against the wall, the breath driving out of him, scrabbling for his own weapon. It all kept happening like a bad dream that goes on long after you wake. The quiet exploded. He saw the other two arch and twist in flashes from the rifle. They screeched like pigs at slaughter. Spouts of blood leapt from them in dark ropes. Their innards splashed across the walls and him. He tasted them.

—Can't think, oh, Christ, I can't, I can't—

They told him later that he finally killed the Argie with a single bullet from his own rifle. He was sure they were correct, but the end of it was lost in his mind. It seemed to him that it was endless, that it was still going on somewhere forever and ever.

Support arrived. He was unable to speak, so violent that when an officer ordered his rifle to be taken away, they needed four men to hold him down. He broke the arm of one and fractured the skull of another. The officer kept saying: "What's wrong with the idiot? He's not even scratched." True, he had never received more than a slight injury—during the bomb attack on his patrol back on the Irish border. Physically, he never had a problem. Training, which pulled the muscles, broke the bones of other men, was just an extension of what he had been doing for years on the island. Physically, he was untouched.

But he had seen his mates wiped out by a bomb that was bigger than anyone needed to kill one little patrol. He had been frightened every hour of every day for months. The red-house incident had removed new mates. Both times, he walked away from things no one else survived. It was too much. The constant fear in Belfast, the redoubled danger when they waded ashore at San Carlos. He had seen too much, and the little Argentinian scrambling in his corner in the house that was meant to be empty, blasting away at them, was the final straw. The rattle of the gun in the tiny room, the flashes from the muzzle, the guts and blood and the raw stink of smoke. The taste of agony and panic and hate like a dry, rotten peach in his mouth. The ragged little tears and rips in his mind suddenly pulled and grew, yawning wider and wider until the red darkness was like a pool in his head and he fell into it, screaming.

They kept him sedated all the way home, packed below

decks with the seriously wounded and dying. On arrival in England, he missed all the flags and cheering and bands playing. He was taken to a military hospital.

Dad came to see him. Embarrassed chatter about stupidities while Harry lay on a bunk, not replying.

Transfers to other hospitals. Psychiatrists asking him to go back over his experiences—things he did not want to relive. He told a pudgy-faced doctor that he had lived it once and that was enough. Some of the psychiatrists were military, but they understood him no better than the civvies. It was all a load of bullshit anyway, he said. "How can we help you," they asked, "if you won't accept?" He didn't want help. He would be fine if they let him alone to forget it.

At nights he was back in Belfast, trotting down the Falls Road, trying to see in all directions at once, because he could not be sure of any window or alley, and the kids across the street might be about to chuck petrol bombs at him. Or it was San Carlos Water in the foul light of a gray, drizzling day. Or watching the Argentinian Etendard jets sweeping in to punch holes in the ships in the bay. Or it was the red house.

Waking up with that arid fruit in his mouth again. Filled with the certainty that his body was nothing more than a filthy bag of guts and blood that somebody was about to burst.

Letters from Dad, telling him things were fine, that there would be a bed for him when he was well again. Letters with a strange, dead quality behind the usual jokes and news. He did not take this in at the time because his entire world was the battlefield in his skull. At some point the paper the letters were written on changed from hotel stationery, but he did not see this either.

Dad visited once more while they had him. He looked as if he had been drinking more than was good for him, and the flesh of his face and neck had slackened, taken the gray pallor of a moth's wing. He talked about Baldrick and how things were at the Edinville, but it was like he spoke of people who had died. When Harry said he would be glad to come home to breathe good air and go out in the boat, his father nodded and said he should just think about getting himself better.

More doctors. The medication was reduced bit by bit, and he did his best to show them he was fine. He tried to keep up to scratch physically. He used whatever facilities they had, or did his own routine of exercises. He would not get sloppy, he would be fit for his return to duty.

Then one day something one of the nurses said made him realize he had been locked away for years—not months but whole years.

At his next meeting with his doctor, he asked when he would be going back to his regiment.

That was when he realized. He had not thought of it before, but the doctor sitting there, avoiding a straight answer, made it plain enough. He concealed his fury from the doctors. He concentrated on getting out, knowing that nothing mattered now but to go home. He continued to be good until, one day, their report on him said that he was, if not cured, at least fit to go back into society. Honorable discharge from the service, grateful thanks from the government. They gave him his back pay and a small pension, asked him where he was going. "Home," he said. They gave him the address of a hospital in Glasgow where he must attend as an outpatient for a while, so they could see how he was getting on. Fine, anything so they let him out.

He walked back into the world one August afternoon when the sun was shining like an arc lamp out of a clear blue sky. Dad was meant to be there with a taxi and two train tickets to Glasgow. He thought of the car trip home, going up through Dumbarton, along the shores of Loch Lomond, the stretch down Loch Fynne and the hills of Kilmichael Forest. It was a hell of a route to take, but lovelier than the easy way, and he would drink in every mile of it, every little burn and each rolling hill.

Dad was not there. Harry wandered down the high street of this town he had never really seen before, found a public phone. It was not like the old ones he was used to. He had to put the money in first. He pushed the buttons, remembering the number of the Edinville as he knew his own age. A voice he did not recognize answered. He asked to speak to his father.

"Who would that be, sir?" the girl asked. Some snooty English girl.

"Mr. Waterhouse," Harry said. "This is Harry."

She went away for a moment, then was back. She said: "I'm sorry, sir. There's no one of that name staying here at the moment."

"He's not a guest," Harry said blankly. "He's the manager."

"Ah," she breathed. Suddenly he was talking to someone who called himself the manager. An educated Edinburgh voice. The voice told him that Mr. Waterhouse had left the hotel some time ago, after the takeover.

Harry could not speak. He was conscious of his breath misting clammily in the mouthpiece of the phone.

The voice gave him a phone number and address. The guy did not even sound curious. He reeled off the number and said he hoped this would sort things out.

Harry stared at the address. Glasgow. He bought a ticket and traveled up, sitting in the airless quiet of a 125 as it raced north. The country beyond the glass was like the moon to him. His suit itched on his body. People watched him over their newspapers as he sat there, mumbling and talking.

All he wanted was an explanation.

Glasgow on a humid evening. The noise and lights of Argyle Street scared the hell out of him. He stumbled into a taxi and gave the driver the address. Smell of fake-fur seatcovers and cigarettes. The driver blathering on about Rangers' chances in the new football season.

The address was a terraced Victorian house near Govan Road. A pair of red curtains hung over the front window, too small to shut out the light. Harry saw a couple of kids playing between the cars and smelled Indian food. Carrying his cheap suitcase, he walked across the road and pressed the doorbell. It did not work. He knocked. Flakes of paint fell off the door. Shuffling footsteps came up the hall. He shivered.

Dad opened the door. He was drunk. He did not look surprised to see Harry there. He did not try to explain. He burst into tears.

That was how Harry discovered what had happened to his home, what Goldman and the others had done to his father. The old man with his eyes poached in whisky, rambling on about how they had pushed him out without a second thought, how his lovely Georgie had helped.

Oh, yes, that became very clear. The girl Dad had trusted like a daughter, offered a permanent job to, had jumped at the Yank's money and power, then helped him to destroy the Edinville, Harry's father, and Scorba.

When Harry got angry and asked why he had not been told, Dad sobbed: "I couldn't tell you that, not the state you were in, son. What good would it have done?"

Harry felt as if everything had been pulled out from under him. He had gone off to one island to protect the citizens of his fair land from terrorists and bombers, then to a godforsaken island on the other side of the Atlantic to save more civilians from a bunch of fascists. And while he was gone, some bastards came in and destroyed everything he knew and loved. His island.

Dad was a wreck. Living on the first floor of the peeling slum with some weirdo old bastard downstairs who listened to the World Service with the volume full up at all hours. The place had scarred lino on the floors and threadbare imitation Persian carpets strewn about under ugly prewar furniture.

"It's just till we get straight," Dad said. But Harry knew that he no longer cared a bugger where he was as long as the bottle at his elbow was full. He did not seem to be angry with the Yank and his company for what they had done. He was too shocked.

"One month to get out," he said, licking wet lips. "Had to sell up most of our stuff, son." He had saved a few mementos, and a tea chest in the small room at the back contained all of Harry's military memorabilia. "Sum total of thirty years," he said. "I wrote and told Georgie, but I haven't heard from her in a while." A snapshot of the three of them on that last summer stood on the mantelpiece. Dad and him with the girl in the middle, showing off her tits in a tight yellow sun top. Her eyes were covered by sunglasses. Big smile on her face. How could he ever have thought she was nice?

Traitorous bitch.

Harry tried to rip the picture up. Dad protested. He could not see how she had helped them to ruin him.

"She screwed you, Dad. She used you."

"She did not. She's not to blame."

Harry sensed the carefully gathered pieces of his control beginning to fly apart again like a fragmentation grenade in slow motion. He had expected to be with Dad in the clean, open spaces of the coast. Fishing, climbing, walking, getting back some idea of the life that had passed him by.

He moved into the tiny back room with his father. He had very few belongings, but he put up all the pictures and charts from the tea chest. He was on social security, no chance of a job. He attended the outpatients' clinic once a month for the next year.

And perhaps he could have persuaded himself to forget, even with Dad dissolving in alcohol on the bed settee in the front room. But if he picked up a paper, there was Goldman, flashing his money and success for the cameras. And there was his grinning face on the television, driveling about some bloody French food. You could not get away from him.

One day he picked up the local paper, and there it was, the greatest insult. A long article with pictures. "Goldman's Game." A shot of Scorba from Kinlosch Ferry, Williamson in the foreground next to a sign saying, SURVIVAL GAME.

He knew of the game. It was increasingly featured in the gun magazines he bought. He called it a joke in his own mind. A sick joke for people who never fired a real gun in their lives. He had heard that, in America, Vietnam veterans were playing it too. He could not understand that. You had to be sick to do something like that for fun. And much sicker to think of making money from it.

"It's a little light relief for people who get tired of driving their desks," Goldman said in the interview.

Light relief?

Harry's headaches got worse after that. Like the pounding of Oerlikon cannons in the dark of his squalid room. He brooded over pictures of Goldman. Finally, he drove the secondhand Ford Escort he purchased with back pay up to Baldrick to see what had happened there. It was late summer then, so he slept in the hills outside the village, walking in and talking to people who barely remembered him. They were all cashing in on the invasion. New shops along the high street, the pub down on the harbor tarted up for tourists. He listened to the locals chat. They were pretty pleased with things as they were.

He found out a great deal about the survival game by writing to the Edinville for details. They sent him a glossy brochure meant for businessmen to drool over.

He returned to the coast in the autumn, holed up in a disused sheep farm out in the hills by Langa Sound. Every day, concealed in the rocks above the ferry, he watched the traffic to and from Scorba. Minibuses came with parties of fat civilians dressed up in camouflage jackets. They sailed across to the island, laughing and joking, returned later in the day, exhausted but elated with their bloodless killing.

Harry took the quiet times to prowl around the cars, checking for the wardens' names. He got to know all their faces; he drew detailed maps of the island from memory. He prepared himself, although he did not know what for until one night in the pub, he listened to a couple of the wardens—Ellis and Richardson—complaining about their lost weekend.

"I was going to take myself to Glasgow," Ellis groaned over his pint. "The last time I had any real fun was April."

"What sort of fun you talking about?" Richardson asked.

"You know what sort, man. Lord, it's like being a monk up here, boy."

"Never mind. Think of the extra pay."

"What good is it here?"

"You could always visit old Mary." Old Mary was a youngish widow, living up on the Hill Road, who was said to be a fair bet if you could afford to entertain her. Harry swallowed the bile that rose in his throat and listened.

"I don't see why he needs all of us for the four of them," Ellis said. "Season's supposed to be ending, isn't it?"

"I don't care," Richardson grunted, finishing his beer. "As long as we get a good bonus, Mr. Goldman and his pals can fall off the cliffs for all I care."

Harry nearly cried out. He stayed in his seat by an effort of will.

More eavesdropping gave him details of when the American was to visit. As he took it all in, he began to see what he had been preparing for. It was so simple and so beautiful that it came into his mind fully formed.

On Thursday he bought the guns.

His head screamed with the bombardment.

Why had the bastard Yank ruined everything? It was all out of order now. Goldman was supposed to go last. But they had screwed it up, sending poor, fat MacNeice in to attack him.

Well, they would discover what it was all about, the girl and the old man. They would see that it wasn't any game. Goldman was dead, night was here, and he had plenty of bullets left for the last two.

He rose, shaking his head violently. The headache receded a little. He glanced out of the doorway. The rain was slackening. It might set in and go on for hours yet, though. No way to tell up here.

He pushed his shoulders back. His body was aching; he had not slept for a long time. Sleep was not important to him anymore. He had not really had peace since the day in the red house. Six thousand miles and a million years away.

He stood in the lighted doorway, rubbing his chin.

Something clattered in the yard. He ducked quickly. A heavy stone struck the wall above his head. He watched it bounce away and splash in the puddles outside.

He lunged inside, grabbed his rifle. Another stone whizzed down and smacked on the floor of the corridor.

He roared with anger, fired an indiscriminate burst into the rain.

No sound from out there.

—Bastards.

He put the hood of his jacket up and sprinted out of the lodge, heading for the trees.

34

GEORGIE DROPPED THE LAST STONE AND RAN. FEAR WASHED through her veins, making her legs suddenly weak. She made the mistake of glancing back down the hill, and that made it worse. He was racing out of the blazing lights like an animal. The kid who shyly explained to her the natural history of the coast and tried not to stare at her.

She put her head down and scrambled up the bank. The rocks and grass under her hands felt like the hard spines of a hedgehog. She left specks of blood wherever her fingers touched now, and she thought about the scars she would have later. Her hands would never be smooth again.

It was completely dark. She moved fast away from the lodge, plunging into blindness. It all depended on keeping her feet high as she ran, on remembering the terrain accurately. The rain was still coming down hard, and her clothes were twice the weight they had been dry. She broke out onto one of the paths that led toward the moors and crept along it. No time anymore to check for pursuit: she had to assume that Harry was after her.

—Oh, no, you don't. If he realizes what we're up to he could just hang on at the lodge, wait for Peter to turn up, and shoot him, too.

The idea of being alone on the island with Harry was more frightening than forcing herself to stop. She ducked off the mushy path into the trees, burrowed in under the ferns, tearing her jacket, snagging her hair. She waited.

Peter listened to his heart beating. It was a Buddy Rich solo.

—There's no need to worry about getting shot here, he thought. I'll have a heart attack before he can plug me.

The area was clear. He had seen the man he now knew as Harry go running hell for leather into the forest. He climbed over the ridge and slid down the slick hillside to flat ground. First, he had to do something he did not want to do. He ran low across the yard, feet splashing in the puddles, and knelt by Dan. He hoped he would find the knife in a back pocket but it was not there. He grasped the shoulders and turned him over, grunting at the dead weight. Dan's chest was a mess of blood and dirt. Peter looked at the ragged holes in the stomach, chest, and left thigh, then at the face.

Dan's eyes were closed. He looked quite peaceful. He lay with the rain pattering on his grazed face. He was younger, relaxed in a way he had never been while alive.

Peter leaned over him, touching the face.

"I'll get him," he said. "I promise you, I won't let him hurt her." He took the knife and binoculars from the body and put them in his pockets, then lifted the body under the arms and dragged it to the lodge. The rain streamed in his eyes, pasting his hair down. Dan's mouth opened, drinking the rain.

He thought: —My old friend. My friend. After all the deals we've done, I thought you'd see me buried when we were both past eighty.

He placed the body in the guest room near the smashed radio. It took a moment to fold the arms and straighten it out, but he could not bear the idea of Dan being found as he had fallen. He left it, uncovered, and checked the other rooms.

It was a shock when he found the wardens, but he had already accepted that something terrible had happened. This was no worse than what he had imagined. He was past the point of really feeling any more horror. Besides, he had much to do; their survival now depended on outthinking the opposition, on forgetting that death was something you ordinarily saw only a few times in your life.

He knelt beside the two bodies least damaged and removed their coats and trousers. He gagged several times but did it. The dead men, whose names he recalled only by looking at their name tags, seemed to resist the outrage. They were awkward and heavy. He could not face removing socks and sweaters from them, but ran to the storeroom and began hunting through the shelves. He found a rucksack. There were several changes of clean clothes, probably for those who got soaked or filthy during the game. He bundled two pairs of socks, a couple of sweaters, and some underwear into the sack.

Food? Some tins by the door. He swept an armful into the sack.

—Think, think. What else do we need?

There was nothing like a genuine weapon in the place. Not even a blade. He had expected something, tools for clearing the undergrowth, but there was nothing. So it was back to his original idea. He snatched two gallon cans of petrol from one shelf, took a pack of cleaning cloths from another, and a large bottle of washing-up liquid because he remembered something he had read in a thriller once.

No bottles. No bloody bottles. He stared at the provisions shelf again. There were some nice, tough plastic containers of cooking oil. —Once upon a time, he thought, they'd have been made of glass.

He ran through to Williamson's office, threw open the desk drawers. There were two bottles of McKay's; one empty, the other half full. He unscrewed the cap of the full one and started pouring it away, then realized what he was doing. He lifted it to his lips and took a drink. The whisky burned in his mouth, trickled fire down his throat.

He poured the rest of it out, listened to it pool on the floor with the water dripping from him. Both bottles went in the rucksack, as did a waterproof matchbox, a can opener, and a roll of insulating tape from another drawer.

He leaned back, breathing hard. The office was a nice, safe place; so was the storeroom. The storeroom had no windows and one small door that could be neatly barricaded with shelves. The walls were thick enough to stop any bullet. What if he just walked in there now, closed the door, and sweated it out?

Very unworthy thought. He was disgusted with himself. Georgie had gone out there, risking her neck to give him this chance, and he was thinking of deserting her.

"It's a natural human reaction," he said quietly, "because I'm scared."

The fear was a constant companion now. It was there so much that he had begun to operate on some level above it. He had to; otherwise he would be paralyzed. But now and then it crept up on him and whispered such things to him.

Anyway, if he locked himself in, the maniac out there would probably settle for burning the lodge down to get him.

—Burning?

Now, that was an idea for the signal beacon. If anyone was going to be out there to see it, then the lodge was a good place for a fire.

He returned to the storeroom, got all the petrol cans off the shelf. It took a minute to open all of them; then he carried them around, splashing the petrol into each room, soaking walls and floors. It was the only real shelter on the island, but if he and Georgie could not use it, neither would the killer. The sweet, acrid smell of petrol filled the lodge.

He stuffed everything he could into the rucksack, put the jackets and trousers into Bob's camera bag. The petrol cans and bottles clinked heavily against his back as he hoisted the sack up. He checked his watch.

The rain had all but stopped. Georgie would be in more danger. He stepped outside under the dripping lights. He struck a match to a bunch of old papers from Williamson's office. The flame spread over the paper; he felt it scorching his hand. The petrol glistened in a trail down the corridor. Dan and all the others were in there, but there was no time now. He tossed the paper down the corridor.

A great cough of flame leapt up and flared through the rooms. The air, heavy with fumes, blew back, slamming doors and searing his face. He jumped back, watching the flames.

—Like a Viking warrior, he thought, remembering Dan peacefully sleeping in there. Warrior's death. No gradual decay for him. He was going up into the air. And if the Vikings were right in their belief that the only immortality was the fame and reputation you left behind, then perhaps Dan had a little of that too.

The walls caught light. Glass cracked in the rooms. The floodlights suddenly went out. Now illumination came from inside, flicking through windows, casting shadows on the trees nearby.

Peter grasped the bag with the clothes in it. He had thirty-five minutes to rendezvous with Georgie. Thirty-five minutes to prepare.

She saw the glimmer of light through the trees, knew she was close to the edge of the plantation. She was well north of the lodge, about halfway between there and the shore. She glanced up. A few stars showed through the branches, washed by the last of the rain. That was magnificent, that was wonderful. If the stars came out she would be easy meat for fully trained Harry.

She crouched into the sodden ferns, trying to catch her breath. She wondered how long it would be before she started to suffer from exposure—not knowing that she already had. She was cold down to the bone even after running so hard, and her stomach was a hollow pit. Sixteen hours could seem a very long time in conditions like these, and she wished she could just have a cup of coffee to get some heat inside her.

The ground in front of her sloped gently away to the right. Above the wet sounds of the forest, she heard the crash and tumble of the burn. Old cottage about half a mile northwest, burn dead ahead. Bob was still there on the floor of the hut. Her main problem was getting across the moor. In the pitch dark it was okay, but with stars coming out, the hills and long stretches of scrub were turning to silver.

She thought that she did not really stand much of a chance. It was stupid to have imagined she did. Little Harry was out there with his fistful of grudges against them. She wondered if Harry knew the real reason she had left the Edinville, whether he cared. Had the old man told him what happened that evening? She did not flatter herself that Harry nursed a personal hatred for her, but he could easily see her leaving to work with Dan as one more betrayal of the old man if he did not know it all.

It did not matter anyway. Not any more. Bob was dead, so was Dan. And so would she be if she did not keep her mind on the job.

Footsteps. She jerked round, trying to locate them. She forced herself to stay still, stopped her teeth chattering. She waited.

A figure went by less than ten feet away.

She ceased breathing.

It was Harry. The rifle was a long shadow thrusting forward. His head was down, searching the ground. He moved so softly in the heavy boots.

She felt her center of balance waver. She was squatting, all her weight on the soles of her feet, and she was swaying.

The shadow passed.

She wanted to put a hand down to stop herself from falling. A twig scraped under her boot. It was so loud in her ears that she knew he would hear it.

He turned slowly, sweeping the rifle's muzzle toward her.

Peter returned to the feeble shelter of the trees and emptied the rucksack of bottles, petrol, and other ingredients for the bombs. He stood the empty bottles in the earth and unscrewed the petrol cans. The cans had wide necks and petrol splashed all over the place before the bottles were two-thirds full. He uncapped the washing-up liquid, squirted it into the bottles until both were full. Next, he rescrewed the tops on both bottles and took out the cleaning cloths. He rolled one into a tight tube and pulled a length of tape, stuck the rolled cloth to the side of the bottle, splashing it with more petrol. He repeated the operation with the second bottle. He picked them up and shook them hard. It was still too dark to see much. He tipped the bottles up to see if they were tight. They went into the rucksack. They were not

much against a rifle, but they were more than he had possessed a few minutes ago. Maybe they would save some lives
before the night was out.

He stood up. He had the rope and Dan's knife. He wondered whether the killer was still following Georgie, whether
he had turned back yet, suspecting something. To his left, a
lurid glow showed in the night, and the thick odor of petrol
smoke wafted on the dank air.

Georgie saw dull red flashes in front of her eyes. She drew
a very slow breath while her lungs ached for oxygen. The
muscles in her thighs twitched with fatigue and strain, but
she kept quite still.

Harry stood as before, his gun aimed in her direction. If he
decided to fire a couple of shots as he had done at the lodge,
she would almost certainly be hit.

She let the breath go. It burned in her body. She did not
feel afraid, not as the others had been. Because this was familiar. She knew it from years ago. Her chest was full of a
sick weight, her stomach churned with disgust. She remembered unwillingly, but remembered: at home alone one night
with her father. Her mother had gone to some night class.
This was after that first time, and she already knew what her
father was thinking when he looked at her. Knew that it was
wrong and terrible without knowing exactly why. She wanted
him to love her, not to be angry or upset with her, but surely
other fathers didn't ask their daughters to do the things he
wanted? So she avoided him as much as she could. When she
came in, she tiptoed up the stairs to her room. Barefoot on the
rough staircarpet. She made it to the landing before she heard
him calling: "Georgie, is that you?" She kept moving silently, slipped into her room, and climbed inside the wardrobe. Her summer dresses hung from the rail. Soft cottons
and textiles blowing on her face. They were all new because
her figure had developed so fast in the last year, but the
wardrobe smelled of musty corners.

She heard the door open, her father speaking in the playful voice he used now when they were alone: "Georgie, you
in here? Where's my Georgie Porgie?"

She crouched with her hand on a pile of cardigans and sweaters. The hand he always begged her to touch him with.

"Georgie? Georgie, love?"

Then his frustrated sigh as the door closed, and she recalled the touch of his fingers in places mother said were dirty, the prickle of his stubbled cheek on her face, and she could not stand it. She threw up in the wardrobe, still silent, still overwhelmed by the sick, black weight in her body.

The memory faded. She gulped vomit back from her throat.

Harry's head was on one side, listening. She imagined she could see his face. His thin, pale face like a younger version of the old man. She recalled that they both wore the same expression when they watched her body: mouth slightly open, eyes flat as windows.

She heard his tongue clicking in his throat.

—He knows I'm here, she thought, but nothing's telling him that. Suddenly, she knew all about the animal instincts sociologists were always talking about at university. She had known Harry was approaching and he knew she was there, but his mind wanted proof.

—In a minute he'll smell me out. Dogs smell fear, why not human beings?

His head tilted farther, the way a dog's head would tilt when listening for prey. She could not breathe anymore. The blackness inside her was spreading. The dog had her scent. He was sniffing her out. She thought of how she would try to run, and how he would shoot her as she tried to get away.

The night exploded with a noise like huge doors slamming. The air lit up ruddy and orange.

Harry twisted round. She saw him palely outlined by the fireball that rose from the south. His teeth were bared, eyes staring. A growl came out of his mouth and he leapt toward the fire, which flickered in the sky above the trees.

Georgie lost her balance and sprawled in the mud. She buried her face in it, a laugh spluttering in the filthy water. She got up into a crawl and dragged herself away from the place where she had come close to dying. She had no idea what Peter had done to the lodge, only hoped he had not blown himself up in the process. The thing now was to reach the rendezvous point, as they had planned. Harry might be turning back to pursue her even now. She could take nothing for granted anymore, and there were no second chances in this learning game.

Harry ran all the way back to the hills on the north side of the lodge. He stared down at the blazing hulk of the building, saw the roof begin to fall in with a groan of twisted wood.

They were trying to fool him again, splitting up, destroying the island behind his back. He knelt down, smacking the rifle butt in the earth. A tear fell. He kept playing fair with them, never damaged a thing that belonged to the island, but they went on smashing things up the way they had been ever since Goldman got his hands on it.

They could not realize that it only made him more determined. Every lucky stroke they pulled meant they were closer to death. Every desecration they committed put them further down in his mind.

He wiped his face. There was no point in going down to the lodge. In another hour, there would be nothing left of it. He checked out to sea, but there were no lights on the water at all, no sign of life on the mainland. They were dreaming if they expected anyone to be there at this time of night. And with luck the rain would return and douse the flames. He glanced at the stars beyond the veil of water.

—Oh, no, Miss Lawrence, it's not done with yet, not for you or your friend. I'm going to blow your insides all over the hills. They'll need a good seamstress to put you back decent enough to be buried.

The water shrine lay on his right as Peter came out of the small plantation. He blundered into a narrow burn before his eyes adjusted to the dim light. The long, high bulk of Cruach Scorba lay like a bruised cloud bank to the west. He moved quickly but did not run. He could not afford a twisted ankle at this stage. He no longer had trouble breathing. If he was wet and tired and hungry, he had also passed through some personal barrier to a place where his feet did not hurt, where the last thing on his mind was checking for blisters. It was probably fatigue combined with shock, but as long as it kept him going, he did not care.

The bottles clinked in the rucksack. He was careful also to save them from breaking. It was laughable, of course, to think you could combat a gun-toting psychopath with a couple of Molotov cocktails. If you had a few more, perhaps you stood a chance—but two? It was a working example, so far as he could see, of "Where there's life, there's hope." Perhaps he and Georgie had gone mad with grief, but he had made the decision, some time after watching Dan flop into the dirt like a discarded coal sack, that he was not letting himself be taken. Never mind poor old Harry and his motives—he had spent his life fighting to get his head above the tide and keep it there; a different battlefield, where the enemy carried briefcases instead of guns, yet it was the same struggle in the end. He had survived on his wits for nearly fifty years, and he was still equal to the struggle if he had to be.

He scanned to the left in the hope of spotting Georgie as she crossed the moor. She would be a mile away, by the water shrine, or had already passed it. If not, though, he stood a good chance of setting up an ambush. Then he would see just how effective one Molotov cocktail could be, if thrown accurately enough.

She came to the burn, tried to jump it, landed in the freezing water. Swearing numbly, she clawed up the bank, keeping low to avoid being outlined against the big plantation. She stumbled toward the trees, aware of the fact that she was nearing the end of her rope. The draining effects of the confrontation with Harry had told on her reduced strength. It was getting to be a mechanical process to put one foot in front of the other. She thought, ludicrously, of a coroner saying: "The victim's last meal was three squares of milk chocolate," as he put her stomach in a metal dish. Now that was funny. The family would go into shock, and the police would call Mother to identify the remains. It would be the first time mother and daughter had been together for years. She saw Mother refusing to look at the body—Mother had always disliked naked bodies that were alive, so it was unlikely she would be able to face a dead one. She would stand there as they pulled the sheet back, and she would look bitter and disbelieving—the expression she always wore when there was something terrible she did not want to know of. She would stare at the face with the hair brushed back off it—and perhaps it would have an ugly wound in it by then—and she would break down with the great, wracking sobs Georgie remembered like a saw in her mind, and the policeman with her would think: She must really have loved her. And the policeman would not know the half of it.

She tried to stop it. She was close to the big plantation now, and she risked a glance back. The moor seemed empty, but anyone could hide in the bracken and gorse that clogged the lower parts by the loch. He could be training the rifle on her right this moment.

—Pray he doesn't have a nightsight, girl.

She dodged aside in reaction to the idea and made it to the trees. She ran along the tree line, staying in the deep shadow.

The vision of white rooms with shiny metal equipment returned. At least when she was there she would be clean. Now she reeked of dirt and every part of her was grimed. The jacket weighed on her shoulders; she would have got rid of it but for Peter telling her that, even wet, the clothing was some kind of insulation against the biting cold. She had no idea what the temperature was, cared less. All she knew was that if Peter was not there when she reached the rendezvous point, she would keep going until she reached the cliffs and throw herself off. Better than that creepy little bastard shooting her down and probably drooling over her body afterward.

She heard falling water, saw the burn coming up again. This was the pool where it came down off the hill. She skirted the rushing flow and leapt the narrowest part of the burn without mishap.

She heard the distant crack of the rifle. A moment later the bullet flicked through the trees above her. She did not throw herself on the ground, since he could only be a few hundred yards away. She saw the rise ahead that would give cover and sprinted over it as another shot whined past her ear.

Below the rise was the long, dish-shaped hollow that contained the loch. It was thick with gorse and bracken coming out of the wet ground. She dived into it and crawled fast into the thickest part of it.

Peter turned back and dumped himself behind a fist of rock. He snatched the binoculars and passed them over the faint landscape to the north. Nothing to see, but the shots were close.

He reslung the rucksack and headed back toward the loch.

She cursed herself for not heading into the trees. The run to them had seemed more dangerous because she would have been retreating in a straight line from the gun, but at least that way she would not have been trapped. The gorse was good hiding, but to get out of it meant running up the shallow sides of the dish, which, even in the dark, was like strapping a target to your back. Anyone standing on the edge of the hollow would see the entire thing.

She raised her head. She turned, straining her eyes against the gloom. The loch shone faintly below, its surface disturbed by the moaning wind. The loneliness of the place was incredible. Finally there was movement on the northern edge. He was running low and easy to find a position. She saw him throw himself down; then he disappeared into the background.

Great. She began to crawl away from him toward the southwest edge, near the big plantation. She was in the undergrowth again, making things easy for him.

Thorns like nails pulled at her jacket, scratched her face. The setup reminded her of the old Br'er Rabbit story, and she laughed. It was almost silent, but what there was had a ragged edge.

"Don't throw me in the briar patch," she whispered in an

Uncle Remus voice. Well, she was in the briar patch all right. Safe enough for the moment. Trouble was, Br'er Fox had a gun.

She paused, raised up again to take a look. Some clouds were pushing across the sky now, but not enough to kill the gleam of starlight. Any movement would be easy to spot.

"Let's have a diversion," she said. "Something to take his eye off me for a second."

She tried to pick out the position of the hands on her watch. Maybe Peter would come soon. When he did, she was unsure what exactly they could do. She sank back on her haunches, cursing her stupidity.

Just then, something moved in front of her. She slipped quickly down, thinking that somehow Harry had circled her. The gorse ripped her face. She tasted blood on her lips.

Bottles clinked. She thought of Peter, did not call out. She gave him time. The shadow on the rise appeared again, gliding silently to her left. Peter was a little distance back, coming toward her. She bit her lip. Any moment now, Harry might spot him too, but if she gave warning, she could end up with a bullet in her back. She reached in her pocket and touched the broken compass, took it out and lobbed it toward the open ground. It struck rock, tinkling. There was a flash from the north and she heard Peter's grunt as he hit the ground. Then silence.

She knew two things now: first, that Peter was still moving around; second, roughly where Harry was. She moved out closer to the edge and listened hard.

The sea boomed far away on a cliff to the south. The night sky roared with the breeze going through the plantations.

—We are seven miles from civilization, eighty miles from a major city, she reminded herself, and this is really happening.

No movement from either side now, not for several minutes. It began to get on her nerves more than the fear. She had to remember Dan's advice that most of a battle was the waiting around. In a situation like this, the loser was usually the one who lost patience and tried some stupid move.

Her fingers clenched and relaxed in the soil. There was no

kindness in this earth. Where it was not hard, it was wet and treacherous.

Then something was happening to her left. She took the risk of sitting up, saw nothing. The rifle cracked again, sounding loud and vicious in the peace of the island.

Peter rolled over, knowing he was in full view of the killer. He fetched up against the gorse, the heavy bottle still in his hand. Rifle fire whacked the earth nearby, and the killer made a sound that was like the whoop of triumph at a football match.

—Lost the element of surprise, he thought, scrabbling into the relative safety of the gorse. Now we're both stuck here, and he's out there with the world at his command.

"Got you, you bastards."

Peter froze. The last thing he had expected was for Harry to start talking. He clutched the bottle to his chest, sweating and shivering uncontrollably.

The voice was quite soft. A note of hysteria poisoned the gentle lilt of the Scots accent.

"You listening in there, *Miss* Georgina? You listening, old man? You're in the shit now, see? You're up to your fucking necks."

Georgie, in her place, felt her stomach convulse. She leaned forward, retching noiselessly.

"Why not talk to me?" Harry said. "That's what all you people're good at, isn't it? Chitchat, talk a feller to death while you rob him blind."

Peter was aware that his legs were still out of cover, but he did not move an inch. He felt no desire to answer back. Only rising anger.

"You made a mistake today, didn't you?" Harry continued. "Teach you to go licking the boss's ass, won't it? Safer to give him a round of golf now and then, not come out to play soldiers. You're out of your league here, whole fucking bunch of you. You can run things back on the mainland, but you're useless out here."

Georgie wiped her mouth, exhausted by the spasms of sickness.

"I'll kill you," Harry said. "Finish the job like they trained me to. See, I really know what it's like to do this. You people need to understand something . . . It's no fucking game."

—Go on talking, you arrogant little bugger, Peter thought, pushing his way through the gorse now, parting the undergrowth without a sound. The more you talk, the less you listen, and the angrier I get.

"You listening, Georgie—Georgina? I remember you, oh, yes. You really gave Dad the lot, didn't you? Softened him up nice and easy, didn't you? You fucking whore, flashing your tits around all summer. I know what you were after—if he'd had any money, you'd've got your hands on it, isn't that right?"

—Sick, she thought. You are so sick.

"Sold him out for that Yank and his dollars, Georgina. You and all of them . . . Don't think anyone's coming to help. No one's coming. They all think you're having a great time. You're having a good time, aren't you?" The rifle blasted again. "I'm having a fucking marvelous time."

—All right, Peter thought. All right for now. He reached in his pocket for the cigarette lighter.

The voice was close. He had worked in as near as he dared, and when he lit the flame, Harry would probably see it. When he threw, he would have an instant to target on his man. In that time, he could be dead too. Never mind. What was that old saying the Norsemen had? "Fearlessness is better than a faint heart for any man who puts his head out of doors. The length of my life and the day of my death were fated long ago."

True enough. What made it better was that he could not imagine himself dying yet. He was filled to the top of his head with the knowledge that he was not at the end of his life. He had many years to go yet. Fifteen years more of work, getting gray and fat and slow on his feet, grumbling over the state of the world and the fact that the *Daily Telegraph* was no longer what it had been. Years of watching Sarah and Liz grow up, get married. Grandchildren and using all that retirement money to travel about the world, making things hot for hotel staffs. Being with Vickie, not noticing how old they were getting, still seeing her the way she was on the day she walked into his life.

He knew all this was to come, so he was not scared of dying.

"I'm going to get you," Harry said. "You can't sit in there forever. When day breaks, your time's up."

Peter took the lighter out. He only hoped it had not taken on water during the rain. He pressed the button. The smooth yellow plume was frighteningly bright. He hunched over it, hoping he was smothering the light from Harry. He spun round quickly on one knee, searching for the target. The cloth taped to the bottle began to char, pieces of it fell sputtering on the ground.

Harry turned to look at him, gun rising.

Peter drew his arm back, knowing the glass of the bottle was thick and would need a good impact to break it.

The rifle went off, he felt a rush of air go by him.

He flung the bottle as hard as he could.

35

THERE WAS A PETRIFIED MOMENT AS IT CURVED THROUGH the darkness, trailing its little fistful of flame. Peter had a last glimpse of Harry's face, contorted in the growing light; then he was down on the ground and starting to crawl.

The bomb fell a few inches short of its target, striking the hard ground in front of him. It disintegrated completely. The petrol-detergent mixture splashed out, taking fire in a sudden bright wash. He snapped a hand to his face, and the sticky gobbets of flame landed on his chest and legs. The detergent made sure the petrol stuck where it landed instead of dribbling away. It was a makeshift kind of napalm.

Harry staggered back from the explosion with his hair and clothes on fire.

Georgie rose out of the gorse, saw him beating at the flames.

Peter sprang from cover and ran toward her, yelling to get moving.

She looked back at Harry. He was down on the ground by the small bonfire of broken glass, rolling over and over to put the flames out.

"It hasn't stopped him," she said.

Peter grabbed her hand and ran with her up the slope out of the hollow. "Next time," he said. "Next time, don't you worry." He was laughing. He snatched up the rucksack, gave her the bag of clothing. They ran to the trees, found a path and climbed it for fifty feet before cutting off to the left into the tangled darkness.

Below, the fire went on burning for some time.

They rested in the shelter of a hollow that went so deep into the hillside that it was almost a cave. In all but total darkness, Peter opened the rucksack and found the tinned food. Georgie went through the garments in the bag by touch, picking out the things she needed.

"There's holes in the jacket."

"Don't ask," he said, slipping the can opener onto a tin.

"The only problem with this is, there's nowhere to change," she said, struggling out of the clammy fatigues.

"Can't see anything anyway," he said, piercing the lid. "I don't know what this stuff is."

"As long as it's not macaroni cheese."

"What?"

"I hate macaroni cheese."

"*What* are you talking about, girl? We haven't eaten for about twenty hours, and you're fussy about food. Ah, that's it."

She left only her panties on, ditched everything else and put on the socks, vest, sweater, and fatigues he had brought.

"Beans," he said. "Cold baked beans. I can't remember the last time I ate baked beans."

"Give them to me."

"Wait and see what else there is."

"Change your clothes. I'll do the rest."

He fumbled his clothes off in the dark. She found it difficult to grip on the can opener.

"It's a combination of cold, fear, and lack of food," he said. "What we could do with now is a few hours' sleep."

"Can't we take them now, while he's out of action?"

"The only way we're going to beat him is by staying ahead. We have to use whatever time this has gained us to set something else up."

"I don't know whether he was badly hurt."

"Just a little singed, my dear. What's in the tins?"

She sniffed, dipped a finger in one. "New potatoes, I think. This one's pineapple."

"There we are, then. Carbohydrates, protein and fiber, glucose, all in three tins. Pass the first course."

She raised a hand to her forehead, staring at the food. Her eyes glistened.

"Eat," Peter said. "Don't think about anything else now. You can't afford to."

"Peter . . ."

"No," he said. "The best way we can grieve for them is by surviving. We can't do that if we go hungry and get weak. We're bucking for exposure and pneumonia as it is. We've been shot at, hurt, seen our friends killed, been scared out of our minds. We either keep going or we break down. So eat."

They ate quickly, surprised by the taste of the food and by how hungry they were. Georgie forgot about listening for trouble. She chewed a mouthful of beans and potato, washed it down with juice from the pineapple.

"Peter?"

His mouth was full. "Mmm?"

"Are you scared now?"

He thought about it for a second. "I'm scared out of my mind. But I'm more frightened of dying than of having a go at him."

She touched his hand. "Thank you."

"What for?" he said, surprised at the contact.

"I don't know . . . For saving my worthless neck down there."

"Thanks for taking all the risks." His fingers squeezed back. "And it's not worthless. I think it's rather precious. So do Vickie and Sarah and Liz. So did Bob and Dan. Anyone with a fan club like that can't be all bad."

She leaned forward and found him in the gloom. She kissed his cheek.

He coughed. "Need a hug?"

She started to say something flip and clever. Then she stopped. She slid into his arms and held him. Tentatively at first, then tighter and tighter.

She was amazed to find herself crying. Weeping hard and like a child on his shoulder.

"I'm sorry," she said, choking on the tears, pushing away from him.

"It's nothing to be ashamed of," he said. "It's all right, it's all right."

The resistance flooded out of her. The tears came harder. She sobbed as if her heart would break, or had broken.

Rocking her gently in his arms, he pushed the hair back from her forehead and kissed the feverish skin above her brow. It was a kiss with nothing in it but tenderness and love.

She cried even harder.

Harry sat by the dancing iron of the burn, trying to wash the petrol-detergent mixture from his hair. There was an irregular patch of singed hair over the top of his skull, and the petrol stung raw flesh as he tried to get it off.

His clothes were scabbed with ragged holes and scorch marks. The jacket's thick lining had saved him from serious harm, but his body trembled with shock. As he went on his knees to plunge his head in the gun-cold water, he swore and muttered to himself, promising that the girl and the old man would suffer for it.

He saw now that he had not been thinking straight since Goldman. Thinking was difficult when the pain in his head was so bad, when the guns were pounding continuously. He had let himself go because of the anger.

He shook his head. Drops fell in the water like coins. The ground was made of needles where his hands had been burned.

It was 0330. Sunrise was a few hours off and, with it, all the threat of people coming to find out what was going on. He could not let them arrive until the job was done. No matter what happened, the two who were left must be dead before the morning light. The ants had to be completely stamped out. Then it would all be his again, and nothing else would matter but to defend the island, to keep the infestation down.

He coughed into his hand, feeling loose and angled from the rage and shock. He proceeded, by touch alone, to check the rifle and handgun for damage. He took his knife, which had not been used, and wiped it on the grass. It glimmered like the burn. He stood carefully and looked back at the gorse where the girl had taken refuge. He blinked rapidly, trembling. He recalled something that suddenly seemed very important. When he had returned to the lodge to see it blazing, Goldman's body was no longer there. He knew the spot where it fell exactly; it would have been easy to see by the firelight, but it was not there. At the time, if he thought about it at all, he assumed that whoever burned the lodge also moved the body. But now a sneaky, glassy suspicion began working into his brain: Goldman was not dead. He had got up, leaking from the holes drilled through him, and come back into the game. A dead man in the field, helping the two who were left.

—Stupid, he thought. But it nagged at him. He started walking toward the big plantation, muttering "Fucker's dead," at intervals to reassure himself. He could see Goldman sitting up slowly, wadding a cloth into his wound, stumbling off to find his party. The air that he should have breathed through his mouth wheezed and sucked through the holes, frothing blood at the wounds. His eyes were sharp with that weary humor he always showed in photographs, and the grin was painted on his face. He lumbered awkwardly through the forest, coming to help his friends.

Harry shivered as he reached the path. He turned his head this way and that, listening for footsteps. Why? Dead men did not walk.

He swallowed hard, and sweat broke out on his body. He moved into the dark, telling himself it was not possible. He knew when a man was "neutralized," as the Boss called it. He knew that nobody ever walked away from wounds like that. Still it gnawed at him, the feeling that the dead man was out there, thinking up more plans like the petrol bomb.

He stumbled into a clearing, vaguely recognizing it. There was a humped shadow on the ground, like someone crawling toward him. He fired into it twice before he could stop himself. The shape jumped slightly when the bullets struck, and he cried out in a horrified gasp. It was only when he gathered the courage to approach that he realized.

Williamson. Of course. He had killed the man early in the morning, hadn't he? And Williamson was just as dead now as then. Harry sniggered nervously, more from relief than amusement. If Williamson could not rise up and join the battle again, neither could anyone else. Goldman was dead, he was gone.

Harry stood over the body and poured another six rounds into it.

Georgie's head flicked up.

"It's all right," Peter said, climbing ahead of her. "He's not shooting at us. Too far away."

They were going up the south side of Cruach Scorba toward the folly, going straight up instead of taking the snaky paths that made ascent easy.

"What *is* he shooting at?" Georgie said.

"Might be trying to scare us a bit more. He's still not after simply wiping us out, is he? He could've done that in a few minutes early this morning. We're dealing with the kind of mind that enjoys pulling the wings off flies. Now stop talking and keep climbing."

Several minutes passed in silence. Despite the ache of cold and weariness in her bones, Georgie began to feel a little better. The food they had eaten was working into her system, the tears had emptied out the pressure in her head.

Climbing was hard. The south side of the cruach looked gentle and smooth from a distance, but the trees that gave that impression clung at bad angles to precarious outcrops and crevices. It was steep, and without the tree trunks as footrests and handholds, they probably could not have done it. Georgie was wearing the gloves Peter had brought to protect her hands from further damage, but they had stiffened up badly in the cold.

Peter, by contrast, had taken new energy from the little victory over Harry. He went up the steep, irregular incline as if the game had just begun. When she got into trouble he paused to help. She could not see his face most of the time but, when it appeared from the gloom, it was smiling and encouraging her.

She dug her fingers into a cleft of rock and pulled herself level with him.

"Must be nearly there," he said.

"And then what?" she asked.

The darkness parted before them. Peter raised a hand, brought them to a halt. He went down on his belly and slithered up to the crest of the hill. He beckoned. She went forward, stepped out of the quiet, dripping forest into the open, hushed roar of the distant sea. In front of them, reaching high into the faint phosphorescence of the night sky, was the tower. She heard the wind groaning softly through the arrow-slit windows above.

"What a place for a fortress," Peter said. He walked into the wide clearing where the folly stood. He looked to left and right but did not try to hide himself. "We're safe enough at the moment. He's not that close yet. We've got a few minutes."

They walked around the folly; then he climbed the steps to the heavy old door.

"Give me some light, will you?"

She took his cigarette lighter, cupped it to provide a chink of light that he could use. In the feeble glow, he ran his fingers over the door.

"Damn it, they made things to last, didn't they? Hasn't been opened for years. Look at the padlocks. Rusted solid."

"Williamson said it was unsafe anyway."

"I wouldn't mind risking it, would you?" He snuffed the flame with his thumb. "If we had a good tire lever we might be in with a chance."

The rain-heavy trees shivered in the gusting wind. A big wave disintegrated on the cliffs below.

Peter slid Bob's knife into the top padlock, trying to force it apart, but the padlocks were old and well made. The blade snapped off in a shower of rust. He stared at the ruined knife and swore. Three inches of blade remained on the haft.

"All right," he said, "so we don't take refuge in the tower. I was hoping we could sit up there and throw things at him till dawn. Can't even build a signal fire after all the rain."

He took her hand again. They went toward the cliff path. "What's the plan, General?"

"Any ideas?" he said. Then, to himself: "Think, you damn fool."

They went along the path. She left him and moved cautiously to the cliff edge. There was little to see. The dim outline of the cliff showed as deeper black against the blue-gray of the ocean. Far off to the northwest were the jagged outcrops of the Gorvellachs. The sea was a rioting crowd, and she felt the hard updraft of the wind climbing from below. She got closer to the edge, heard a papery rustling close by.

"Birds," he said. "Come on, we'd better not stay here. He's hardly going to oblige us by stepping off the cliff."

She glanced back at the trees. At this point, they were some five yards from the sheer drop. She peered down the path. "The path goes all the way round, doesn't it?"

"If you can call it a path."

"Let's see the map again."

He pulled at his nose, gazing at her curiously.

Harry tracked southward through the forest until he found evidence of their meal. He stood in the hollow, kicking the empty cans with the toe of his boot.

Someone was cleverer than he had supposed.

He knelt, running his hands over the earth, up over the foliage. He found the broken stems where they had climbed out of the hollow. He clambered up, squinting into the dark. He flicked a mint and sucked on it. This was interesting. He had expected them to head for the shore again, yet they were climbing the hill. Perhaps they had some idea that being at the top was safer. Silly idea. Look what it did for King Harold at the Battle of Hastings.

He swayed, clutched at his head. Sweat all over his face. He wished he could get rid of the stink of petrol, lose that scorched smell from his clothes. It was too much like the smell that had come wafting up from the *Antelope*, burning down in the bay.

—Got to be careful this time, lad. Too much riding on it to mess it up for want of a little control.

He licked his lips. The trees leered at him. The hill was a breathing animal above him. It was so big, and the enemy was so small. He put his beret on to cover the itching flesh of his burned scalp and started up the hill.

It took them a while to find the place. It was half a mile from the folly along the south path. They had to go carefully because the path was never more than four feet wide, and the trees occasionally stuck out across the way, making it difficult to spot the drops that littered the way. Sometimes it wandered inland for several yards, other times simply stopped at the brink of a long fall. Twice they came within inches of stumbling over a precipice, but Peter kept saying: "Any minute now, we'll find a spot."

Then the way narrowed and came up against a curving promontory. The path turned sharp right to follow the line of the coast. It climbed the back of the outcrop, and the trees bunched up in the shelter, their branches reaching almost to the edge of a sheer vertical face. In the blue-black night, it was hard to see the exact configuration of the rocks, but it was clear that the path was dangerously close to the edge here. The trees were a wall, and the path was no more than two feet across, and then there was a steep incline, then nothing but the empty space.

Peter went along beneath the trees, testing any branch that projected over the path. Not far from the curve, he found one that was long and straight and quite thick. It blocked the way at about waist height.

He began to laugh quietly. Georgie came closer as he took the knife and cut back some of the other branches, then trimmed it down. He crept under it to face the way they had come, grabbed the branch and, using his weight, drew it slowly back. He pulled until she heard a faint crack inside it and raised a hand for him to stop.

"Get the rope," he said, bracing himself to stop it springing forward.

She cut a length of rope and lashed the branch securely. She tied the other end to a stout trunk a yard away.

"If it doesn't slip before its time, we should be okay."

"It'll be fine," Peter said. "The real problem is getting him here."

"Can't we just wait?"

"He's no fool. He covers ground smoothly and methodically. He's trained to look out for traps. If he's going to step into this one, he'll have to be running, ignoring the danger. And he'll have to come down the path, not from inside the forest."

"Not the decoy job again?" She slumped down. "Peter, I can't."

"You don't have to. You've done your share of target practice today."

"That path—"

"It's pretty hairy." He nodded. "And it needs someone sure on his feet, someone nimble, not an old sod in tight boots with the first twinges of rheumatism in his bones."

"That's not what I meant."

"Yes, it is. But you're not looking too spry yourself. I'll get him down here, don't worry, but it's up to you to cut that rope at the right moment."

She touched the tautly drawn rope. "You think it'll work?"

He rubbed his nose. "Have faith. At least it might knock the gun out of his hands, give us some kind of advantage. It's the gun that makes him so powerful here. If all we do is deprive him of that, we'll accomplish something."

She gazed at the path, at the yawning drop below. "Why should he chase you all the way down here?" She pointed to the rise they had come over just before reaching the promontory. "He could stand there and take a shot at you."

He paused, then said, "Something'll turn up, as my mother used to say."

She grasped his arm. "It's not going to work, is it?"

"Not if I don't get back up there, it isn't. I've got to attract him to the right place before we can play follow-my-leader. Come on, Georgie. Just be sure you cut that rope dead on time."

"Don't let him shoot you. I don't want to be here with him by myself."

"I'm not Sherlock Holmes on the Reichenbach Falls, believe me. I'm just too angry to be chased anymore. Pass me the rest of the rope, will you?"

She gave him the rope.

"I'll try to give you some warning when we come down," he said. "But you should hear us anyway." He stood up. "Getting light, isn't it?"

She jumped up and hugged him, took him by surprise.

"What's got into you?" he said, finally breaking her hold.

She shrugged. "Maybe I'll tell you afterwards."

He looked at her. "Do that."

He climbed the path, watching the edge as if looking for something. She saw him go over the rise out of her sight. —If he dies, she thought, I'll finish the job. But then she realized that she could not bear the idea of him dying. She knelt down by the rope, the broken knife in her hand.

Close to the summit, Harry saw a light. He hit the ground, zeroing in with the rifle. It was far off, a blurred pinpoint. He took a look through the field glasses, saw that it was a fire. He covered the last thirty yards very slowly. The fire wandered in and out of sight. It was a feeble thing. He could see the wind blustering it almost flat. What good did they think it would do, if the whole lodge burning did not bring anyone?

The smoke from it darted down on him as he reached the edge of the clearing. The fire, lonely before the steps of the folly, was already dying away. It looked like a small pile of clothing; they were so damp they had failed to take the flame properly.

He sucked hard on the mint. What good was it; who would see it? He waited, suspecting an attack. They couldn't be in the tower, but what if they were, with another of those petrol bombs? He could not run the risk of another one.

He worked his way round the clearing inch by inch, expecting to come upon them any moment. He slung the rifle over his shoulder and used the handgun to give himself more flexibility.

But they weren't there. He turned, staring up at the tower. It was diagonal in his sight. His fingers went into his pocket and found a loose cartridge case for the pistol. He flicked it toward the tower, heard it chink on the steps and clatter on the stone skirting.

Nothing happened. Were they being clever again? He could not decide. Going into a darkened, enclosed space like this worried him too much. It was full of memories he had spent too long trying to lose.

Time was passing. Too much of it, if he wanted to finish this before daylight. The tower was more distinct against the sky than before. First warning of sunrise: a reflection in the upper atmosphere. The tides that swept the island were at their height and he was standing on a little piece of his homeland that had become his kingdom again.

"Don't feel bitter," Dad had said, pouring himself another glass. "It's no one's fault, lad. Just the inexorable march of progress." He stumbled over "inexorable." "It's no more the American's fault than it is the family's. They sold up, did they not? You can't blame them for stepping on us little fellers."

But who else was to blame, and who said they were the "little fellers"?

"Least of all is it young Georgie's fault," Dad would say, closing his eyes. "She was a young girl who wanted the world on her plate. I expect she'll write when she finds out my address."

Poor old fool. He never stopped believing the good in

people, even when experience showed him the truth time and time again.

Harry made up his mind to do something, sprang up and sprinted across to the tower, kicked at the door, felt it as solid as ever. A moment to check the padlocks told him that no one had entered. The tower was secure from them. It had not been taken.

He backed down the steps, circled the base. As he came round the western side of the triangle, he saw the gap through the trees that led to the cliffs. If it had still been completely dark, he would have seen nothing till it was too late. But picked out in grainy silhouette against the distant ocean, he caught a flicker of movement.

—Shit, he thought.

A little dash of flame arched out of the shadows toward him.

36

AT FIRST HE WAS SURE THAT THE THROWER HAD LOUSY AIM. It was far too high to touch him. But as he started to dive, he realized the purpose.

The bottle struck the wall of the tower some eight feet from the ground. A hundred gobbets of flame rained down on him with the jagged flowers of glass.

He was already into his dive as the hot storm fell. He came out of a neat roll, smothering the fire with handfuls of earth. He continued his course and got back in the safety of darkness.

The petrol sputtered and began to go out, flames falling to a dull blue. He watched them sink to nothing, until the gloom was restored; then he was up and running out of cover, straight across the clearing toward the path, yelling his head off as he had been taught to, firing the pistol in a wide arc.

No attack was made. In a couple of moments, he was through the trees and out on the gentle slope down to the cliffs. The sea shone like oil, heaving slowly in the starlight. He was struck by the beauty of it even as he checked each quadrant for a sign of the enemy. He breathed the salt spray.

A pebble skittered off to the left. He swung and saw the old man stagger as he went down the path. It was the man all right, tall and bony and running with surprising agility.

Harry fired once as the old man ducked out of sight. The shot whined off rocks and spent itself over the sea. The man was really moving. That was pretty brave when he could not be very familiar with the path.

But Harry knew it, and he was not about to lose another chance to plug the bastard.

Peter ran as he had never run before. He did not suffer from a fear of heights as a rule, and he could not see much to his right anyway, but knowing how great the drop was would have frozen his nerve if he had been given time to think. He had to be fast and nimble at the same time. If he lost Harry, he would fail. The gunman had to stick with him all the way down to the promontory.

A rock caught his boot. He swayed out over the drop, arms windmilling to regain balance.

—Blast and damn, think about it later, will you? This is no time for deep thought.

He climbed again as the cliff rose, felt the exposure of the position. He crouched low and prayed not to hear the rifle's distinctive crack. He leapt over the rise, skidding round to check the situation.

Harry came on like a black dog running. He suffered no problems with the path, had probably spent his boyhood jumping around the cliffs like a goat. He drew up short, lifted the handgun. Peter threw himself down the other side of the spur as a bullet hissed by.

The ocean thundered below. Peter made the mistake of looking down as he edged along a narrow shelf, saw the glimmer of distant water, the luminous nets of foam surging at the cliffs. It was three hundred feet down at least.

The gun fired again, a shot whistled over his head. Difficult to hear anything now for the wind and the sea.

He wobbled along a stretch of the path that was like a paper streamer in a high wind. It twisted round a spur, no more than a perch on a vertical wall, like the roads to be found halfway up sheer rock faces in the Alps. He clung on and heard Harry coming.

—Too close, too bloody close.

Maybe he had miscalculated, left himself too little start. That would be funny: Georgie would sit there in the trees, waiting for the chase to end, while Harry caught him half-way there.

He stopped being careful, let go of the meager handhold the rock provided. He felt the safety go out of his position and suddenly began to enjoy himself. Really to delight in the sense of danger. He felt as he had once in Austria, driving the tortured thread of the Villach–Lake Bled road into Yugo-slavia. Flat out, with a promise to himself not to use the brakes. He'd done it on impulse, for a dare, almost. He had scared himself spitless, but never felt so alive as he did when he was throwing the car around those high turns.

Now, on foot in this unfamiliar ground, that pleasure surged back. It was because of the fear, part of it, and he saw with a great clarity that all the petty worries that had nagged him for months were nothing beside this sweet, clean feel-ing of being alive. He used his momentum to keep balance, telling himself he could no more fall than he could be shot.

He knew he had gained some ground because the foot-steps faded. He cleared the cliffside path and came out onto the top again. The trees bunched up and he tried to remem-ber how much farther it was. That bastard Harry was well behind now. Not a sound from him. Peter eased off just a lit-tle, still hearing absolutely nothing behind, and the alarm bell went off in his head.

What if the killer had not followed him round the path. What if he had gone over the top and arrived first?

He stopped dead, instinct driving him to his knees.

Lucky move.

The night blew up. He felt the heat of the pistol flash as Harry lunged out of the trees five yards ahead of him.

He still possessed the beautiful knowledge that he could not die, that he was going home to Vickie and the kids and Sunday papers in bed and all the other things that made life worth living. It gave him the power to do what he next did.

The killer was homing in for another shot. Everything was down to fragments of a second. Peter launched himself from the ground, arms spread wide, head up, roaring at the top of his lungs.

The gun went off, numbing his ears. He smelled the hot rush of gas from the barrel. An instant later he collided with Harry and sent him sprawling back into the trees. Harry screeched like a terrified animal: "Don't touch me! Don't you fucking touch me!"

Peter regained his footing. The killer was on his back, the pistol was lost in the gloom, and Harry was fumbling with the rifle on his shoulder. He decided not to risk it, swung and headed down the path, partly terrified, partly exalted by what he had just done. He heard the killer yelling after him and the words were lost in gibberish.

—He's mad, Peter thought, belly churning with the adrenaline pumping in his system. —He's absolutely crazy.

More gunshots—the pistol had been found—like fireworks in the vast emptiness. He was already out of the firing line.

"Come on," he called back, gasping for breath. "Come on, Harry. Can't you do it to an old man? Come on, you little bastard."

That worked all right. The pistol barked again, and this time it was a little too close. A couple of slugs pinged off the rocks below him. He hardly heard them. Since the two close shots, he was almost deaf.

Perhaps another hundred yards to go—over the next rise, then down to the promontory with the path narrowing and Georgie sitting in the undergrowth with the knife raised.

He tripped, went down. A white pain flicked through his head. He climbed up immediately and went on, dimly aware of Harry shouting nearby. He never believed for a moment that he could be hit, not now, not so close.

He lurched down the incline toward the promontory and the trees, could actually see it now in the cold, colorless light preceding dawn. The cliff below the turn dropped away out of sight. It was a perfect place. Perfect.

He put on a last spurt. Passed the first of the trees that hung over the path, smacking the branches aside. Under the tight-drawn bow of the branch that could not be seen until you were upon it. Past Georgie, huddled in the shadows, eyes bright and terrified.

He dived into the trees at the curve, rolled, smacked heavily against a tree, and turned swiftly to watch Harry fall.

Georgie's fingers twitched on the knife, free hand resting on the rope. She squinted through the branches and saw Harry coming. He was no longer very human. He was covered in scorch marks and blisters from the petrol bombs, blood seeping through the dirty bandage on his forehead. She saw his lips drawn back over his teeth and the way he ran. He did not care about falling or meeting resistance. He had one thing in his mind now. He came over the rise and hurtled down the path toward her.

She put the knife against the rope.

He came on. She could hear his ragged breathing now. It was a snarl.

She gripped the rope, felt the tension in it ready to go.

He was almost there. Almost.

Knife pressed to rope, cutting the fibers.

And Harry stopped.

Harry stopped.

Body heaving for breath, he planted his feet on the hard, uneven surface of the path. He raised his head, trying to hear above the pounding of the guns—the hammer of his heart and the wash of the sea.

The path curved to his right along the promontory. The trees clustered thick and dark.

The enemy had to have taken cover in them.

He stared at the path, looking for them, wanting to know why he had stopped. Hesitated.

Peter did not move. He was pinned to a board. He could not move, Harry was too close. Even breathing could give him away.

Georgie began to shake. She let go of the rope before her trembling disturbed the branch.

—He knows I'm here. Christ, he can smell me.

All the while, Harry waited, an expression of bewilderment on his face.

—Come on, Peter thought. Two more steps'll do it. Come on . . . Anger surged again. He could not believe all the dying and the fear had been caused by this burned and blistered youth. They had to get him moving again. But how? Yelling so close would be disastrous. The killer would know they were up to something. He would be off the path before the trap could be sprung. To convince him, it had to sound accidental.

Peter leaned forward slightly until the weight resting on the soles of his feet passed over the center of balance. He commenced to fall. Full length, flat on the ground. Slender branches cracked under his arms. When he struck the forest floor, breath went out of him in a choking gasp.

Harry reacted without thought, leapt forward, starting for the curve.

Georgie grabbed the rope again, gave him half a second to be sure.

She drove knife through rope.

And, lifting her head, saw him glaring straight at her.

Stored tension in the branch snapped the rope in two.

Harry heard it, saw it in the tiny points of time before the impact. He saw the girl there behind the tree with the broken knife in the downswing from slashing into the rope. In reaction he brought the gun up and his finger yanked the trigger as the branch whipped toward him.

She screamed. A red mist blossomed around her and she jerked back into the trees.

—I did for you anyway, you bitch.

The branch swept across and struck him square in the chest. Stumpy points of growth that had been cut off pierced his flesh. He was thrown backward and fell, half on the path, half over the edge. The pistol sailed out into the dark.

For just a moment he thought he was going to be all right. He had not fallen off the path, he could get up and finish the job. Then he saw the old man coming out of the trees, and the old man was furious and scared. Harry tried to get at the rifle. The old man grabbed his boot, got hold of it and twisted Harry toward the edge.

Harry's eyes reflected the empty, distant sea. Harry's fingers scrabbled at smooth, damp rock. He kicked at the old man who was pushing him toward death. Loose cartridge cases slipped from his pockets and went clinking down the slope like old pennies.

He clawed the air, cried out for something to help him.

Then he was gone.

37

PAIN.

Wind strengthened and came off the ocean like a salt blade. It gathered the tide and threw gray waves harder against the unmoving cliffs. Birds below Cruach Scorba fluttered in the dawn light. Sun began to redden slowly from the east. The cliffs were still in deep shadow. A great black-backed gull, lonely as the end of the world, swooped upward to the clouds.

He groaned. Blood filled his mouth. It trickled down his chin and splashed on rock.

Pain.

He tried to move. Needles jabbed in his chest; he almost cried out. After that he took it very carefully. Tested the fingers of his left hand, made sure they worked. Spread the palm flat on the rock, exploring the area around him. He pressed against it, levered himself up, over, as gradually as he could. The needles turned to lances, tore him again. He cried out, but quietly.

Harry knew he must be quiet. Someone might still be up there, waiting.

He rolled on his back, rested a moment until the burning subsided. He opened his eyes and looked up. The clifftop overhung him about twenty feet above. The overhang gave some shelter from the brief shower that began to fall.

Despite the pain that seemed to be working through every part of him, he tried to laugh.

They had fucked up again. He supposed that, in the dark,

they could not have seen the overhang or the ledge below. It made no odds. They had messed up again. Chucked him off the cliff believing he would plummet three hundred feet into the sea. It was almost pitiable.

He moved the right arm; it seemed to be all right. He prayed he had not broken his back in the fall, tried his legs. They moved too. He attempted to sit up. The fire hissed through his insides again. He slipped back, banging his head. Some ribs were bruised, maybe broken, but considering the fall, he was lucky not to have come down on his head.

—You're still on my side, he thought, and stroked the little shelf of rock that had saved him. It was still his island; it was looking out for him.

He got up more carefully this time, keeping his back straight. The ledge was no more than three feet by six, an irregular crescent. It gave little room for mistakes. He gained a sitting position, legs hanging over the edge, and leaned back against the face.

The bandage came off his head. It was not enough. He eased his jacket off, then the sweater, wincing whenever a wrong move gave him more pain than he could hold on to. He got down to the green vest, used the knife to cut it off and make a long, wide strip of it. Then he bound his chest with it as he had seen the medics do it in the field hospital at Ajax Bay. Blood dripped on the material as he wound it tight. He dabbed his nose and realized that it was probably broken. It gave him a sick, squeezing sensation in the front of his head. He sat up straighter and cinched the makeshift bandage as tight as he could bear. It stabbed him worse than before and he stifled a scream. He knew it would have to be tight to keep him in one piece for what was coming.

One more to get rid of, that was all. Just one more crummy bastard to neutralize. He thought about how the old man had run out to tip him over the edge, and the memory gave him strength. He pushed himself up by cautious stages. He hurt like hell, taking a deep breath was just about impossible, but he could move all right.

He turned and studied the cliff. It rose above him like two

walls of a room. He was near the corner. He couldn't go straight up. For one thing the overhang was a killer, for another the old man could still be there, mourning over the girl. To the right, it went into the curve and was not good. The left was a few degrees out of vertical with some snatches of grass growing in the clefts. He chose the left, because he could work along a distance and get away from the overhang before he came up. Not too hard for a man who knew the island.

He recalled that his pistol was over the cliff. The rifle remained, slung over his shoulder. He checked it quickly, making sure the mechanism had not been damaged.

It was going to be all right. It was like the island had put out a hand to save him, to give it back its dignity. It was on his side, as it had always been.

He moved to the edge of the shelf and put out his hand to the time-worn stone. Every movement was pain. His fingers touched a fault and slipped into it. He glanced up. Twenty feet was nothing at all. He stepped off the ledge, touched a foothold. The steps were there for him. He was going back to the battlefield, and wouldn't that bastard get a surprise? Wouldn't he shit himself when he realized that Harry had come back from the dead? It would be so good.

He fumbled the next hold, slipped sideways. His chest burned with sudden, deep pain. Vision blurred. It took a moment for things to clear before he was hanging on safe again. He rested, breath wheezing, eyes closed to stop the swimming of his thoughts.

—So you're not so well as you thought. Mustn't lose this. Got another chance to finish the work. Mustn't lose it.

He took the next hold, lifted.

By the time he reached the top he was soaked with sweat. He swung an arm over the edge and pushed himself up the slope. He stayed there, clinging to the rocks, head touching the cold surface, murmuring quietly.

He crawled into the trees and got to his feet. His entire face was beginning to throb with agony from the broken nose. He kept moving, though, to get away from the cliffs, to be safe for a moment. He noticed his left leg was hurting too, but gave it no attention. All he wanted was for it to keep working a little longer.

His watch had smashed in the fall: the angle of dull light told him that it was something over forty-five minutes since the old man had pushed him over the edge, which gave him maybe a mile start. A mile. He did not feel as if he could cover a hundred yards, but he had to do it now. There was more of a score to settle with this one than all the rest. He had dared to put up a real fight, had cheated with his petrol bombs and the rope tricks. He was the one of them who had succeeded in fighting. But he could not be allowed to think he had got away with it.

Harry dabbed his nose with his sleeve, gingerly wiping the blood away. The aching made thought harder.

—Three down, he thought, to give himself an extra boost. Three down, one to go.

He found a way of loping along on his bad leg that gave him more speed than walking pace but was also as comfortable as possible under the circumstances.

Time passed. He lost track of it and was unsure of anything except the repeating chant in his head: Three down, one to go. Three down, one to go.

He went straight over the humpback of the hill, then joined the path. He was sure that the old man, thinking the battle was won, would head for the burned-out lodge and the jetty, to be there when the Seventh Cavalry turned up. He intended catching up with his man before that, long before they even reached the moors. Harry did not want any more close contact with the enemy; he was uncertain how well he could do if it came to more dodging around. This was to be a straight, no-nonsense kill with the rifle.

He noticed a spot of blood on the ground. It gave him confidence. Not only was he going the right way, but the old man was hurt too.

A quarter mile from the summit on the east side of the hill, the ground leveled slightly. It took a couple of steps; two large plateaus that relieved the steep downward plunge. Some hours before, he had watched the players of the game from the northern end of the lower step. He paused above the first and scrutinized the view over the trees. To his left he heard the splashing waters of the burn on its way to the moor.

He spotted movement below. At first he thought it was a bird. Two hundred yards or so, no problem for the rifle. He waited, saw another flash of green combat jacket.

This was it.

He went down on one knee, took up the firing stance. Peering down the scope, he located the old man coming through the trees on the edge of the step. He walked slowly, limping. Even from the back he looked dog-tired.

Harry breathed quicker, groaning with anticipation. He took aim very carefully, centered on the back of the old man's head. Old man? He wasn't that old, really. Not as old as Dad. He saw Dad's drunken face, the pleading eyes in their tears of alcohol. He concentrated again. He pulled the trigger.

The shot rang far off across the hillside, over the moor, over the ocean. Its faint echo returned from the small plantation and the loch. Harry opened his eyes as the rifle jumped in his grasp. Through the scope, he saw the old man clutch spasmodically at his neck and fall. The shot had gone low but it seemed effective enough. The old man disappeared from view.

Harry lowered the rifle. He covered his face with one hand and cried silently. The pain was worse, but he could not stop it. He was happy. The tears came. He slipped over, hit the ground, kept crying or laughing. Whichever it was.

After a minute he got up and stumbled down the path toward the lower step.

The body was there, lying on its back. It was in a pool of blood. A hand was still clamped to the neck as if it could have stopped the flow. The body looked pale and shrunken.

Harry slung the rifle on his shoulder. He did not need it anymore, not until the "rescuers" arrived. He took one last look at the body, thought about kicking it to shreds, but he was too tired. Besides, the old man deserved a little respect for staying alive so long.

He went off the path to the burn. It trickled over slick brown rocks here. He knelt and dipped his head in the rusty, frozen water, drank about three pints of it. It tasted good, always had done. He sat back and wiped his face, touching the gash on his forehead. Soon be time to go home, or Dad would be worried. No, that wasn't right. He reminded himself dully that this was now, and the only thing left to do was defend the island for as long as he could.

The forest was coming alive now. A hooded crow labored up into the air, some rock doves cooed to each other nearby. He took out his field glasses, found they, too, had been smashed in the fall.

No matter now. He had done what he set out to do, for Dad and for the island. He could make his way back to Silver Cove, where his food was hidden, eat a little, prepare himself for the next battle. He had no idea how long he would last, but there would never be a survival game here again.

He stood up, glad to be breathing the clear, sharp air.

The clouds began to clear as he left the big plantation and started across the moor. A ray of gold struck down across the small plantation, lighting the trees with fire. He trudged over the spongy earth toward the water shrine a quarter mile distant. He found the packet of Tic Tacs and flipped one into his mouth. Everything was fresh and reborn this morning. The island was cleansed.

He saw the ruined stones of the water shrine, nodded toward them as he passed. He turned south for Silver Cove. He wanted to sing, but his face hurt too much. He laughed about it, dragging one leg in front of the other.

Then a voice spoke close behind him.

"Hello, Harry."

He spun round, staring at the water shrine.

Georgie raised her gun and fired.

38

HE NEVER HAD TIME TO REACT. HIS HANDS WENT UP TO protect himself too late. The gun made its soft, whacking report and a pellet exploded full in his face.

He stumbled back, blinded. Fumbled to bring the rifle down off his shoulder. No good.

Georgie came at him from the water shrine, screaming.

Something drove into him, deep and low in his belly. He howled as it went in, kept going in, felt it tearing into his guts, all the way through. Then the girl twisted it, and there was more pain than he had ever known before. He groped feebly to stop her but she hauled the spear upward, transfixing him on a nail of agony.

He couldn't stop screaming.

No longer aware of any sensation but the pain, he collapsed, crying out again when his body jarred on the ground.

He could see a little through his stinging eyes. He blinked at the paint, trying to locate her.

She stood over him for a moment, mouth curled in disgust. Then she sat down next to him, pulling the hair back off her face. It was a face that had almost no resemblance to the photographs in the papers or the girl who had arrived the day before. Drawn and colorless and marked with weariness.

He tried to grab her, but that was stupid because he could hardly do it at all, and anyway, she reached out and pushed at the stick in his belly and he screeched and felt everything dissolve in fire again.

"Don't do that," she said. Her voice was quite flat and ordinary. Her eyes were neutral. "What's the problem? Oh, I see. Let me . . ." She leaned over and wiped some of the paint from his eyes.

His fingers scraped nervelessly at the stick where it was buried in him. Blood welled around it. His heart thumped erratically in his ribs and sweat beaded on his forehead.

She held up the pellet gun and smiled at him. "I thought you'd like that little touch," she said. "After all, you did so much to liven up the game for us. It only occurred to me a little while ago, but I thought it was sort of suitable."

He tried to speak. A thick clot of blood burbled from his mouth. The question: "How?" came with it.

"I could ask you the same thing, couldn't I? As my dear mother used to say. We were so sure we'd got you that last time. Never thought to check the cliff afterwards. Stupid of us, really, but there you are. We weren't experts like you, were we?"

She tossed the pellet gun away. Her face creased with pain.

"Oh, don't worry, you did hit me. Left shoulder, as a matter of fact." She drew her jacket aside so he could see the bloody material cushioning the wound. "Hurts a lot, doesn't it, getting shot? But I think it went straight through. Anyway, it's stiffening up now, but it lasted long enough to fix you."

She glanced at him and saw the eyes rolling back in his head. She nudged the stick and waited until he stopped crying before she continued.

"After you fell, we thought that was it. We thought we'd done for you, all by ourselves. Peter—that was his name, by the way, if you didn't know. Peter and Dan and Bob. He helped me up and tried to stop my bleeding. Then we decided to make for the jetty, wait for someone to come. Peter wanted me to stay where I was, but I wouldn't. I wanted to be with him. So we staggered off, him supporting me.

"You know, we were really happy there for a while. We

were laughing and joking, knew we shouldn't be, after what you put us through, but we couldn't help it. It didn't matter that you killed everyone. I suppose we would've gone through that later, but just then all we cared about was being alive.

"Halfway down the hill we stopped a minute to get a drink from the burn. I sat down and started mopping my face and neck to clean them up. He went to the edge of the path to see if anyone was coming from the mainland. He said: 'This is a mess, Georgie. A terrible bloody mess.'

"Then you shot him.

"I think what was worst about it was that he didn't die straight away. Because of the fucking awful way you shot him. He fell down, and there was blood coming out of his neck like a hose. He started grabbing at it, and I tried to close the wound to stop it coming out, but you screwed any chance of that. His neck was torn so badly I couldn't make it stop.

"And all the time he was lying there, jerking around, and he kept saying: 'Help me, Georgie, help me.' He couldn't talk properly. Then the blood wasn't pumping so fast and I stopped trying to hold it back because he put his arms around me. He knew what was happening to him, and there was nothing we could do about it. I just held him until he stopped."

Harry whimpered and coughed more blood.

She pushed at the stick in his guts again.

"I don't know how long it takes for someone to die like that, do you?"

He tried to shout the pain out. All that came was a gasp.

"So, Peter wasn't with me anymore," she said. "And you were. I had to do something about it. I don't know where the idea came from. It just seemed the natural thing to do.

"I cut off the path and found Captain Williamson, and I took his gun. Then I found a nice, straight sapling and sharpened it to a point . . . Dan was right about that, after all. Then I crept out to the shrine to wait for you. I would've waited all day if I needed to. Even if the police had come,

I'd have found a minute to get to you and kill you. See, you've made it so easy. Twenty-four hours ago I didn't know a thing about killing, but I've learned a lot from you."

She leaned closer to him, looking hard at his eyes.

"You're starting to die now, aren't you? That's all right, that's fine. I just hope they're waiting for you, the wardens and the boatman, Bob and Dan . . . and Peter. I hope they're all waiting for you. I suppose when this is long past, I'll understand why you did it, and I might even be able to see it from your point of view. But they don't have the time anymore. You try explaining it to them."

She rose on her knees over him. He was too weak to do anything more than swallow on the dryness in his throat. She grasped the stick in both hands.

"I hope you burn," she said.

And twisted. And twisted.

And twisted.

39

The men who came from the Edinville found her sitting on the jetty, dangling her feet over the water.

They had seen the charred ruin of the lodge from a long way off. Now they saw her ragged, bloodstained clothes and the expression on her face.

The manager of the hotel clambered out of the boat first.

"What happened, Miss Lawrence? Where's Mr. Goldman? What the hell's going on?"

She would not answer him, but one of the men, who wrapped her in a blanket and persuaded her to get into the boat, saw her clutching a gold pocket watch with an ornate cover. He asked if it belonged to her.

She flipped the cover and scratched her thumbnail over the marks within.

"It was my father's," she said.